LOCKWOOD

A HULL GANGLAND LOVE STORY
CHRIS SPECK

Copyright © 2024 Chris Speck
Flat City Press 2024
All rights reserved.
Cover photos by Specky

'You only got power over your mind, everything else just happens. Once you get that, you'll feel a whole lot better about everything.'

John 'Hannibal' Smith
The A Team

ISBN-13: 9781739330859

This is a work of fiction. Unless otherwise indicated, all the names, characters, businesses, places, events and incidents in this book are either the product of the author's imagination or used in a fictitious manner. Any resemblance to actual persons, living or dead, or actual events is purely coincidental.

PROLOGUE

Hull
Summer
2012

It's late July and three weeks into the summer holiday. Gaz's mountain bike has a flat tyre. He's pushed it along the path beside the drain from Beresford Park because there's no point being out if he can't keep up with the other lads. Ryde Street has cars parked on both sides and black wheelie bins stand outside front doors. The sun belts down from a clear blue sky. At the alley between two terraced houses, Gaz wheels the bike down towards his backyard. There's the smell of drains and cut grass.

Gaz's mum won't be able to help him with the flat tyre, he'll have to sort this himself. He leaves the bike on the grass that needs cutting, and goes into the kitchen through the thin glass door that isn't locked. Inside, there's the smell of cold grease from the chip pan on the stove. The bin overflows with rubbish and there's the faint whiff of his mother's flowery perfume. Gaz stands on the tacky lino floor and listens upstairs – he hears a man's voice. This is not unusual because Gaz's mum has a lot of friends and uncles who visit her, and despite his age, Gaz is aware of what she is doing. This is why he has a bike, and why he's got a Mega drive in his bedroom too, and why they can get takeaways on a Saturday night. She entertains men, and they pay her for it in crisp twenty-pound notes, sometimes in envelopes, there are gifts at times too, boxes of chocolates, bottles of wine, perfume, pairs of knickers. He's in secondary school now, he's old enough to know what goes on. He takes a glass and gets a drink of water from the tap. Gaz has been told not to come back until six. That's the rule when his mother is working but he has a knackered bike. It'll be okay. Gaz has returned on other days to get a drink and she hasn't even noticed.

From upstairs there are voices once more. Usually it's giggling, sometimes creaks as they sit on the bed, sometimes grunts, but this afternoon with the sun hot in the sky over the city, a man's voice is explaining something in level but muffled tones. His mother's answers are clipped and to the point. Gaz walks to the bottom of the stairs so he can hear better. If the man comes down, he'll dip into the living room - he just wants to make sure everything is alright.

Gaz doesn't like men. They smell of sweat or fags, they make a lot of noise and they do whatever they want. There's always a mess after they've been anywhere as well. Sometimes they shower upstairs and leave their hairs clogging up the sink. Gaz does not have a father but his mother has explained three possibilities, Gaz knows that she's lying, but it's fun to imagine. He could be a toned rugby player, or a thin and intelligent professor at the university or an airline pilot with shiny dark glasses and blond hair. Gaz wouldn't know and his mother is never straight about where he came from.

The man's voice upstairs is getting louder. It's irritated. There's a big bang on the floorboards as if he is stamping or something has fallen:

"You're not listening, love," comes the voice as Gaz creeps up the stairs. It's deep and level with the authority of a schoolteacher or a policeman, just like a man, all noise and arrogance. "It all belongs to me, all of it. I look after you, and so the money belongs to me, I pay you from it. There's no negotiation." Gaz has got halfway up, and he can hear the voices more clearly. It's his mother:

"I don't belong to you," she says. "I've set up on my own. This is my house that I rent, I pay the bills and I run the punters, I run the risks and that's why I keep the money. You've got nothing to do with me anymore – that's all done. I bring up my son here, and if you don't want anything then you're free to leave."

"You've got a nerve," he bellows. "It was me that took you

in all them years ago, and it was me who looked after you. Now I'm here to get the return. You don't get to set up on your own – that's not how this works."

"Well, it is in this house." His mother is a strong lass. You have to be in her business. Gaz has moved up to the top step and goes to just outside her bedroom door. His heart is banging in fear.

"Do I have to show you how it is, woman?" The man is not shouting now, but his voice is raised in anger.

"You'll not hit me," she answers.

"I've been bloody good to you in the past," he snarls. "From this minute, I'm back, and whatever you make belongs to me like it used to. I'll show up when I like and I'll collect when I like, and I'll do what I like to you whenever I like. Do you understand?" His tone is cold.

Gaz stands behind the door and the voices are crystal clear. His mother sits on her bed and the man stands over her. The sun shines through the curtains, Gaz can smell his mother's perfume. Like she has told him many times before, whatever happens, they are together. When they sit on the sofa downstairs with a blanket round them both in front of the telly, when she takes him to Hornsea for a day out and an ice-cream on the beach, when they sit on the wall outside the chip shop on a sunny day – 'it's me and you, Gaz,' she says. The woman tells him about one of his three possible dads and he looks up at her eyes twinkling with mischief, 'they're not here now though, Gaz, are they? It's just me and you.' That's why he's here. They look after each other.

"Close the door on the way out," says his mother and her voice is steel cold. "I've got nothing else to say. I've told you already. The business has changed. I'm on my own, and you'll just have to suck that up. Go and find yourself another poor lass to pimp out like you did me." She's tougher than most. The air prickles around Gaz's head. He can sense something is about to happen. The hairs on the back of his neck stand up and his hands go into fists at his side.

"I never wanted it like this," whispers the man. There's an almighty slap, and Gaz's mam begins a scream that is cut short almost immediately as the man gets his big hands around her neck. Gaz's mum would tell him to run. He should not be opening the door quiet as a mouse and peeping inside, but he cannot let this happen. The man is wide rather than tall and dressed in a black shell suit, Gaz can't see his face and he has the woman's neck pushed down on the bed below him so she cannot cry or breathe. Her hands claw at the powerful arms in silent desperation.

Gaz Lockwood is not considered a bad kid. He doesn't cause trouble at school and is neither bright nor dull, he's not overly noisy or boisterous, he likes video games and riding his bike when the chain doesn't keep coming off. He's an uncomplicated lad, and so, with the sight of his mother being strangled on her bed by a stranger, he does what an uncomplicated lad would do - he attacks. If he was thinking straight, he'd pick something up to help, but adrenaline fires through him; he dashes forward and shoves at the figure with his two outstretched hands. The big man in the black shell suit looks over his shoulder, turns slightly and delivers a backhand slap across Gaz's face. His knuckle catches one of the lad's front teeth, and although it doesn't come out right away, it will later on that day. This staggers Gaz and he smashes his head on the long mirror of the wardrobe while the man in the black shell suit goes back to strangling his mother.

His head swims. Gaz's mother manages to bite at one of the man's wrists, so he slaps her before he returns to strangling and pushing down on her throat while he grunts with the effort.

Gaz watches him do it. This is all he does. A man murders his mother and he watches, in stunned silence with his mouth bleeding down his chest. His eyesight is blurred, but he can hear him calling her names through gritted teeth, and the gurgling she makes under his big hands. Gaz does not know if this man is brown, black or white, he does not know what colour his hair is or what his eyes are like. The memory is vivid and blurred at the same time as he is frozen to the spot in fear and shame and weakness. He does not even remember the man leaving, but it is Gaz who calls 999 on the phone in the hallway. He doesn't remember that either.

Gaz cannot tell the police much about the man in the interviews he has in the days that follow. The world changes quickly, and there are a string of clean, well-meaning social workers who try to make him feel better. He's not allowed out on his bike, and then he's moved into care faster than he can blink. Gaz does not forgive himself for what he didn't do that day. There are so many should haves, he should have run next door for help, he should have picked up a knife from the kitchen. He should have attacked once again, he should have yelled and screamed.

He talks to a counsellor for a few years but doesn't tell her how he really feels – that's guarded. Gaz is not one to make a fuss or be fussed over either, and in the teenage years he spends in foster care, he comes to be outwardly at peace with what happened, even if he is not. He manages to hide the sleeplessness, and the rage too.

After he does badly in his GCSEs, Gaz goes to college to study uniformed services with the promise he will resit maths and English. He hopes he can be a firefighter or a copper, but the other kids are rowdy knob heads. The work isn't difficult enough and so he stops going. Because he's five foot eleven and doesn't smile, he gets a job bouncing at the pub at the end of Holderness Road. It's easy. It's where he learns how people move and fight, and how to stop them. Drunks don't feel pain, so you have to be rougher than you might otherwise be. Gaz is good at it because he's careful and spots when trouble will start. He doesn't drink and he's reliable, so he gets given better shifts. Bouncers can be as much trouble as the punters at times, they sell drugs, intimidate the customers, hit on the pretty girls and for some, the arrogance of power makes them insufferable. Gaz is not like this, by the time he actually is eighteen, bar managers can rely on him to control the door at the karaoke place on Newland Ave where gangs of girls drink and dance; and when there's a fight between two big lads from the university, Gaz gets rid of them both out the backdoor into the car park behind. Word gets round.

He works the door at the new Brewhound place in the shopping centre, but Gaz does not want to be in this line of work. He gets his GCSEs in maths and English at college, then applies to become a teacher, but his time working doors is not desirable experience. The man in the fire brigade office doesn't think firefighting is suitable for him either, especially when Gaz has a big bruise on his face where someone clobbered him with a stool. He leaves care and gets a single room in a shared house with men in their fifties. He knows this is not what he wants so he works harder.

Gaz gets a one-off job at Leeds Arena bouncing for a band and their manager is impressed with him because he can drive and isn't a dickhead. He moves up. Not because he wants to, but because there are so many in the protection game who cannot cut it, they are men who are angry, or arrogant, needy or just arseholes to work with. Next he gets paid well to work a strip club in central Leeds, and there's less trouble than you might think, people don't go there to drink usually. He makes money and as always, the managers like him because he does his job, doesn't hurt anyone, and doesn't give them any shite.

Out at Leeds there's a security firm, they have an office in a posh tower block and Gaz is invited to apply for a position. He buys a dark suit for the interview; they like him for the same reasons as always – he just does the job and doesn't smile or natter, he's focused, on time and he's got good references. He trains for close protection work. It's not as exclusive as most people think, and you don't have to be a black belt in karate or be ex-forces or know how to use a handgun. Turns out the most important quality they want is to be able to trust you, and you can trust Gaz. For a while he works twelve-hour shifts protecting a man out at Clarence Dock in Leeds – the new flats are posh and expensive. He's Chinese and the job is easy and Gaz does it well. The company like him and, because he's from Hull and he knows it, they send him back. He spends six months patrolling a big house out at Kirkella on the outskirts of the city where they have huge lawns and employ gardeners. Gaz does eight-hour night shifts checking the cameras and walking the perimeter of the grounds. A few years back the billionaire's daughter was kidnapped and ransomed. The police got them in the end but she suffered. Gaz is vigilant and on point.

After a year or so, on the balcony of an expensive Leeds restaurant overlooking the river, one of the managers introduces Gaz to someone important, he says. The man is a wide fellow named Rose with a beige suit and massive shoulders under a grey, ratty beard and bald head. He is ugly, but charming in the northern sense of things with a heavy Leeds accent littered with swear words, and a no-nonsense attitude to business and money. He interviews Gaz for another kind of protection job but it's more an informal chat. Rose has a fledgling protection company called Sandersons that's expanding. He wants Gaz to protect someone on the quiet back in Hull. There will be more in it for him if he can do the job right. Rose talks of expensive cars and holidays to far off places but he can see that Gaz is not like that at all. That's why he likes him. That's why he knows he can use him.

To begin with, they give Gaz Lilly.

CHAPTER ONE
Ela

Hull
Summer
Present Day

This is Richmond Street Garage. Gaz is here to buy a car. Our Dave suggested it. Gaz could try his luck on eBay or social media, but you know where you are with Barry. The garage is unique. If you didn't know better, you might think this is just a ten-foot-wide alleyway behind some of the posher houses off the Avenues. There are cars and vans parked all along the left side and even a rusty caravan at the end. Richmond Street don't advertise, they don't have a Facebook page or a website, you can find the number on the internet somewhere but it's not a mobile and there's no answering machine. It survives on pure word of mouth and because Barry here with his flabby face, 1980s glasses and dark-blue, greasy overalls, is an honest man. He's not the best mechanic, but the lads who work for him are. Like his stepfather explained to him, if you treat people right, that's just how they'll treat you.

Gaz has looked at a few motors already. An Audi that Barry wants nearly ten grand for and a ford Focus that's too pedestrian. Gaz wrinkles his nose at the black 1982 Capri Lazer 2.6 in front of him. The body work looks good for its age. It's a huge poser's car from the eighties.

"The colour's charcoal black," says Barry. He has a bald head with bits of hair growing just above his ears and flabby jowls. "It's just been resprayed. I've gone over the engine and it's clean enough to eat your dinner off. The tyres are new, the transmission is fine, it's got a posh original interior – she's a beauty." In truth the Capri will only start once every so often, Barry himself has never got the engine to turn over, but the work experience kid from last week who's quiet and nervous could start her every time. Barry continues:

"I won't lie to you Gaz, there's no power steering, she handles like a bastard and the fuel economy is shite - as soon as the petrol gauge gets to empty you have to fill her up right away. You've to keep an eye on the engine temp gauge as well, it a thing with Capris her age. She sounds and looks amazing but it's not your day-to-day kind of car. You'd be better off with something newer like that Focus. It's awful to reverse park too." Gaz walks around to the front and looks at the huge hood. He's driven something similar in Grand Theft Auto. The number plate reads B500 ELA. He puts his palm flat on the smooth charcoal black metal of the hood, and he doesn't know why, because Gaz isn't the sort to do anything mystical. This is just a car, but there's an energy to her. Her name is Ela, and although Gaz will never know it, she has been looking for him all this time, from owner to owner for more than twenty-five years. Ela's been resprayed many times, crashed, abandoned, refitted, and abandoned again. Children have been conceived on her front seats, blood has been spilt on them, and tears and whiskey too. She has history. It's he who is meant to find her.

"Where'd you get it?" he asks.

"It's a left over job," says Barry. "The lad who asked us to respray it has gone to jail. I just can't keep motors lying around, I haven't got the space. Time was you know, Gaz, that people loved classic cars like this, it was a hobby, now they're either skint or into racing bicycles and wear spandex shorts."

"Can I try her?" Barry nods and fishes round in his overall pockets for the keys. He hands them over. This is where the sale will end, the Capri only starts when it feels like it. There's no rush as Gaz unlocks the car door and gets in, he puts the key into the ignition, and gently turns, patiently, like this is something he already knows. The engine catches and dies. Gaz checks the gear stick and looks at the retro dashboard, he turns the key gently again and the twin banks of cylinders fire up under the bonnet in front. He gently revs her, and the sound is smooth and powerful. Gaz should really buy the Ford because he wants the car to commute to Leeds and get to jobs around town. He doesn't need anything flashy or fast, just something functional and normal, he wants to blend in like he always does, but there is more to this car. He looks over the passenger seat and down to the gearstick, then runs his palm across the worn leather of the steering wheel. She is familiar somehow. This is Gaz's car however much reason may suggest it's not.

"Two grand, was it?" asks Gaz through the open door. He knows it was four. This is a game you have to play when you are buying a second-hand car, especially from Barry.

"I've got a bad heart you know, Gaz. I take pills for it." He always says this sort of thing when faced with a price he doesn't like. Barry wipes his forehead with a handkerchief from his pocket. He must play this carefully, for he wants rid of this big Capri that doesn't start as often as it should.

"I've got cash," says Gaz.

"You can have it for three eight, Gaz, but you can't bring it back. I'm not a specialist. If it blows up or seizes then it's not my problem." Gaz nods, gets out the car and closes the door gently behind him. He pulls out his wallet. Gaz knows that cash works much faster than anything else, and so he brought enough with him.

"I'll give you three thousand five hundred right now," he says. Barry sighs. This is the best offer he is going to get without sticking it on the internet and dealing with all manner of enquiries.

"Go on, then," he does a big huffing sigh. Barry really is telling the truth about the Capri. The owner of the car has gone to jail, he got twenty-two years for rape of a minor, so the car will probably be the last thing on his mind. Barry doesn't have any of the owner documents, but Gaz won't give a toss. Barry likes cars, and if he had the space and the time, he'd keep her. Gaz hands him over a wad of twenty-pound notes which Barry will not count right away.

"Are you going to look after it?"

"Maybe," he says. Gaz doesn't strike Barry as a petrol head who would buy a car like this, he's not a poser either. It worries Barry a little. He knows Gaz is a bouncer and Our Dave has told him that he's someone you can trust. Barry shouldn't worry so much, Ela is not that kind of car anyway, she's powerful, choosy with who she trusts, and careful with those she cares for.

"One day you won't be allowed to have vehicles like this, you know, they'll all be electric. It'll be like driving a dodgem at the bloody fair." Barry always says this sort of thing when there's an old-style motor around because he thinks it makes him sound whimsical.

Gaz gets into the car, closes the door, and starts her up first time, his feet find the pedals below and he slides the gear stick into first. It's like he's driven her before. Ela edges out into the alley, and then Gaz eases his foot off the clutch to drive out of Richmond Garage through the big iron gates. Barry watches him go. It's a weight off his mind that the car is gone, and even though he let her go for less money than she's worth, he feels like he's done the right thing.

Gaz works the car out as he goes. He's driven enough to know what's where even on an old car like this. The dashboard is small, and the dials have a retro feel to them, the indicators take a bit of getting used to, and the windscreen wipers are vigorous and quick. The windows are not electric and there's an old-time smell to the springy, brown leather seats. Ela is well put together and solid, Barry was not wrong about how she handles, there's no power steering and the bonnet is long so it's hard to judge where you're turning. It will take Gaz a bit of time to get used to driving her, but perhaps not as long as he thinks. He parks the car halfway down Westbourne Ave and gets out so he can look at her from a few paces away. He doesn't know what he thinks.

Sometimes, when Gaz is not sure about something, he channels his dads. Like his mum told him all those years back, there were three possibilities: the stocky rugby player, the slim professor from the university and the airline pilot with a blonde quiff and sunglasses. You don't get through the care system without having a fantasy world you live in sometimes, even though Gaz doesn't seem the type. He knows that his real dad was probably a punter who had a condom split while he was at it with his mum, but there is no comfort in that story. Gaz can do what he wants in his own head, and he would never dream of telling anyone.

He considers the car through their eyes. His rugby playing dad would be happy with her, there's speed and aggression along with muscle, she'll be fast. The university dad would approve as well for the body work is sleek and educated, it's pleasing to the eye and Ela has history as well as grace. Gaz wonders what his pilot dad would make of it. He gets in again and drives down to the end of the street, the engine generates noise in gravelly revs, it's louder than is really necessary. He turns right into the busy traffic of Princess Ave and waits at the zebra crossing near the church where a male couple, arm in arm, walk across the road in front of him. The smaller one with the short bleached blonde hair, tight blue jeans, and a swagger, gives Gaz and Ela a beaming smile as he passes:

"You can take me for a ride in that car, love?" he yells in a deep voice. Gaz grins. His airline pilot dad would definitely approve as well.

CHAPTER TWO
Lilly

This is Grove Street off Beverley Road. Lilly looks at herself in the mirror in the little bathroom upstairs, she has long, voluminous black hair with huge curls, big eyelashes, and fake lips. The make-up is heavy, but well applied so it doesn't look tacky. She gives herself a wink and a little smile to reveal the white veneers. You could put Lilly on the front of a posh magazine.

This is a new place for her. It's a little end terrace opposite a convenience store supermarket and just off the busy traffic of Beverley Road. Grove Street is a dead end and there's usually a place to park. This is good for the punters and it's just busy enough for nobody to really take any notice of you. Normally Lilly struggles to find a property to work from because anyone who knows what she does will not want her there. She's a working girl, but not your average working girl. Lilly is pretty and smart enough to charge way more than others, and, for the last month or so, she's had protection. He's called Gaz. Working girls don't get protected, they do business alone, and if a punter gets nasty they have to deal with it. Gaz has done protection work before and Lilly has been told to look after him, she works for Sandersons too, kind of. They will have a bigger job set up in the future for him. He's tall enough with black hair, dresses neatly in clothes you might find at Topshop, and he's quiet with light blue eyes. Gaz has powerful shoulders and his legs look strong in tight trousers. Surprisingly, Gaz is not at all a dickhead. He's meant to be there during the day while she works but sometimes he stays the night in the little box bedroom because it's easier than driving back to his flat on the rough side of the city. Lilly is not used to working with men like this. He makes her cups of tea and cleans the kitchen, he'll pop to the shop. He listens to her chatter away and despite the many half openings she has given him over the last four weeks, he has never tried it on with her. She likes him.

Gaz has set up the box bedroom with his laptop on the clean white desk. He plays Rocket League and Fortnite while she works because it takes his mind off what he's hearing. Lilly deals with the punters that message her through a website, Gaz doesn't get involved, he's there as an insurance policy only. The truth is, Lilly can handle the men, usually. She is a modern version of what some folks call the oldest profession although she hates this description of it. The business is the same but the arrangement has moved online, Lilly only sees punters who have feedback on their account. She has a medical once a month and never has unprotected sex, she only does certain acts at her discretion, and doesn't work after six in the evening. Lilly is a Hull lass, she got work as a teenage stripper in Leeds and then London, but dancing is hard and grueling with nasty, seedy managers - life is much better with a string of regular punters who have dull lives. She can be her own boss and set her own prices even if she does take orders from the men in Leeds. The overheads are relatively small, just the rent on where she is and her phone, her beauty upkeep too. It's not like an underworld film with gangsters who force young girls to fall in love with them, nothing like that, this is a service industry - she works for the men she meets.

Of course, it's not that simple.

In the clean kitchen of the terraced house, Gaz boils the kettle for a cup of cocoa and looks at himself in the round mirror on the wall. He has the top button on his white polo shirt done up. Gaz is clean and smart so you won't notice him, as if he's not there, that's how he likes it. There are only a few minutes because Lilly is between punters so Gaz will have to go back upstairs into the box bedroom. It's half two on a Friday afternoon and he wants to be well out of the way.

Lilly clacks into the little kitchen and is dressed in a very short skirt with fishnets and a low-cut top that shows her cleavage. The punter has requested that she look slutty. She has big pumped-up lips and long orange square-ended nails. This look works for lots of men, she has a spray on tan every so often too. Gaz has spent time around these types of women in the Leeds strip club, his mother was the same as well. The smell of the perfume makes him feel safe rather than turned on. Lilly looks at her big white phone.

"This is a new one," she says. She has a down to earth turn of phrase despite her glamour. "I've not seen him before. Will you keep your ears open?" Gaz sips his cocoa. Coffee makes him nervous. He will keep his ears open, it's his job to look after Lilly.

"What's up with him?"

"Nothing. He's a new punter, that's all. You never know."

"I'll be upstairs. You just yell." Lilly likes having someone around when she's working and if she's in other places she'll travel with another girl just for someone to talk to between punters. Gaz hasn't helped her yet, and probably won't have to. In all honesty, Lilly does not know why he's been asked to be here. She likes that he looks after her and does not want anything back. It's refreshing. She'd like to look after him as well.

"You'd make a good husband, Gaz," she says. He's not as quick at irony as she is, and he nods. Gaz goes through into the lounge and moves up the stairs two at a time with the cocoa mug in his big hand. Lilly goes into the front room to wait.

Before he sits down, Gaz goes to the window of the box room and without showing himself to anyone outside, peeps down into the daylight. There's a light blue muscle car, probably a Merc, at the end of the street and a man gets out the passenger side. He has a leather jacket zipped up even though it's warm. Gaz pulls his head back out of the way and considers what he's just seen. From his days on the doors, he knows that preventing a situation is preferable to dealing with one. He wonders why the man wasn't driving and why he had his coat zipped up on a sunny afternoon. He'll listen out for this one.

Gaz sits down at his computer and wiggles the mouse so the screen flashes into life. It's all colour and movement. He turns his head to listen for the exchange below. Lilly has let the punter in and there's his low tones with the loud voice of Lilly as she leads him upstairs. Gaz hears them cross the landing to the bedroom, he picks up the man's aftershave through the closed door. It's sharp and cheap. He stands and goes to the closed door to listen.

There's no stereotype for the men who visit girls like Lilly. They are rich or poor, handsome hunks who work out, ratty business types, they are married or single, old or young. They're educated or stupid, tall or short, flashy or quiet and everything in between. Most have been vetted already by Lilly or the other girls she knows, some are new with feedback on the website – that means other working girls have marked them as OK.

Lilly giggles in the other room and the sound is muffled through the closed doors. The man's voice is hushed. Gaz blinks as he listens. Lilly's chatter cuts through the thin walls asking if she should get undressed and how he likes it. There's silence. Gaz swallows and narrows his eyes. The pause is a little too long to be comfortable. You get a sense of people and situations when you work doors in pubs and nightclubs, sometimes you just know that it's going to kick off, you can be wrong, of course. There's definitely something not quite right, the fact that Lilly has gone silent is the real giveaway. Gaz swallows. If he's got this wrong, Lilly will be angry and the punter will be pissed off. He listens again and hears nothing. Better to be safe than sorry.

In three steps, Gaz is out his room and he pushes open the

door to the master bedroom. There's a big mirror in the fitted wardrobe showing the bed with Lilly on the end of it and her eyes wide. The dark-haired punter has unzipped his leather jacket to show a tight black t-shirt. He's got a wild look in his eye like he's on something. In his hand is a four-foot machete.

The world stops.

It's started lightly raining outside. The landlord from the Bull over on Beverley Road is pulling a pint through the pipes to clean them out. The traffic is beginning to thicken. Two underage lads have bought a three-litre bottle of cider from the supermarket on the corner. A cyclist stops at the pedestrian crossing for a Sudanese woman in a dark purple headscarf to cross.

This is what Gaz is paid for. Many years ago, he hesitated in another room with a man and a prostitute. From his bouncing days, he knows it's much better to attack first than try to talk your way out of a spot. If you see a weapon, or someone puts their feet into the right position, the situation is a long way from being resolved peacefully anyway, and this man has a machete. It's not a video game or movie. There's no replay if he gets this wrong. Gaz launches at the punter in the black leather jacket, the man notices him, just, and his eyebrows raise, but he doesn't get chance to turn properly before Gaz is on him; his heavy right fist connects with the side of the punter's head, and Gaz is already following up with the left. This is street fighting. There is no grace or second chances, it must all be aggression and speed and hatred. Gaz's left fist hits his face at the same moment as his temple crashes against the mirror. Then he works his punches into the man, one after another in controlled anger. People are capable of getting up after a beating, Gaz knows this, and he must make sure this punter or whoever he is, will not be causing them any more trouble. It takes about twenty seconds. That's a long time in a fight, but he did have a machete. It's not a toothpick.

When it's done, Lilly looks up from the bed at Gaz with

her nostrils flared, there's nothing to say. He's come over a light sweat under his black hair and the knuckles on his right hand are bloodied. There's no telling when someone has a knife – it's not like a nineties action film where you can kick it out of his hands. Gaz has seen people stabbed before in night clubs, you wouldn't believe how much blood there is, like a washing machine leaking stinking, sticky red paint.

"You didn't have to kill him," she says in shock.

"He had a machete," comes the flat reply. "Who is he?"

"I dunno. He had feedback on the app." Gaz steps over to the window onto the street and peers through the net curtains at the cars parked below. There's the light blue muscle car a few yards down, in the front seat is a fat man with dark glasses smoking a cigarette out the open window. Gaz takes a deep breath through his nostrils. He returns to the body. The man is still conscious but drunk from the beating, Gaz drags him up by the collars on his leather jacket, manhandles him into the landing and lets him fall down the stairs. About halfway down the man gets kind of snagged with his legs trapped against the wall, and Gaz has to knock him down with his heel. The bloke lands in a mess in front of the door. He's bled on the carpet on the way down.

"You didn't have to kill him," says Lilly again from the top of the stairs.

"He was carrying a machete," repeats Gaz. Lilly can be sentimental and she doesn't like people getting hurt. Neither does Gaz. At the front door, Gaz grabs the man by his collar again, and, like he is taking out a bin liner of trash, he walks down the little path with the man sliding along the floor behind. He goes out into the street and struggles with the body to the light blue muscle car. The driver's door opens, and the blubbery man with the dark glasses steps out, he's imposing and tall, more than six feet easily. He removes the shades as he watches Gaz drag the man towards him and then dump the body in front of the car. Gaz could make some sort of comment, but he's learned to let his actions do the talking.

The big man has a bald head and a flabby face above a tight white t-shirt that shows off his tits. The blue muscle car is tatty now Gaz is up close, there's rust around the wheel arches and the windscreen is filthy. The two men stand looking at each other. The big one's lack of speech and his calm demeanor mean he either thinks he's someone hard, or he actually is. Neither frightens Gaz. He's thought of something to say.

"Your mate fell down the stairs."

"How'd you know he's my mate?" comes the reply.

"You look like you might fall down the stairs as well," sometimes Gaz surprises himself with this kind of comment, it's like the city is answering for him.

"Do you know who I am?" asks the big man. There's no trace of irony on his voice, as if he's a famous football player or a mafia boss. In fact, this is Cod and he resides on the great and sprawling fifties council estate to the north of this city called Bransholme. It has a reputation, and like all reputations, some of it is true, but most of it is shite. He's called Cod because his eyes bulge out of his head like a fish. Ironically, he's from Scunthorpe. People from south of the mighty Humber River are sometimes called yellow bellies and they refer to those from Hull as cod heads. On the Bransholme Estate, Cod has a medium to small reputation as a thug and a money lender. His sister, Shell, is a heroin addict and she's in the process of setting up weed production with the money he makes. She's also in the back seat of the light blue muscle car. It's low-level stuff, but not to Cod, he could be one of the gangsters from a Guy Ritchie film, only without the humour. He's not sure what to make of this man who's just battered his associate and then dumped him in front of the car. There's going to be a fight and Cod feels his stomach rumble in mild fear – he doesn't swing his fists unless he's sure he can win. Although this man is smaller than him, there's a sense of steel calm in his buttoned up white polo shirt and sensible trousers.

Gaz is about to knock him into next week.

Lilly steps out of the house and walks down the tiny path to the wrought iron gate. She's covered herself over with a pink dressing gown and bellows in her best fish wife shout:

"Leave it, Garry. They've had enough." She never calls him Garry because that's not his name. He looks over his shoulder and then back to the big flabby man. The rear passenger door opens and another much smaller lad gets out. Gaz didn't notice him previously. He's ratty and thin with rotten heroin teeth and black hair.

"This is Cod," says the rat man. Gaz grins at the information though he's not supposed to. "People know him round here." This is not technically true. They are on Beverley Road, and not Bransholme Estate. Nobody knows who he is, not the Romanians who sell knock off cigs on the corner, or Evan from the Bull across the road or even the coppers from Clough Road police station. Cod is hoping to expand his operation into Hull and he's decided to start by threatening and then extorting whores because it's easy and they are usually alone. He's frightened a few working girls already, usually he does it himself with the rusty machete, but he has had this lad from the estate do this one, because he had some feedback on the app that Lilly uses. Cod's attempts have not worked today. It goes to show that people in this part of the city don't know who he is. Cod's rat man had to call his name like some sort of herald.

"Whoever you are," says Gaz. "You'll have to get your lad to hospital." Cod blinks in the afternoon haze. There really is a lad bleeding into the pavement on Grove Street at 5.34 on a Friday afternoon. Gaz steps back and Lilly comes up behind him with her arms folded. The pink dressing gown has fluffy collars and cuffs. Cod goes to the front of the car and looks down on the battered man, his hand goes to his bald head in worry at what he sees. It looks like Gaz broke his jaw, and his temple is bleeding.

"This isn't over," calls Cod. "Not by a long way." A black kid with a square blue delivery backpack passes on his ebike, a man with a Jack Russell dog crosses the road to avoid Cod's car. People do have fights in the street and shout at each other around here. You ought not to get involved.

"He shouldn't have brought a machete into the house," shouts Lilly back, "that's what you get, you're lucky he's not dead." Cod picks up the man's shoulders and the ratty lad grabs his legs then they move him without much care onto the pavement and then to the open back door of the car. They stuff the body inside and Cod swaggers back to the still open driver's door with his feet splayed out in his size 15 trainers. Cod delivers a message:

"I'll be back for you," he warns. "You can't do that sort of shit to me, you'll get what's coming, lad." There's a fatalistic quality in his voice, as if it was not his idea to send a man armed with a machete into a house to threaten a woman. Like lots of things that have happened to Cod over the years – they are not his fault, and it's a cruel world that conspires against him, he must stand strong against it.

Gaz likes the silent response. Lilly has a gob on her:

"You might as well send your mam next time," she yells, "at least she's got a pair of bollocks." Cod gets back into the rusty muscle car with a grimace, he will answer in kind when the time is right for it. Gaz watches him drive away and Cod holds a middle finger up as he passes. In the back, sat next to the man he just battered, is a woman with a pale thin face and hollow eyes like a ghost, her hair is scraped up into a topknot. This is Cod's sister, Shell. She looks ten minutes away from an overdose as she stares through the car window at Lilly.

Gaz has a bad feeling about all of them.

Back in the kitchen of the end terrace, Lilly is standing at the door and having a cig as she looks into the little garden. Her fluffy slippers have got a little scuffed from walking outside. Gaz goes to the cupboard under the sink where there's a bowl and a cloth, he'll have to clean the mess in the bedroom upstairs. He hopes there's not too much blood on the carpets, the mirror will be cracked, he can replace that. The smell of Lilly's cigarette comes through into the kitchen, and into Gaz's nose. It reminds him of his mother.

"I shouldn't have battered him like that," says Gaz.

"You did the right thing," she calls over her shoulder. Normal people would have phoned the police over an incident like this, some folks would be in floods of tears at being threatened by a man with a machete, but Lilly and Gaz have been toughened over the years and events. Even though she is a premium quality working girl, Lilly still has sex with men for money, and they can be rude at times, she's danced in strip clubs, had men touch her up, fought off advances from club managers and failed to prevent these attacks in the past. Punters grunt and rub themselves off on her, they grip her arse and call out through gritted teeth. This is the life she leads. She tosses her cigarette out into the backyard, steps in and closes the door. Gaz has the bowl of cleaning materials on the floor and is rooting through the cupboard under the sink to look for stain remover.

"I'm glad you was there, Gaz," she says. He looks up.

"It's my job," he answers.

"I know, but I'm glad just the same. What are you doing?" she asks.

"I'll have to get these stains up before they dry."

"Leave it," says Lilly, "do it tomorrow. Have a drink with me, it's been a rough day. I'll make you some tea." Gaz stands up and looks down on her. She has wide eyes with full eyelashes and white teeth. Lilly is pretty.

"I won't settle if I don't sort it," he says. Her big eyelashes blink at him.

"Ok."

"It'll take me five minutes, you can make me something

then." Gaz needs a minute on his own as well.

Upstairs Gaz wipes the blood from the broken mirror, he works on the splats on the wall and on the beige carpet. There are dots here and there. At the top step he finds a big patch and he scrubs at this as well. Gaz does not like hurting people. He hopes the police will not be involved and he hopes that he keeps his job. A few months ago, Gaz did a Saturday night bouncing job at the Piper club on Newland Avenue, it was a favour. In the gents' toilets at the end of the night he found a blister pack of pills on the cubicle floor, ordinarily he would have handed them in or thrown them away, but he put them in his pocket. In the lonely one-bedroom apartment that he rents on Hessle Road, he fished them out and Googled the name. They are ADHD tablets called Adderall. Five of them will put a person to sleep for good. Gaz put them in the drawer in his bedside cabinet. You never know. He might need them someday.

By tea, Lilly means an evening meal, and she will not be making anything special. For a start, there is nothing wholesome in the fridge, only butter spread and some cheese. Lilly attends to business first – from the freezer she pulls out a bottle of expensive looking vodka and pours herself a reasonable measure in a tall glass before adding ice cubes and some lemonade. Gaz takes a seat at the little table for two in the kitchen. Rush hour is just beginning outside and the traffic on Beverley Road some twenty yards up the street is slowing. Lilly takes a sip on the vodka as she opens the cupboard door:

"Do you want beans or spaghetti hoops?" she asks. Gaz narrows his eyes in thought.

"Spaghetti hoops."

"How many toast?"

"Two, please." Lilly is not at all as daft as people would like to think. The slutty outfits do not mean she's a fool. She has to listen and watch her punters because that's the only way she can do her job. For those regulars, Lilly figures out what they want and how they want it, she watches their eyes when she moves her hips, and feels the tingle of their bodies when she nibbles on their ears. Most men aren't as kinky as they think, they like to hear her giggle so they think they're funny, they like to talk a lot and be listened to as well. It's a simple enough game to learn. The ones with mild kinks are the easiest of all because they are clear what they need, they wear lingerie themselves or like feet or shoes, they want Lilly to scratch their backs or pull their hair or call them names. She doesn't mind at all.

Gaz is a little more complex because it's clear he doesn't find her attractive. He's spent lots of his life around women covered in make-up with strong perfume and short cut dresses, so the look is mundane. Lilly has begun to work him out too, she's gathered that his mother was important to him, but he doesn't go on and on like most men do so it will take her time to get to the bottom of him. He has no significant other and as far as she is aware, Gaz does everything for himself and nobody looks after him. He values and notices small things, so, she will take care of him – just for ten minutes, and nothing too special or he would suspect she is trying to play him. Lilly makes spaghetti hoops in a bowl in the microwave and puts two thick slices of white bread into the toaster between sips of vodka. She would do more if that was what he wanted, for Gaz is pleasant to be around, he is mindful; he can take the initiative too, as he did today.

Lilly butters the bread heavily, pours over half of the hoops, and delivers the meal, then sits on the chair in front of him with the ice clinking in her drink. She gets up again to grab the tomato sauce from the fridge – where Gaz thinks it should be kept, then watches him eat. He gives her a smile.

"Thank you, Gaz," she says in a soft voice. "You're a good lad to me. I appreciate it." He is a little boy again, sitting at the table cutting into his two pieces of hastily buttered toast covered in cheap spaghetti hoops and tomato sauce. This is all he wants. Lilly has tried to get him to talk, men love to tell her things they would not mention to their wives or best friends, but Gaz is not like that. She knows he has a foster mother in the city somewhere also, and that he works out at the boxing club on Orchard Park but doesn't fight there. He's straight, he says. Perhaps Gaz won't tell her anything because he doesn't think she wants to know. Lilly likes him and she wants him to like her, so, this is how she looks after him, as a friend, no fuss just her sitting with him as he eats. In weeks gone by, she has left the bathroom door open when she showered, she's asked if he will zip up dresses that she can't reach and got him to rub fake tan into her back. He doesn't take the bait. It makes her feel warm.

"You'd make a great husband," says Lilly. Like always, she means it and like always, Gaz knows that she is taking the piss. He gets up and takes his plate to the sink where he will wash it up along with the rest of his dishes.

"Shall I make you another vodka?" he asks.

"Yes, please," she says.

She's done all she needs to do.

CHAPTER THREE
Kasia

Not a great deal has changed at The Dairycoates Inn since Ann Leatherhead went on holiday a few weeks back. The regulars are still the same, the beer is still good, the narcotics operation out the back door of the kitchen still goes on, the warehouse just off the old docks that Leatherhead kept is still in use. The product comes from Amsterdam or The Hague through Asia, probably Afghanistan, and the same guys Leatherhead used, chop and cut it with other white powders and chemicals. Then, the dealers get it out onto the streets or they just sell it out the backdoor of the pub to those they are sure they can trust. Since Kasia became Leatherhead's assistant, the place has always been clean and organised, but now the old woman has permanently gone away, it has taken on a sanitised feel. Kasia still comes to the pub on her shopper bike with flowers around the edge of the front basket, she still has her hair dyed dark red, she still does the early morning clean too; but upstairs has changed. Leatherhead's eighties style kitchen has been replaced, and the big wooden table has been chucked in a skip. Now at the top of the stairs where the carpet has been swapped for polished floorboards, there's a sleek white kitchen with black worktops and an island with stools around the edge. Kasia sits at her open laptop and there's a light cough from the top of the stairs. She looks up. Bang on time at eleven in the morning, as arranged. This is Our Dave.

"Come in," she says. As Our Dave walks into the room, Kasia climbs down from her stool and goes over to him, she holds out her hand and they shake. She looks up with her wide green eyes and her hand feels small in his, but she does not smile. This is the first time they've spoken since he got a gun to her a month or so past. That was just before Leatherhead went on holiday.

"Do you want some tea?" she asks. This is what Leatherhead would have said, only with a Hull accent and slightly different grammar. Kasia's voice is smooth and easy Polish. She sits down. She has a proud and delicate nose, high cheekbones and her red hair is swept back into a perfect ponytail.

"I've just had one thanks."

"Please take a seat. Then you can explain why you wanted to meet." Our Dave pulls back one of the stools and sits. It's one of those bouncy ones, and he sinks slightly. It's awkward. Things may have changed, but they are much the same. This might be a new kitchen and though he is seated on a trendy stool and the old table is gone; Our Dave is still opposite the most powerful dealer in the East Riding, she's not a big Hessle Road lass anymore but she's just as smart, and perhaps even more dangerous. Our Dave heard that Leatherhead retired to Florida, but he knew her, she wouldn't survive outside Hull, so she'll be dead, and Kasia here will know how that happened.

"How've you been?" he asks. This is what he would say to Leatherhead. Kasia looks at him with her green eyes, she's calm and level.

"Why did you ask to see me?" Unlike folk from round here, Kasia gets straight to the point. Our Dave does a half smile. He'll have to learn to be direct as well.

"A couple of reasons. I wanted to see if you're ok, and to make sure the agreement I had with Leatherhead is still on with you." He deals in booze, spirits specifically, and Leatherhead used to deal with everything else including heroin straight from Europe and increasingly those new chemical highs you can cook up if you're a chemist. Our Dave supplies the Dairycoates Inn with spirits, for nothing.

"I prefer it if I pay for the alcohol from you. It looks better for the tax. So, you can provide me an invoice and I'll pay. The rest is the same. You leave my business alone and I will leave you alone." Our Dave rubs his short white beard like he does.

"It's easier if I just give it to you, Kasia, like it never existed. A present from me to you."

"It's not easier for me." Our Dave nods. It's impossible to create an invoice for something you have smuggled into the country. He'll have to buy the booze legitimately himself and then make a discounted invoice for Kasia to pay. It will cost five hundred a month or so, but worth it to keep the peace with her and her organization.

"Consider it done," he says. "How are you settling in?"

"With Leatherhead gone? I think everyone is happy that she is on holiday. She earned it after many years."

"Do you know where she is? I mean, will anyone find her? Will anyone find out how she got there?"

"She's safe and cold until we can get her moved out from the fish store, and the gun your driver gave me, that's safe too. Leatherhead is not the sort of woman people come looking for. Business is good, as always." Kasia looks out of the window, the net curtains are gone, the glass has been cleaned, and there's a view to the already busy A1166 going off Hessle Road. "I wanted to say thank you, Dave. You gave me the opportunity to get a better position, and I owe you for that." Our Dave nods.

"You did me a favour too. Thank you." She looks back at him with those green eyes, they are cold and beautiful.

"Why are you really here, Dave?"

"You've got competition."

"Who?"

"A Bransholme lot. A small outfit from what I hear. They use mopeds to get their stuff out. There's a mobile phone number on a Facebook page. A lot of it is homegrown, mostly weed. They're not nice, so I've heard." Kasia gives a smile that has no humour.

"I know about them already, Dave. They're noisy and stupid. It's good for the police to see them and not my operation. They're smoke for me to hide behind."

"As long as you know," says Our Dave. Kasia is streets ahead of where Leatherhead left off. The stuff she is selling is better quality, so he's learned, and the dealers she uses are more professional. Our Dave has also heard of deaths in the heroin flats opposite the hospital, there have been overdoses and disappearances. Kasia is cleaning up like she did in the Dairycoates Inn when she first started work here. Unlike the weed sellers out at Bransholme, Kasia is sober and clinical, this is not a quick way to make money, this is her business, and she is in it forever.

"We will soon follow the Canadian and American model," explains Kasia. "Cannabis will be legal. Leatherhead knew this as well. She tried to set up the infrastructure. This Bransholme lot will burn themselves out, but thank you for the warning."

"I am your friend, if you need one, Kasia," says Our Dave. She considers him with her deep, sea-green eyes. There's no indication that she needs a friend. Kasia seems to have it all in her new and bright kitchen with the shiny black worktops. Her small hand reaches up and closes the mini laptop, almost like she's closing the meeting down.

Our Dave notices something from the corner of his eye in the door leading off to the other upstairs rooms. It's a little girl. She's perhaps seven or eight, dressed in a pink tracksuit and has a serious look on her face with her eyes narrowed. There are the same green eyes that Kasia has. Our Dave smiles at her. He's good with kids.

"Ey up," he calls.

"Back into your room, Alexander," commands Kasia. There's too much force in her voice when she has used almost none to explain serious matters to Our Dave just seconds before. At once, he understands; Kasia will not struggle at all with the running of a pub, or even an organisation that smuggles heroin into the country and distributes it, but she will wrestle with how to control a daughter who is smarter than she is. Our Dave looks down and grins. He's seen it many times before. Family breaks you in the end. The little girl disappears down the corridor and he is left with the calm, cold and professional Kasia with her laptop closed.

"I'm glad it's all working out, lass," says Our Dave.

"Thank you," she answers. "I'll call if I need anything." He stands up and seems too tall for the room.

"Please do." Kasia once again slips off her stool and approaches Our Dave. They shake. Kasia's grip seems firmer than it was.

"Look after yourself, Dave," she says.

It's two when Our Dave gets back to Avenue Cars. He drives his grey Ford into the little car park behind and puts it next to the Berlingo wheelchair carrier that's already there. Our Dave has just the three drivers, gone are the heady and busy days of the eighties and the nineties when people went out drinking and didn't have mobile phones. They just do council jobs these days for kids and folk with disabilities, Our Dave has his other business too, but that's not common knowledge. There's a young blonde woman waiting outside the back door with her handbag over her shoulder and big blue-grey eyes. She's in her twenties and has a gap in her two front teeth when she smiles. Kate works at the library across the road and she also studies psychology up at the university. She's asked Our Dave a favour, and that's why she's here.

"Ey up," he calls as he walks to the back door. She has a nervous smile for him.

"Are you sure this is okay? Are you sure they won't mind?" Kate is looking for some help with her course, and like everyone down this street she knows Our Dave. He told her she can have a word with the drivers at Avenue Cars.

"They won't mind at all," he says. "I'm sure of it."

He walks through the back door and into the galley kitchen to the office and there's the smell of coffee and something sweet as he goes in. Things have changed in the last few months; Our Dave decided to paint the whole back room and get rid of all the old furniture to make it brighter. They needed a change after what went on. The place was a right mess when that lad got shot.

There's a big round table in the centre of the room and the walls are a clean light brown with two second hand sofas and an old armchair. Another desk with a laptop and a phone is against the door to the front of the taxi office. The grate is still there for you to speak to people who just walk in off the street, but that doesn't happen anymore. Dilva and Liz sit at the white table with an open Tupperware box with biscuits between them and cups of coffee in mugs that don't match. Bev sits on the desk in front of the laptop. They all turn to look at Our Dave and the blonde lass in her twenties behind him with frightened eyes. If there was any conversation previous, it stopped as soon as these two walked in. Our Dave frowns as he stands there. It's not normally frosty. They're friendly girls.

"Who's this?" asks Bev. She's a bleach-blonde with heavy makeup on her blue eyes. You have to be careful around her if you don't want your head bitten off.

"This is Kate, she works at the library." The Kurdish girl called Dilva gives her a smile and a nod. Liz stands up and steps forwards, she holds out her hand for Kate to shake.

"She's not another bloody driver is she, Dave?" asks Bev. He feels Kate next to him go stiff with fear.

"No, she's not another bloody driver. She works at the library across the road. I just told you that."

"Well, what does she want?" Bev doesn't like anyone she first meets. She especially doesn't like young women who are attractive and smiley. Our Dave looks back to his guest and does a kind of apologetic grin. He didn't think it would go this way.

"She's studying psychology up at the university," says Our Dave. "She's looking for volunteers, you know, people who would like some therapy and what not, all for nothing, she's in her second year. It'll all be confidential. It might be good, if anyone of you wanted to take her up on it." The mood in the room darkens when Our Dave mentions the word therapy. Kate takes a step back. The woman who she shook hands with called Liz, wears a scowl to replace the smile – the thought of anyone getting under her sweet and innocent looking exterior is not welcome. At the table, Dilva looks up from under her loose headscarf and her eyes are mistrustful, she's come so far, the panic attacks are under control, she feels safe, she does not want anything to unravel what she's built these last few months. Bev stands up from the desk, she's just over five foot and still has the curves in all the right places, things haven't worked out with the man from Holland, as if she ever believed they would, and her Amy has gone off to university – that's no reason for her to go and blabber everything she feels to a woman half her age. Bev isn't going to let anyone into her secrets, she's buried them, like people in this city do with their problems.

"Why don't you try the pub down the road, love?"

"It was just a thought," says Our Dave in defence. He really did not expect this reaction. "We're all on the same side, you know." He gives Bev a mid-level angry glare because she, out of all of them, knows what it's like when you need a break.

"I'd have nothing to talk about," says Liz as she sits down. "I've just done a course on mindfulness and I'm not sure I'd have the time." Liz has begun a parent help group for those with disabled kids like her, she's good at it.

"I'm okay," says Dilva. She's learned that this means 'no thanks.' Dave realises his mistake. These girls aren't friendly to outsiders, they've been through too much on their own and they've only just warmed to each other. He looks back at Kate in apology. It was naïve for him to have brought her into the office.

"Why don't you talk to her, Dave?" calls Bev.

"I'm too busy," he says. Kate looks embarrassed.

At the back door to the carpark, Our Dave follows the girl from the library outside. She turns to him and looks relieved to be out of there.

"I'm sorry," he says. "They're not usually like that."

"The idea of therapy frightens people," says Kate.

"Well, I'm just pleased that everything is going well for you up at the university. How's the course?"

"Great. I feel like I'm meant to be there."

"You've come a long way," says Our Dave. Kate has a complex past. Her father used to drive lorries off the docks, he was a good fella, but a piss head till the end. He propped up the bar in the Avenue Pub across the road and when he lost his driving licence, he didn't go anywhere else. Her mum disappeared a long time ago and Kate looked after the old man, in exchange he taught her how to drink and she was good at it too. Our Dave used to see her staggering down the road when she was sixteen, and that was fine, but it happened every Friday and Saturday. When her old man died, she moved in with a poncy car salesman who had a big Doberman dog twice her size, he used to belt her, and the dog would drag her along the pavement when she took it for a walk down Chants Ave. They lived nearly opposite Avenue Cars down Perth Street back then. Our Dave once saw her in the street without any shoes at two o'clock in the morning, she was pissed up and covered in sick with bruises on her face, in November; the car salesman had shut her out for the night. Our Dave let her sleep in the office here. Funny how things happen. The car salesman lost his job at the Hyundai showroom just off the motorway out of Hull, and his car got repossessed. The RSPCA took the dog, and he must have said something wrong to someone, because he got filled in on his way back from a night out. A couple of weeks later it happened again, some lads bounced his head off the litter bin on the corner outside the graveyard. He got the message that he wasn't welcome down Chanterlands Avenue. Like Liam from the chip shops says:

'it's funny how folk always get what they deserve.' Kate got a job at the library and luckily for Our Dave, the house that he owns on Belvoir Street needed someone to look after it while he got the garden upgraded. She's a good tenant. It took her a long time to get counselling but when she did, she knew it was something she wanted to do in the future.

"How's the house?" asks Our Dave.

"Yeah, all good. I won't be there forever, just so you know. I'll get myself sorted and buy a place one day."

"Stay there as long as you like for me, lass. You pay the bills and look after the place. I imagine you'll meet someone and move on one day though, that's what you young ones do."

"I'm not in any rush," says Kate. "I've had enough of fellas to last me a lifetime." She still has a sense of humour, a lot of folk wouldn't in her situation. Men in general have caused Kate a great deal of grief over her short life so far.

"We're not all like that," says Our Dave. She gives him a knowing grin. He is someone she can trust.

"You pretty much are. I'll wait till the right one comes along, and if he never shows up, then that's fine as well. You have to be happy in yourself first, I guess." This is the kind of thing Hazel would have said to Our Dave when they first met, full of wisdom and sunshine as well. "You don't know anyone do you?" she asks. It's a joke.

"I'll find you someone," says Our Dave. Kate cocks her head as if she doesn't quite know what he means. "I'll find you someone who'll help with your studies, someone you can interview." She smiles again:

"I owe you."

"Pass it on," he says.

"I will." Kate means it as well.

CHAPTER FOUR
Kate

It's Monday. Like hairdressers, Lilly has the day off. She texts Gaz very early on Monday morning with a picture of her in the blow-up hot tub at her mother's house. She has a wine glass in her pale hands with long fingers and orange nails. Lilly looks washed out and her eyes are crossed. She will be in bed until Tuesday at the earliest. Gaz texts her back at seven in the morning when he wakes up telling her to have a good time and doesn't expect a reply. He stayed at the house last night rather than the grotty flat he rents above the motorcycle shop. He ran to the gym too.

In the bathroom, Gaz brushes his teeth while looking in the mirror. There are hairs in the sink and around the shower plug left by the punters from the day before. The towels are used. Gaz cleans out the bath and sink and has a wash himself. He doesn't like men.

In the kitchen, he looks out the window to the backyard with plastic, vivid fake green grass while he boils the kettle. His phone buzzes on the kitchen table, Gaz never has it on anything but vibrate just so it doesn't bother anyone. It's Wilkinson. This is the foster carer who he doesn't talk about much. He puts it to his ear.

"It's me," she says.

"I know from the number. It says your name on my phone screen when you ring."

"It's our coffee morning," she says. She knows that Gaz does not drink coffee but invites him round once a week to catch up.

"It's usually ten thirty, isn't it?"

"Make it one o'clock today. I've got someone coming round."

"Ok." The woman on the other end puts the phone down. Ten years ago, when he was fourteen, Gaz floated through

Hull's worst and busiest care homes where he kept his head down and his mouth shut. His social care notes read that he was dull and docile and quiet, so they sent him to a big flat just off Pearson Park. The lady who runs it is a tall, pin thin woman with short blonde hair and dungarees. She's sardonic. Unlike the other foster carers, Wilkinson says she does it for the money. She likes Gaz. They are still friends.

He puts on his dark pants and shoes with a grey t-shirt, anything that looks normal and won't make him stand out is good. In the street, Ela grumbles but starts first time and her engine is loud in the morning. Two kids on mountain bikes with North Face coats and grey tracky bottoms admire the car as Gaz eases her up to the junction. He takes off along Beverley Road, goes slow down De Grey Street and over the speed bumps, past the New Adelphi club and onto Newland Ave with the bustle of folk about their business. He's driving to Chanterlands Avenue. Gaz has someone to see there before he visits Wilkinson. There's a taxi office with a yellow sign opposite Dundee Street fisheries. This is where Our Dave runs his business. Gaz parks Ela on the street.

In the little car park, there's Our Dave reading his phone with the screen close to his eyes. He's dressed in jeans with a checked shirt tucked in and his sleeves rolled up to show his arms, he might be in his sixties or late fifties with a short beard and his bald head. He's old to Gaz. There's just the VW transporter van parked up, this belongs to Our Dave but Gaz has driven it lots of times before.

"Thanks for coming," says Our Dave. Gaz does not like men, but Dave is an exception, although he would never go as far to say that he likes him. He respects the man. Back when he first learned to drive, Wilkinson introduced him to Our Dave and he started doing odd jobs for him behind the wheel. He didn't pick up passengers ever, there was no insurance for that, but he'd drop packages off, get things from the shop and deliver bits and bobs to Our Dave's allotment. It didn't take the man long to find out you could trust Gaz. Periodically, three or four times a year, Gaz drives that electric VW van parked up in the corner to Scotland for Our Dave. He carries locked briefcases which he knows contain money, and delivers them to distilleries right up in the highlands where the roads are thin and the air is clean. It's lonely and sweet to drive there. Gaz brings back a case of whiskey sometimes and Our Dave trusts him because he doesn't ask any questions, drives steady, and if there is a problem, Gaz can handle himself. Our Dave has booked Gaz in to go up again at the end of July. Gaz doesn't know why he's been asked to come this morning.

"It's just a quick job, Gaz," says Our Dave. "To the docks to collect, and then back here." Gaz is not going to ask what he'll be collecting. It could be anything.

"When?"

"Now?"

"How long will it take?"

"An hour tops, there and back." Gaz nods, he won't ask for any money. Our Dave pays too well for the Scotland runs, the van is nice to drive, it's modern and electric, easier and sleeker than Ela but without the power or the spirit. Our Dave hands him the keys and Gaz goes to the driver's side, opens up and gets in, he winds down the glass. Our Dave explains the trip through the window.

"Head down to Albert Dock. There's a container there on the dockside with the back open. Get as many of the boxes as you can before they get taken to the incinerator." The Albert Dock is just to the right of Hull Marina, it's a working facility still, but the boats that arrive don't bring the silver gold in anymore. The fishing days are gone. Gaz nods. He's picked up stuff from there before and he's not going to ask Our Dave what the boxes are. They could be anything.

"How will I get in?" asks Gaz. A barrier before the docks proper stops any idiot driving too close to the boats.

"There's a kid called Josh on the gate. He knows the van.

He'll open up." Gaz nods. Our Dave leans into the window, so he is closer to Gaz and the young man can smell his aftershave. This is where he explains the details. "There's someone coming with you," he whispers. Gaz narrows his eyes. This is not usual and he already doesn't like it. "They'll help." Gaz wrinkles his nose. He has visions of a middle-aged man wearing Adidas Samba with a mod haircut who never shuts up.

"I do things alone," he says. Our Dave nods.

"I know but, this isn't one of those jobs, Gaz. She's from the library across the road. She'll know which boxes are worth getting." Gaz should not ask his next question.

"What am I picking up?"

"Books." says Our Dave, as if six hundred thousand in used bank notes to Scotland is normal, but loading up with books is not. "It's a stray container, Australian, God knows how it ended up in Hull but it's full of books – reading books for the third world. Classics and stuff. The council are off to bin them. I thought we could grab as much as we can for the library across the road." Gaz takes a deep breath. He doesn't understand Our Dave at all. One minute it's no questions asked and the next, Gaz is asked to deliver furniture donations to the Red Cross shop in town or pick up books.

"Why can't you get one of your drivers to do that?" Our Dave runs a taxi office, but they're private hire these days with three lady drivers not including himself.

"It's Monday, they're on other jobs. I'd go myself, Gaz," says Our Dave, "but you know it's not a good idea for me to show my face at the docks." Gaz nods. Our Dave has an operation that very few know about in this town, he brings in booze, spirits mainly from Europe in the back of trucks carrying furniture or grain, and it goes off to nightclubs and pubs across the UK. It is much better for everyone if he doesn't get spotted near where it all comes in.

"Right."

"You can pick her up from outside the library, now. I'll text her." Our Dave does not step back. He looks at Gaz and swallows, it's as if he wants to say something but he can't quite get it out. Gaz isn't going to rush the man. "Her name's Kate." Our Dave still doesn't back off. "She's a nice lass, Gaz. She's had a few problems in the past, but she's over them now. She's looking for someone to talk to." He is telling him something, but Gaz is not sure what it is and there's really no need to go into this level of detail. For a fellow who runs a complex and at times dangerous smuggling business, Our Dave is a bit daft sometimes. The man steps away from the van window and Gaz starts the engine. "Outside the library," calls Our Dave, "she's blonde, called Kate." He said that already.

Kate is waiting outside the library on the other side of the road. Gaz spots her because of the blonde hair falling over her shoulders, he pulls in down Marlborough Ave and parks up on the double yellow lines to wait for her. She sees the van and walks towards the passenger side. Gaz gets a clear view through the window as she approaches. She has a black vest that shows off her smooth shoulders and neck, long wavy blonde hair, sixties style sunglasses, and a tattooed line of writing on her upper left arm. She gives a big grin as she approaches the van and Gaz can see the gap in her two white front teeth. She's got that kind of indie vibe. His stomach gurgles. She opens the van door and gets in. There's the smell of light hairspray and the coffee she's just been drinking. She takes off her glasses and smiles. He likes the gap in her teeth and that she is not wearing any make up, Gaz sees her hands as she puts on her seatbelt – they are strong and well defined with a thumb ring. He swallows.

"You must be Gaz," she says. Her voice is level and calm.

"That's me," he answers. Normally he would simply say yes. He feels his palms are instantly clammy on the wheel and his throat is dry.

They drive into Monday traffic, past Walton Street Car Park and the stadium. At the lights on Anlaby Road, they join a line of waiting traffic. Kate opens the window slightly and the sweet smell of weed drifts into the van from the skatepark. Gaz hasn't said anything for fear of sounding like a fool. If you're quiet, most people will start talking anyway. Not this Kate. He can feel her eyes examine him.

"How do you know Our Dave?" she asks. Gaz is not great at small talk. He tries.

"I do him favours sometimes."

"Thanks for doing this for us."

"No problems." Gaz is better at talking to women, not in terms of chatting them up, but they generally have less to prove. "I just do what Our Dave tells me to do."

"Do you work for him?"

"For favours, aye. I'm his delivery man, as well as other things." You have to follow up with a question. Gaz does this because it's much better to have people talking. He's a listener. "How long have you worked at the library?"

"About a year. I used to work at the pharmacy next door," she says. "I kind of like books, and I like people too. I do a psychology master's part time. So, it's books in the day with the studying and the clients at night." Kate has been off the booze for a year now. She feels more together because she doesn't have a constant, anxious hangover and she doesn't have to worry about when she'll get her next cider.

"Sounds hard."

"I love it. It's finding out about people that I like." Gaz drives steady, the traffic is thin. He looks down and across at her. He doesn't want to notice, but he can see her smooth collar bones and the perfect curve of her shoulders.

"Have you known Dave long?" she asks.

"A few years, he helped me out one time. I kind of owe him."

"What did he do?" She's quick with her questions. As they

drive towards the hospital, they join another queue of cars waiting at the lights. He slows in the line of traffic and stops. Without knowing why, Gaz comes out with the truth, as if he can't stop it from jumping out of his chest.

"He kind of saved my life once." It has humour in it, so it's not to be taken too seriously.

"Me too," says Kate. Her answer is not serious either.

"We both owe him, then," says Gaz. He is not normally humorous, especially with someone he doesn't know, but there is something about her, perhaps it's Gaz's airline pilot dad speaking through him. Kate asks questions. It used to be that Kate wanted to fix people's problems, now she's older and more educated she realises all she can do is help them see and mend the issues themselves. At the same time, it might help her fix herself.

"Is this your van?"

"It's Our Dave's." Kate likes the muscles in Gaz's legs against his tight trousers and the smell of his aftershave, she likes that he seems nervous around her. There are big red marks on Gaz's knuckles from where he punched the man carrying the machete a few days before.

"What did you do to your hand? she asks. Her questions are good for conversation and people who are happy to reveal themselves, but bad for Gaz. He does not want to tell her much about himself or his life. He wishes he'd worn his driving gloves.

"I hit a fella."

"How come?"

"To stop him hitting someone else."

"You're a fighting lad then?"

"Not if I can help it. I'm in security." This answer, he hopes will explain that he is not a thug. He searches for a question that will keep her talking. He should ask her something. His mouth is dry and he looks ahead at the line of traffic waiting at the lights.

"Our Dave doesn't trust everyone," she comments. Gaz wonders if she knows that his business is not really the taxi office opposite Dundee Street Fisheries. "He kind of told me about you."

"What did he say?"

"He said you were a nice lad, and that you'd had your problems, but you were over them now." Gaz grins at this. Our Dave would have had the same awkward talk with Kate as well. It makes him more nervous. "Do you live down the Avenues?" The lights change to green in front and the traffic begins to edge forward. This is not what he is used to. This is not how a conversation goes. Ordinarily with Lilly or the guys from the gym, Gaz can ask a few choice questions and they will run with it, rambling on and on so that he can drift away and just listen. Kate asks questions. If this is the way it's going to be, and if she asks anything too personal, Gaz is going to have to lie.

"Hessle Road, above a motorbike shop."

"Our Dave told me that you're reliable. He said you were reliable and quiet." Gaz does not know how to respond. He wishes he could channel his airline pilot dad on the spot, but Gaz can only think of clever things to say in retrospect when the events are all over. He'll have to rely on himself.

At the end of Neptune Street there's a barrier. Normal cars can't get up here but the security guard knows Our Dave's van, like he said, so the red fence goes up and they drive along the side of the dock. He doesn't go too far, just up to a big, rusted metal container with the back open and inside, there are boxes stacked up and some fallen over. Our Dave gets to hear about things that are free here. Kate from the library has first pickings. Cancer research will be here later. Then they'll go off to be burned.

Kate picks through the boxes of books. They're sets of classics meant for the developing world with Charles Dickens, Chinua Achebe, Steinback and bibles too. She goes through and looks for the books she thinks people will want to read then puts them at the edge of the container for Gaz to put into the car. She's a good worker. Her baseball trainers are sensible for the job, and without socks, Gaz can see the back of her ankles. She is strong too, in a wiry way, she lifts and shifts the boxes and there is no fannying about. Gaz takes her in as he moves the boxes to the van. He sees the line of text in a tattoo on her forearm in detail but he can't read it, he sees her smooth wavy hair is more strawberry blonde with slightly dark roots. He likes her. He's not sure why.

In twenty minutes, they are back on the road driving to Chants Ave. Gaz puts the radio on so she can't ask him any more questions - he likes the questions understand, but revealing himself is against his training. She talks over the loud sound of radio 4 – this is Our Dave's van so that's what it's tuned to.

"You work in security then?" she asks.

"A private company. Some people are proper horrible."

"Why do it?"

"It pays the bills." In fact, Gaz is not sure how he would handle a real job, there'd be too much stress and people talking, too much muck and mess as well. There's a silence between these two, space and time that normal folk would fill with chatter. Gaz is not the kind to go on and on, and Kate is not afraid to be quiet.

"You don't talk a lot, do you?" This is more a statement than a question.

"I'm not used to it," says Gaz in his defence.

"I like that," she says. Kate senses in this man, a challenge. Lots of people are wide open, and if you listen, they'll spill the whole of their story. They'll tell you it all, that their husband cheated on them, that they were fired from their job, that their parents' divorce affected them and all the rest – just as long as it's not their fault they'll tell. Kate is in the second year of her psychology master's and so, she has two clients who she works with for free. In order to find out about them, she must also offer up herself. This is how it works. Gaz here, driving the van with his bruised knuckles on the wheel, is a closed book. Kate is a closed book too, but you wouldn't know it because she'll tell you all sorts, she'll chat and ask questions, she'll listen to you as well, but you won't find out about what makes her tick. Gaz here doesn't care if you know he's quiet, but Kate would rather you didn't find out that she's got something to hide. They drive back along Walton Street with the big, deserted car park on the right-hand side and the stadium lonely behind.

"You know that Our Dave set us up," she says. Gaz takes his eyes off the traffic to look over to her for a second.

"Set us up for what?" he asks, and realises his mistake straight away. He is too naïve at times.

"I need people to interview for my psychology course." Gaz waits for a gap in the traffic. The transporter is smooth and electric under his feet without the fuss of gears or a clutch.

"Why can't you use Our Dave?"

"He said Hazel would kill him if he started talking to me, besides, he's too old. I need someone younger." Gaz drives over the railway tracks and the wheels of the transporter hardly rumble, he turns left down Chants Ave.

"Don't you get people referred to you?" He knows more about counselling than Kate might think.

"We do, but I was looking for local people."

"Okay," says Gaz. This is a good way of saying he heard, but doesn't want to give an answer. She makes him nervous.

Gaz parks the transporter on the wide path next to Chants library on the corner of Marlborough Ave. They unload the books from the back and Kate works as hard as Gaz does. There are no fingernails to snap or high heel shoes to wobble on. He sees that she breaks a sweat. Outside when they have finished Gaz closes the back doors of the van and Kate returns to talk to him. She smiles and he sees the gap between her front teeth and her smooth blue eyes. She's worked hard. Our Dave was right about her, she is a good lass.

"Did you think about what I said, about being interviewed. It wouldn't take long. You might not be what I'm looking for." Gaz doesn't smile back at her. He thinks about the blister pack of Adderall in the drawer of his bedside table. He doesn't want to get involved with anything, not even a friend, and not someone who wants to ask about his problems – he's had a gutful of well-meaning counsellors to last him forever. Kate has cool blue-grey eyes that examine him. She wouldn't like him anyway if she really got to know him, but Gaz cannot help himself, it's as if someone else is speaking through him:

"What are you looking for?" he asks. Kate might as well be honest.

"Someone who needs help, I guess."

"Is that me?" asks Gaz.

"I don't know. You don't say a lot."

"You said you liked that."

"I do."

"We could just meet for a coffee," he says. It is the best possible answer he could give, then he can fob her off if she ever does follow through with it, but he knows he won't.

"That sounds like the best idea." He nods and is about to step round to the driver's side. "You better give me your number," she says.

CHAPTER FIVE
Wilkinson

Gaz has swapped the transporter for Ela. This is Pearson Park, opened first in 1860 as a place for working people to be outside. The homes of stature and merit around the edge were to keep wealthy people living in Hull. Those big houses are homeless shelters now and care homes, or they've been carved up into flats like Wilkinson's. Gaz is here to show her the car as well as chat. Wilkinson likes things that are quirky because she's quirky too. The both of them stand outside the big house where she used to run a foster home for teenagers on the second floor. Wilkinson is tall with short blonde hair and one long earring, her face is wrinkled from all the smoking, she's wearing denim dungarees with a black roll neck jumper and battered Doc Marten shoes.

"How much did you pay?" she asks as she looks at the car.

"Three and a half grand," answers Gaz.

"You'll be shafted if anything goes wrong, it'll cost a bomb to get it fixed." Wilkinson swears like this with whoever she speaks to. She is genuine Hessle Road originally but with a sexuality that wasn't considered normal in the seventies or the eighties down there. There was a woman she lived with once upon a time, they set the foster home up together. Gaz never did find out what happened with them both and he never met the woman either. You don't ask Wilkinson about things like that.

"If it falls apart, I guess that's the way it's meant to be."

"You don't have to be all fatalistic," she says. Wilkinson is a mixture of cruel and kind, she is half educated and foul mouthed at times too. Just like she never fitted on Hessle Road, she doesn't really fit in with the bohemian types that live round here.

"I think she likes me," says Gaz.

"It's not a person, Gaz. It's just a car." Wilkinson has her long arms folded as she looks down her nose at the charcoal black Capri. "You've always been full of shite." She can say this to him because it's not true at all; people in this city will only take the piss if they care for you. When he first came here at fourteen, Gaz didn't say a thing, she didn't get past 'hello, how are you?' for six months. He gives her a very tiny smile. Wilkinson likes this.

In Wilkinson's kitchen there's a big window that overlooks Pearson Park and she's got a rectangular oak table under it. The kids she used to look after ate here, Gaz did too. The kettle boils and Wilkinson comes to the table with a cocoa and green tea, she sits opposite him. The kitchen has warmth to it, with a line of pots and pans hanging over the big stove and there's a spice rack on the wall with a bookshelf above. Wilkinson likes to cook, she says it saves money. She sips her green tea and Gaz can see that the wrinkles are deeper across her forehead. There used to be three or four teenage lads here, some stayed for a few months and others for years, like Gaz. Wilkinson is good with teenage boys who have attitude because she has attitude as well, it kind of cancels out. Gaz got the feeling that she stole a little of their spirit as well, just to keep her young. The big flat seems empty without the teenagers.

"How's the recovery?" asks Gaz. Wilkinson had breast cancer at the end of last year. That's why the kids are gone. The doctors removed one of them and she suffered although Wilkinson just says the hardest thing was having to give up smoking. She's been for tests and there's another lump on her back. The biopsy came back and the prognosis was not good. The doctor was very kind with her, but Wilkinson will soon be sicker than she has ever been before, and there's no stopping this one whatever they try.

"It's all gone, Gaz," she lies. "I'm better." There's no emotion on her face and the lips are thin and cracked.

Wilkinson wears a roll neck jumper that makes her look thinner even than she is, and the bags under her eyes are darker than usual too. There's no need for small talk. She gets to the point.

"I'm selling the place, Gaz," she says. "I'm moving away."

"Right." At once he wonders why she's telling him.

"You're probably wondering why I'm telling you."

"Yeah."

"There's nobody else to tell." This isn't really true. Wilkinson may be a prickly character at times, but she does have friends in this city.

"Where will you go?"

"Spain," she says. She looks at Gaz to see that he's narrowed his eyes in mistrust. "I've got pals there, in Valencia," she takes another sip on her green tea. "I've done my time here, Gaz. There's nobody left for me to look out for, and so I might as well go. I'll get a few quid for the flat."

"It'll take a while for it to sell."

"No, I've done it cash. You know those companies who pay you quick and it's cheap."

"You've been ripped off then?"

"Not really. It's just a flat. I need to go."

"When?"

"In a few weeks."

"You'll have to get packed up," says Gaz. Wilkinson looks out of the big window to the park outside. Others might have expressed regret or emotion that she was leaving, but Gaz sees right through to the practical problems first. She's taught him well.

"Just a few things, that's all I'll need. It's just stuff. The rest will be house clearance. You can have anything you want."

"I thought you were going to start looking after kids again."

"Me too, but plans change."

"Is this goodbye, then?"

"Not right now, Gaz. You can come and visit me when I get settled." He looks back at her and she is staring at him with her wide green eyes. "I haven't got many years left. I need to live a bit before I go. I look in the mirror and all I can see is an old, thin lesbian with wrinkles." She wouldn't share this with anyone else.

"You are an old, thin lesbian with wrinkles," he says. She grins and shows her straight white teeth. When she smiles the world lights up a little. There's nothing she likes more than the truth. "You're a beautiful lass," he says and she looks away. Gaz doesn't know why he says this. It just came out of him because it's true.

"You shouldn't say things like that to me. You'll make me cry, and I don't believe you anyway."

"I'm too long in the tooth to tell lies, Wilkinson, and you're the smartest person I know." She doesn't look at him because tears will come if she does. She likes that he says he's long in the tooth, he must be all of twenty-two, but there's a strange wisdom to him. The old Gaz, the one that she took in as his last chance, he would never have told her that, he wouldn't have been so brave. It's out of character.

"Something's upset you," she says.

"How do you know?"

"You're easy to read, Gaz. The more you try to hide it, the easier it is to spot." She looks at his hands, the knuckles are split and bruised from when he belted the man with the machete.

"I had a fight."

"It's not that." Gaz has been in too many fights to let them worry him.

"You can't help me, Wilkinson, why would I bother you with it? You never bother me with any of your stuff."

"Talking helps, Gaz. I have folk I talk to, I have girlfriends."

"Well, I'm not very good at it."

"Just because you don't talk a lot doesn't mean you're not good at it. I think you do just fine."

"It's you who called me over here, Wilkinson. What do you really want?"

"I want to know you're going to be ok, and I want to be sure you know that I'm still here for you, even when I'm gone."

"You mean on the phone?" The thin woman swallows. Gaz lost his mother and Wilkinson is conscious that over the years she has become the woman's replacement in some form. It was not at all what she wanted, but the facts cannot be altered. She wants to hurt him as little as possible.

"Yes, kind of. Are you okay for money, Gaz?"

"Aye."

"You know the things we talked about all these years. You can live a life on those lessons, a good one too."

"I'm glad you're going, Wilkinson, after what happened to you last year."

"You know what I'm like, Gaz, I don't need anyone, or at least I like to think that I don't. I'm like you. They cut one of my tits off, Gaz. There wasn't much of it there anyway. Ironic really. When I was in my twenties I would have paid to have them both cut off." There's a coarse humour to this lass. You can hide behind it, and lots of people in this city do. Gaz looks into her green eyes and he can see the fear there, buried.

"You could have told me how bad it was."

"What good would that have done?"

"It might have made you feel better. Didn't you think I was tough enough to deal with it?"

"I know you are, Gaz. There was no need to bother you, that's all. It's over now anyway. That's why I'm leaving. I need to do something different with the time I have left."

"I'll give you a lift to the airport," says Gaz. "You just let me know when." Wilkinson smiles at him and her eyes glow.

CHAPTER SIX
Sandersons

Gaz is in Leeds. It's not his favourite place. The traffic is always bad and the road system is complex. This is a real city with huge, high-rise tower blocks and wide streets rammed with traffic jams that stretch for miles. This is where Sandersons have their headquarters and Gaz is here for a morning meeting with Rose. He's left Ela in the multi-storey car park next to the city. It's a short walk to the curved office tower that overlooks the river Aire and the old docks. In front and around him are trendy hotels and chain restaurants with outside seating, grey glass covers the high-rise office blocks and there are gaudy, soulless coffee houses. It's just past ten. Gaz wears a navy jacket and trousers over a dark polo shirt with the top button done up. He knows the suit is cheap, but it will give these men an impression of him that he wants.

There's nobody else in the foyer of the office complex and he smiles at the receptionist as he walks to the lifts. There's no need to give his name – there must be a hundred companies in this block. On the seventh floor he steps out the lift and walks down the hall, past empty offices to a closed door at the end. The name on the dull metal sign reads 'Sandersons'. He knocks twice, and waits thirty seconds before he hears a loud 'come' from within. He opens the door and steps in.

This is a conference room with an oval table that seats eight or more, there's a large computer screen and an unused brand-new flipchart stands in the corner. Two men sit at the end of the table facing the door, Gaz has met them before. The thin Pakistani looking man in a crisp black suit is Saif, he's small with glasses and delicate fingers that work the keyboard of a laptop. The other is Rose with a grey beard over wonky teeth and his bald head above deep frown lines in his forehead. He's wearing a tight pink shirt that hugs his muscles and fat gut under the grey jacket; he might have been a prize fighter in his day - he's past it professionally, but he can still handle himself, Gaz senses it. He also has a laptop open in front of him and he's wearing thick rimmed black glasses that might just be a fashion accessory.

"Sit down please, Gareth," says Rose. His accent is hard Leeds with a strong r sound. He says he's a recruitment officer for Sandersons, but Gaz knows he's the boss. Saif is second in command and has that laptop permanently open. Gaz heard that he trained in law, he also heard that he taught uniformed services at Leeds College and got sacked for fraud.

"Thanks for coming in Gareth," says Saif as he takes his eyes from the laptop screen. Gaz put down that his name was Gareth on the application form even though his real name is Gary. Just in case. He doesn't know why.

"How are you getting on?" asks Rose.

"Okay, thanks."

"I heard you got a new car." Gaz wonders how he knows.

"It's second hand."

"Lilly says it's a classic."

"It's a Capri." Rose takes off his glasses and smiles. It's perhaps the first genuine emotion Gaz has ever seen on the gruff, solid man.

"I used to have one of those," he says.

"Did you invite me all the way here to talk about my car?" Gaz is not ordinarily combative.

"No." Rose shakes his head. Saif cuts in with his thin, reedy voice.

"We've called you in to talk about the altercation that you had with a client on Friday seventh of July. You reported it in, and the whole event was logged." He uses overly long words to make himself sound more important.

"He wasn't a client," explains Gaz. "He was there to extort money. He threatened Lilly and so I hit him."

"The report says that you did more than just hit him."

"I know. It was me that called in the report. It was me that told you." Gaz can feel his voice rise a little, although Rose and Saif probably won't notice.

"That worries us, Gareth." Rose shuts his laptop as if to speak more candidly. "You're a professional. You can't assault people – even if you think they're a threat. You neutralize, not attack. You were too heavy handed."

"He had a machete."

"Maybe," says Rose, "but you're trained to deal with situations like that. You didn't need to hurt him."

"Let me cut in," says Saif. "This is a legitimate business, Gareth, we're moving what was a sleazy and dangerous activity off the streets so that we can give clients a safe and professional service. You're there to make sure it goes smoothly. As we understand it, the individual that you assaulted does not want to follow this up with the police, but he could, and then we'd be in a difficult position. Nothing we do is illegal - this is not a criminal enterprise. We need our employees to understand that gangster tactics and violence have no place within our organisation."

"I'm self-employed," says Gaz. "You've made that clear in all your documentation. My client was under threat." They are trying to make Gaz uncomfortable. Rose begins again:

"You didn't need to go that far." This big Leeds fella in his mid-fifties has a cold stare and a sense of rigour. "The law is very clear – you can use reasonable force as a security officer, nothing more. We have to comply with the law. Your actions overstepped your duty."

"Is that why you asked me to come here?" says Gaz.

"Yes," says Saif. "If this had been an incident in Leeds or Manchester, or Birmingham, then we would have to let you go. As it is, we're just going to give you a warning."

"In short," says Rose, "you beat someone up again and you'll be fired. The police will also be involved. Lawyers can make up all sorts of lies about people that would be believed, especially if they have a history of criminality like you do,

Gareth." This is an old school threat. Gaz looks into Rose's dull grey eyes across the table, there's the whir of the fan on Saif's laptop. The strip light above their heads flickers. "Do you understand?" Gaz nods.

The law on prostitution is clear. It's not illegal to sell sexual services, but it's against the law to run a brothel, so pimps are prohibited as well as madams. The company that Saif and Rose work for gets around this by saying that Lilly is self-employed. Like many big companies, they twist the law to make that which is criminal legitimate. This is how the world works, modern day slaves have contracts with their employers, oil companies manipulate governments, young men are sent to murder other men in the name of war, and it is all above board, all good and all correct. Gaz wrinkles his nose. He wishes he hadn't told them what happened.

"Is that everything?" he asks.

"Not quite." Rose slides a piece of paper and a pen across the table to Gaz. "Sign this please," he asks. "It's just a record of what we've discussed." Gaz takes the pen and scribbles a signature across the dotted line under a list of points without reading it. He slides it back to Rose.

"We do need people like you, Gareth," says Saif. "This is still a potentially dirty business and we need your muscle, but we need you to be smart about it. You need to control yourself, be a professional."

"Do I get expenses for this trip?"

"You're self-employed," says Rose, "take it off your tax bill at the end of the year." Gaz knows a real thug when he sees one. Rose has big, working man's hands and his beard is unkept, the skin on his cheeks is marked with pocks and uneven. Like the company he works for, Rose is just one step away from the streets.

"No more punch ups then," says Saif. "If it comes to anything heavy, take a step back. Do you understand?" Gaz nods.

This is Wednesday. Lilly has shaken off her hangover from the weekend, and the house smells of perfume and hairspray with an undertone of the fags she's smoked out the back of the kitchen door. Gaz returned late morning, he left Ela at Avenue Cars and borrowed Our Dave's transporter to do a job for the man – he's filled the back with sacks of topsoil for the allotment. Gaz will drop it off after Lilly has finished working.

Gaz makes toasted cheese sandwiches in the frying pan – one with a little chili for Lilly and the other with extra cheese. She stands next to him while she uses her phone connected to the charger plugged into the wall. The long orange nails log into her app and she turns on the green available button.

"Where did you go this morning?" she asks, not in an accusing way either.

"Leeds."

"To see those fellas?" Lilly knows who they are.

"Aye."

"What did you do wrong this time?"

"It was that lad I beat up the other day."

"You were doing your job, Gaz." He shrugs his shoulders. "We don't have to work for them, you know. We could do it on our own." Gaz shakes his head as he carefully turns over the cheese sandwiches in the pan. He heard his mother talk about that the day she died.

"I don't suppose you're going to do this forever." He turns to her and she looks back at him with her big eyebrows and voluminous dark hair over her shoulders, she is already in full make up for the working afternoon and early evening ahead.

"It won't be long for me," she answers. "When I've got enough to buy my sister's house for her, I'm moving in there." Gaz has heard this before. She plans to help her older sister with her mortgage on the house she has out at Hedon where the streets are quiet and clean, then she'll give up the life of a working girl, study level three beauty at college and open up a spa. Gaz serves up her extra hot sandwich on a grey-coloured plate, she takes it and sits down. He knows that Lilly does not save any money at all and that she spends on trinkets, handbags and outfits. Her nails alone cost a hundred quid every three weeks and she holidays whenever she can, her job pays well, of course, very well, but Lilly knows how to spend. Gaz wishes he could help her more. Growing up poor and without his mother has taught him to be tight and careful and prepared. He saves for a rainy day, because for Gaz, there is nobody on the flat earth who will help him. Lilly at least has a legion of family, cousins, friends, and ex boyfriends who she could turn to, she has a big heart and people like her. She eats half her sandwich and takes sips from her mug of tea. Her phone pings, then pings again three times in succession. It'll be punters.

The working afternoon starts.

Gaz disappears upstairs when the men arrive. There's a regular who stays for a good hour, he's from out of town and drives a works van which he parks round the corner. Gaz hears them giggling downstairs. More follow. Next is a ginger kid who looks too young to get served in a pub, then a fat man with long hair, then a bloke in a suit with a beard, most of them shower. There's a workman type who stinks of booze and so Lilly turns him away – it's not uncommon that she does. Gaz plays Fortnite without sound as she works. He hears her dirty talk and her groaning in real or false pleasure, there's the rhythmical banging of the sofa or the bed against the wall and the relief from the back of the punter's throats. He makes her cups of tea between clients, and she smokes a cigarette out the back door while she readjusts her hair and make-up. The last punter of the day is another regular, and has a request for some outfit so she has made time to get ready. She looks tired, for the job is not just about her body, but part of her soul perhaps. While Gaz is listening to this last man finish off on Lilly in the bedroom with loud grunts and gasps, he thinks about Kate from the day before. He thinks about her ankles and the gap between her two white front teeth, he hopes that she sends him a message, but dreads it more.

At seven, when the last punter has gone, Lilly runs a bath and makes herself some toast with the radio on. She's had a fairly steady day and because it's a school night she's not having a drink. She says her stomach hurts. Gaz picks up all the used towels from the day and puts them in the washing basket. He turns off the boiling taps from Lilly's bath. Once she's in it, Gaz says he's going to the gym. She has her music upstairs and Gaz laces up his trainers.

"I'll lock you in," he calls up the stairs.

It's half eight. The sun is just beginning to go down over the rooftops as he jogs back along Beverley Road. Like always, Gaz doesn't go fast, the jog is more of a warm down after the boxing training. They did circuits and used light weights that train your muscles to be quick and strong but not so big, and Wednesday is never about sparring, so Gaz never has to get in the ring with anyone. He doesn't want to hit people - that's what he does in his day job. He's going to drop in and see Lilly one last time before he drives back to his room above the motorcycle shop on Hessle Road. At the house, he turns the key in the yale lock and opens the door. The music is still on in the bedroom.

"I'm back," he calls up the stairs. There's no answer. Gaz goes into the kitchen to get a glass of water and, as he fills a plastic beaker, he notices out of the corner of his eye, that the back door is open by an inch. She must be outside. He opens up and looks out into the darkening sky. There's a chair where she sometimes sits next to a white ashtray on the floor, but the square of paving stones with a rotary washing line in the centre is empty otherwise. He finishes his drink, and goes to the bottom of the stairs. The music is still loud, and suddenly, his mouth is dry. Gaz takes the stairs three at a time and goes into the bathroom, the bath is still full with bubbles and the water is stone cold. In the bedroom, the wardrobe is open and some of Lilly's clothes are strewn on the bed, the little speaker pumps out noise, and Gaz pulls the chord from the back of it to switch it off. In the new silence, Gaz checks the box room with his computer in and - it's just as he left it. He checks the bathroom once more and puts his hand down into the bath water to find nothing but bubbles. In the bedroom again, her house keys are on the bedside table.

It's as if she has just disappeared.

He calls her phone and it goes straight to answer machine. In the kitchen he examines the lock on the back door, the wood around the latch has been forced open leaving the white gloss wrecked. There are marks left by a crowbar on the frame. He goes down the garden to the back latch gate that swings out onto the ten foot and opens it up. He looks one way and then the other, there's nothing but wheelie bins and weeds. On the ground just outside the door, he finds one of Lilly's broken false fingernails.

Gaz's chest begins with horror. His stomach churns.

She's gone.

CHAPTER SEVEN
Lilly

Acting without proper consideration can lead to errors, Gaz has seen videos on scientific methods. He must take this slowly and he must be calm. Lilly would never go anywhere without her phone – it's big, white, and studded with fake plastic diamonds and her name is written on the back in gold letters. Her phone is here somewhere. Gaz finds it upstairs under the pillow, there are two missed calls and lots of messages – he can't unlock it anyway. Lilly has been banned from social media sites so many times that she has back up accounts, and she has a backup phone too, it's an old smartphone. Gaz opens his map application and scrolls down to see if he can see her second icon – it's a picture of a Pokémon, her favourite one, an Umbreon. He clicks the button and the black and yellow cat circle moves along the map towards Leeds on the motorway. He grins. The sneaky cow managed to take her spare phone with her. It must be in her handbag. He zooms in to where the picture is on the map and it is still moving along the M62 into the centre of Leeds.

There is still no need to panic. Gaz must consider all angles and possibilities. It won't be the tall thugs from Friday – this is too professional for that. It could be an ex or a punter even. At the front door he checks the map again. The icon has stopped. He zooms in. Leeds. Near the river – close to where he was the day or so previous. Gaz will need to get there as quickly as he can. He checks the time – it's nine.

Before he leaves the house, Gaz forces the back door lock into place, he makes sure to check the plugs are pulled out the sockets and that the cooker is off. In his little rucksack, there is everything he needs, a spare charger, another phone, aspirin, wet wipes and a twenty-pound note hidden in one of the inside pockets. He also has Lilly's trainers and a cap that she almost never wears. In the top drawer of Lilly's bedside table there's a little taser that she said a punter bought her for protection. It's black with two prongs on the end and a big red button that makes the electricity buzz between them. Gaz doesn't like weapons like this, you can't rely on them at all. He puts it into his inside jacket pocket just in case.

Outside, Gaz remembers that he left Ela up at Avenue Cars and he has Our Dave's transporter which is full of the topsoil he picked up at the garden centre earlier. He takes a deep breath and sighs. He hasn't got time to get his own car. Our Dave won't mind him borrowing the van – although Gaz knows he will. He should send the man a text to explain what he is about to do, but there isn't time. If anything happens to Lilly, this will be Gaz's fault. He'll get her back and return the van before morning, it will be that simple.

The route out of Hull is quiet in the darkness of a summer night. Gaz goes past the big hospital onto the flyover to the main road. The dual carriageway cuts out along the Humber and the lights of the bridge twinkle red and white in the darkness. He drives steady, and the electric motor of the transporter van hums dishwasher soft around him as it picks up speed. Gaz needs the silence. His face is illuminated by the dashboard as he drives with his mouth a straight, serious line across his face. He checked where Lilly's phone is, and pumped the postcode into the satnav, it's a hotel on the river Aire, one of the big multinational ones. There are things that run through Gaz's head as he drives at the speed limit of seventy on the deserted inside lane. What if she's not there? Who's got her? How will he get her back? The darkness of the future does not worry him so much now he is moving towards it. On the seat next to him, his phone buzzes, an unknown number is calling. He presses the button and it connects to the van audio - he takes the call.

"Hello, is that Gaz?" It's a woman's voice, the accent is smooth and well-spoken.

"Yeah?" he answers.

"This is Kate from the library." He gave her his number the other day. He did not really expect her to call. Worry runs up his legs to his knees and he grips the wheel a little tighter. The speedo climbs to seventy-two.

"Hello," he says.

"How are you?" she asks. Gaz does not need this right now. "Are you still on for that coffee?"

"Sure. I'd like that." There's the truth coming out of him again without him being able to stop it. He wants to see her.

"Tomorrow morning?"

"I'm on a job right now. It depends on how I get on. I might not get back till late." Gaz does not want to say that he might not get back at all.

"Eleven then?" says Kate.

"Ok. I'll message you beforehand." The night around him darkens as he drives, the speedo climbs upwards, there's the sound of the wheels on the tarmac below and the rush of air past the driver's window that is open just a fraction.

"Great," she answers. Gaz wants to stay on the line to her. He wants to hear the way she talks and the way her sentences flow.

"I'll let you get on then," he says, because he doesn't know what else to say and the awkwardness of speaking to her is worse than the loneliness of the M62 in the summer evening.

"Are you ok?" she asks. It's an odd question from someone he hardly knows.

"Yes," he lies. "Why?"

"Something in your voice."

"I'm driving," he answers.

"It's not that." What's the point in lying to her? He hardly knows her anyway.

"Something's happened," he says as if admitting it to himself. "Something's happened and I have to sort it out."

"Is it bad?" Kate does not ask what it is, but rather how he feels about it. Maybe she doesn't want to know.

"Yeah, it's pretty bad."

"I don't know you. Gaz, but if it's anything I can help with and if you want to talk, I can do that." He's not used to this.

"It's up to me to get it fixed, and there's nothing anyone can do. It's down to me, but thanks for asking."

"Do you want to tell me about it?" Gaz feels his hands grip the wheel. Kate is good at opening people up. She gives them the space and they walk into it. If she sat in front of him, looked into his eyes and spoke in her smooth voice – he would tell her everything he has kept hidden all these years. Perhaps it's the stress of what he is going to have to do that is affecting his emotions – he must be careful, Gaz must trust the way he's trained himself, to keep it all guarded.

"It's just a job to do," he answers. "It'll be fine."

"You know how Our Dave describes you, Gaz?"

"Didn't he say I was reliable, reliable and quiet."

"He also said you're deep." Gaz shakes his head in the darkness.

"Our Dave doesn't know me, Kate."

"I think that's why he said that."

"Maybe."

"I'll let you get on with it then," she says. He wonders where she is on the other end of the phone, she could be on her couch in the front room, looking out of the window at the street or out the backdoor of her kitchen. He doesn't know anything about her at all, and that part of him he cannot control wants to know.

"Good night," he says.

"You too." She hangs up, and the silence of the motorway returns with the sound of the transporter humming like a kitchen appliance. A road sign for Leeds appears on the left ahead of him out of the darkness. He has eight miles to go.

Gaz follows the Satnav through the city streets to come to

Granary Wharf over the river. It's the Double Tree Hotel. Lilly has stayed here before, she's told him about punters who are wealthy and will pay her for two nights here. The circular building stretches up into the night sky with lights around the roof, the balconies higher up have steel railings. He slows and turns into the little car park at the front, then reverses the van round so he's facing the direction he needs to drive away. You can't park here of course. Gaz fishes in the glove compartment for the blue disabled badges that Our Dave made him, he puts these on the dashboard and gets out. It's not the fine that he wants to avoid, it's the clamp which will stop them getting away.

His legs are jelly as he walks to the revolving door of the hotel. In the foyer there's a wide reception desk in the wall on the right-hand side overlooking rows of leather sofas. Lights hang down from the ceiling. It's empty, apart from a young receptionist with dark hair in a ponytail wearing the hotel's gaudy brown jacket and a red tie. Gaz checks his phone to see where the icon is now. He zooms in. He's on it. The technology might not be good enough to get him as close as he needs to be, so he will have to be patient. He walks to the receptionist. Gaz is shy, ordinarily, but in this sort of situation he will talk to anyone. There's a job to be done.

"I'm meeting a friend, is it okay if I take a seat and wait?" he asks. He's surprised at how clean his accent sounds. She smiles and nods.

"Of course," she says. As a half attractive young white man in sports pants and a training shirt, Gaz is not under suspicion, especially if he is polite. He walks towards the leather sofas and sits down. Gaz takes out his phone and thumbs down the screen to make it look like he has something to do, and the revolving doors turn. He does not look up, but examines the man who walks in past reception out the corner of his eye. He's wearing a dark suit that's too big for him, and smart shoes, in both hands, he carries a pizza box wrapped in a white plastic takeaway bag. Gaz scrolls through his screen. Why would you bring in a takeaway when you're in a posh hotel? Maybe because you can't go out, or you're not allowed to. Gaz notices the floor digit the man presses on the lift, number four, he watches him go inside and the silver doors close. When the receptionist goes into the backroom for something, Gaz makes for the stairs. The place will be full of security cameras, but what else can he do? The quicker he gets Lilly back, the better.

He jogs up the hotel stairs two at a time. He must find out where the pizza box man is going. At the fourth floor he hears the ping of the lift and watches the man with the box as he walks down the corridor away from him and stops at a door at the end. Gaz keeps himself out of sight – there's a chance that the receptionist has already noticed him going up the stairs on the CCTV. The man opens up with his key card and goes in, letting the door slam behind him.

Gaz makes his way up the corridor. He slows as he gets nearer and there's shouting from inside the room, it's a woman's voice and it's not angry, more commanding. Gaz knows the tone even if he can't make out the words she uses – it's Lilly. There's no time to plan this, he has to react as the situation needs. He will not give himself time to be anxious, and he fixes his eyes on the light brown of the hotel room door in front of him as he taps. There are footsteps behind it and voices. From what he hears there may be more than just one of them. It opens and the pizza box man in the big black suit looks back at Gaz, he has balding hair and a rough, slightly flabby face. Ordinarily, Gaz would never hit anyone first, there are legal as well as moral complications to doing so, but here, there is no ambiguity for him. This man is guilty of kidnap, and could hurt someone who is under Gaz's protection; to prevent them coming to any harm, he will do anything that he has to do. Gaz steps in and puts his left trainer into the door to keep it open. He uses his hips to drive a straight punch at the man in the black suit's chest, Gaz is going for his solar plexus just under his rib cage. The man's jaw drops open as he sees Gaz stepping in, but he does not have time to move back and the fist connects with his chest. Gaz has not found the sweet spot of his solar plexus, but hits his ribs instead and the shockwave shatters some of them as it drives him backwards. In years to come, the man in the oversized black suit will tell of this day, he will say that he went to Hull once to pick someone up, and that it is the worst place in the world with its bleak rubbish strewn streets and vicious people. It's not the punch to the chest that will effectively cripple him for six months, but the next move. Gaz steps into the room and grabs the man's head by his ears in both hands, as he pulls him down he brings his knee up to connect with his face. It breaks his cheek and jaw and his nose will be permanently crooked.

There's screaming from Lilly as the man in the suit crumples into the on-suite bathroom of the hotel room. Another assailant charges at Gaz. This one looks bigger and has a red bomber jacket and a bald head. He's wide and well-built. Without looking properly, the silhouette of him moving at speed lets Gaz know that he's both powerful and skilled. He roars as he runs the few steps with his arms outstretched. There's a wheelie suitcase against the wall, Gaz grabs the handle, picks it up, and rams the wheels into the man in the red bomber jacket. It winds him. Gaz draws it back and hits him in the chest with it. This isn't boxing. There aren't any rules. Gaz kicks his legs out from under him and as he falls continues to clobber him with the hard black suitcase until there's a big gash on the side of his head from the metal wheels. In his left hand, Gaz sees the knife the man pulled. He keeps hitting him until he stops moving then stands back, out of breath. The noise of the fight will bring security soon. Gaz looks down at Lilly sitting on the end of the bed, her eyes are wide in fear and she looks different without all the make-up. He takes off his rucksack and unzips it, then removes the cap and trainers which he tosses to her.

"Put these on," he says. "We're leaving." She blinks back up at him and is on the verge of tears. Her instinct is to explain what happened.

"They're going to do something to my mum if I don't go with them, Gaz. They were going to put me on a flight tomorrow." Traffickers would much rather frighten someone into going with them – violence is a last resort.

"There's no time to tell me."

"Gaz, what about my mum?" she asks as she holds her head in one of her hands, he can see where one of her long nails is broken. Gaz flares his nostrils.

"They won't know your mum, it'll be lies. Put on the hat and shoes, now." She senses his urgency and does so. There's a groan from the bathroom. The thug in the over-sized suit must be coming round.

They leave down the corridor and then the stairs that Gaz ran up five minutes earlier. He's lucky to have found her. At the front desk the girl who was friendly before is now on the phone, and her eyes are like saucers as she watches Gaz and Lilly walk to the revolving door. The cameras will have shown her everything.

"The police are on their way," she says as they move past. Gaz doesn't even look at her as he leads Lilly out. The receptionist isn't paid enough to try and stop them, and the police probably won't be on their way. Leeds is a big city. Coppers are a busy lot. He and Lilly walk quickly away from the hotel towards the arches where he parked the van before. There's a voice behind them from the darkness.

"Oi!" and Gaz breaks into a run pulling Lilly by the arm next to him. He knew she'd need her trainers. At the van, he opens the sliding door to the backseat and pushes Lilly in. He turns and there's a man following. He stops a few paces from him and is out of breath.

"The police are on their way." He's security. He's wearing

a black uniform and cap. Gaz waits for a second, to see if the guard is going to attack him but he remains where he is. He won't be paid enough to scrap. Gaz moves round to the driver's side and gets in, he starts the engine and the van moves off towards the arches that he drove under – once he's out of Leeds this will all be over. That might well be a long way off, for coming down the hill opposite in a blaze of flashing blue lights is a long police Volvo. Gaz puts the brakes on and hopes it will pass but the vehicle drives into the dark arches and right in front of him. The silent lights flash. It's a weeknight after all, there can't be that much on for them to respond so quickly. Gaz takes a deep breath. This isn't Grand Theft Auto on his PlayStation. He won't be able to outrun them, and there are cameras all over the city – they'll track him wherever he goes, however, this is Our Dave's van, and if they have an interest in his vehicle then maybe they will have an interest in Our Dave. This is actually the last thing Gaz wants, for Our Dave has helped him out more than most. He swallows as his hands grip the wheel, his brain searches for solutions.

"What's going on, Gaz?" asks Lilly. He turns back to her:
"Put your seatbelt on, lass, we're going for a spin."

Gaz spent a long-time playing driving video games before he ever got behind the wheel of a car. He played Need for Speed and GTA 3, so drifting, handbrake turns and high-speed crashes were all very much the norm. Wilkinson gave him his first real driving lesson when he was seventeen, and he took to it quickly. He passed his test first time and so, by eighteen, he was driving Wilkinson to the folk club out at Cherry Burton where she could get pissed, he took her to do the weekly shop at the big supermarket too. It's natural for Gaz to drive, it's a way he can help without having to talk. He knows Our Dave's van well, he's driven it to Scotland five or six times, so knows how far he can turn the wheel before the tyres skid or how fast the van can take a bend without tipping up. It's electric and doesn't have the raw aggression that Ela does, but it's quick.

Gaz turns off the lights, puts the van into drive, and they burst into movement towards the police car blocking their way. There's a run up of a hundred yards, and the electric motor buzzes as the wheels squeak on the wet tarmac, the space Gaz has to fit the van through is small, but worth it if they can get away from all this.

He accelerates and hopes that the copper inside doesn't open the passenger door. They drive at speed towards the parked police car with its blue lights flashing in the darkness. Gaz is level and calm here in the eye of the storm. His mind is clear. He does not drink alcohol. He's never done drugs. He goes to bed early, eats good, clean food, he worries about the people around him more than himself and he misses his mother even though it was a long time ago that she went. This is why Gaz is rock steady on the wheel and why he can get the 2021 VW Transporter with barnyard back doors through the space between the wall and the police car with less than half an inch at either side. They clear past the police Volvo and he accelerates up the hill.

Gaz sees in his rear-view mirror that the police car is turning round, the coppers inside will be on the radio now calling for assistance with cameras and any other cars in the area. Gaz looks down at the square screen of the satnav on the dashboard – Leeds is hard enough to drive around in the daytime. He blasts up Wharf Approach and turns left, accelerating as he does, there are traffic lights in front and he drives straight through them on red. It's a good job it's late and the traffic is thin. Gaz drives through more red lights, he does not know where he is going as he drives up Great Wilson Street. In his rear-view mirrors and far away, he sees the flash of blue lights. The coppers will catch him. Gaz has only one card to play. Our Dave.

"Siri," he yells to the satnav, "call Our Dave." The female

computer voice, answers back, smooth and calm:

"Call Our Dave." It's late for him, about half ten. He'll be in bed, but he'll still answer. When Gaz works for him on the jobs up to Scotland there are protocols that he has to follow if anything goes wrong. Nothing has ever gone wrong before, but he's following the instructions.

"Is this my van?" asks Dave when he picks up the phone.

"It's Gaz. I'm in Leeds. Safehouse needed." Our Dave takes a second to process the information. He could get angry, but that won't help the situation.

"Central? What's the postcode?" he asks.

"LS10," says Gaz.

"Two minutes," comes the reply and he hangs up. The noise of the engine and the wheels on the tarmac below are calming as they drive the deserted city streets on a Wednesday night in July.

"What's going on, Gaz?" says Lilly from the back seat.

"If we don't get this van off the street, we'll be in the shit." Gaz doesn't normally swear.

"I just want to go home," she says and her voice breaks as she does. That's all Gaz wants too. He sees flashing blue lights coming down the hill in his rear-view mirror.

You wouldn't believe how sneaky people can be, especially when they can make money. Our Dave has connections all over the UK, it's how he ships his booze. Should anything go wrong, then there are places to go unseen. There are garages in Manchester that will hide whatever car you're driving, just like places in Liverpool that will have your vehicle dismantled and separated within the hour so it can't be traced. There are breaking yards in Newcastle that will do the same, as long as you know them of course. Our Dave knows Leeds. The satnav in front of Gaz is reprogramming itself, Our Dave will be linked to it as the map calculates a new route to a postcode he is inputting into it all the way from Hull where he is sitting up in bed on his smartphone.

Gaz watches the blue line snake out across Leeds on the map. He just has to keep the copper off his tail till then. It's not far – just off Low Road and to the right. He drives down a side street with a tyre company on the left and a garden fence company on the right. It's dead quiet. The satnav tells him he's arrived so he turns off the engine and his heart beats shallow in his chest, he looks back to Lilly. In all honesty, Gaz does not know if this will turn out alright – he is out of his depth. There's a tap on the window. A face with a balaclava appears. Gaz gets out and the figure standing in front of him hands him some car keys. Gaz, in turn, gives him the keys to the van.

"A green Yaris, parked in front of the tyre shop. Wait ten minutes until you leave," says the man with the balaclava and a thick Leeds accent. Gaz nods. He opens the sliding back door and Lilly clambers out into the warm night air. They walk back up the street and there's the ratty green Yaris parked lonely at the front behind a little wall. They get in, but Gaz doesn't start the engine. This will be a blind spot for cameras or else they would not have done the exchange here. In a few moments, the 2021 VW van with barnyard backdoors crawls up past them and goes out into the Leeds city streets never to be seen again.

Gaz rubs his eyes without putting the key in the ignition. The silent blue lights of a police car zoom by and they watch it go into the orange glow from the streetlights above.

"I'm sorry, Gaz," she says.

"Please don't be. I'm just glad I got you back."

CHAPTER EIGHT
Our Dave and Kate

Gaz sits in the taxi office on Chants Avenue. It's the next day. He's wearing dark trousers with a black t-shirt tucked in and has taken off his aviator-style sunglasses that he got for two pounds from the charity shop. Our Dave sits in front of him, and the taxi office is deserted. These days Our Dave runs a small outfit of daytime drivers and there are only three of them. He has his booze business too, but very few people know about that. Our Dave has made Gaz and him mugs of tea and they sit looking at each other. Gaz doesn't like to waste words and he has already explained that he had to rescue Lilly from the men who took her. They must unpick this problem together.

"The van cost me fifteen grand," says Our Dave. They both know it's gone now, "and it's another ten for the lads who got rid of it at short notice. I've paid already by the way." Gaz looks at the dark glasses that he set on the table. He doesn't have to say how sorry he is, Our Dave can see it all over his face and in the way he swallows.

"I'll make it up to you. I can do the runs to Scotland for nothing. You can have my car – it's worth a few quid, Barry says it's a classic." Our Dave frowns in worry.

"You nicked my van though, Gaz. If you'd have asked, I would have said yes."

"I couldn't have known what you'd say, Our Dave. I wasn't thinking straight. If you'd have said no then I would have nicked it." The older man sighs.

"What are you mixed up in?"

"Nothing. I don't know. I do security for a lass. Someone took her. I got her back."

"Who are you working for?"

"They're semi legitimate, a Leeds firm. They hire out security for whoever. They're called Sandersons. They find the jobs and pay me to do them. I've been looking after Lilly for a while."

"She's a working lass, isn't she?"

"Yeah."

"Working girls don't have protection, Gaz. That's why it's a dangerous business." Our Dave knows the way the world works. Independent prostitutes take a risk every time they open the door to a punter. It's too expensive to hire security. A pimp maybe, but not a guard. That's why this is odd for Our Dave. "They just have you protecting one lass, do they?"

"At the moment. They say they'll want me to look after more as time goes on." Our Dave swallows. Gaz is a nice kid. He's as tough as they come, but nice, and if someone gets their teeth into him they'll tear him to pieces.

"That's more like a pimp." Gaz looks back at him.

"I wouldn't do it forever, Our Dave, and I wouldn't see anyone get hurt."

"I know, mate. Have you told them what happened?"

"Yeah. I emailed. Nothing back."

"Have you considered that they might not be the best people to work for? I'm just speaking from experience, Gaz. If it goes shitty once, it usually goes shitty again."

"They pay well," says Gaz, as if this is an excuse.

"So do I." Gaz has already apologized but he wants to do it again, his voice is low:

"What do you want me to do? I've messed up. I want to make it right." Our Dave rubs his face with one of his big hands. He's more philosophical than angry because getting upset does not change the situation or get him anywhere.

"You cost me twenty-five grand, Gaz. That's a lot of money in anyone's business." The young man looks down at the floor. It's not the first time he's messed up. He feels like it's all he's ever done. Our Dave can see that the words hurt him, and he does not want to do this. In the great scheme of things, Gaz is potentially worth much more than twenty-five grand to him. "Having said that, do you know how hard it is to find someone reliable to take half a million pound in cash up to Scotland? Either drivers are too bent that they'd nick it, or too straight that they'd need a written invoice. I work with people that I can trust. I am angry with you, Gaz, but only because you didn't involve me – you can't do that again."

"I wouldn't."

"I can't let you drive for me, not for a long while. Do you understand?" Gaz keeps his eyes down on his shoes, gives a sigh, then stares back at Our Dave. It's a shame to lose the gig with the man.

"I understand," he says.

"Maybe we can work together again in the future, but not now, not after this." Our Dave is genuinely sorry. Gaz gives another sigh as he picks up his aviator-style dark glasses from the table.

"If there's anything I can do for you, Our Dave, you'll have to let me know. I wouldn't need to be paid."

"I'll be in touch, Gaz, maybe. You take care of yourself, won't you?" This last line is the most telling, it's Our Dave cutting ties with him as an associate, as if he's going away somewhere for an extended period. Gaz responds in kind.

"You take care of yourself too, Our Dave." Gaz wants to ask where he'll find another driver to replace him, he wants to offer advice about how to get up to Scotland and the roads to avoid - but it's beyond this. Gaz is being let go by a benefactor. "Thanks for the tea," he adds.

"See you soon, Gaz," says Our Dave. He watches as the man walks out the back door of the office at Avenue Cars then rubs his face again with one of his hands, like he does.

You don't always do people a favour by helping them out.

Gaz drives Ela out of the back of Avenue Cars and onto Chant Ave. He feels hollow. It's like when he got kicked out of the first foster home, like when he failed his GCSEs, like when the man told him he wouldn't be suited to a career in teaching, like when the fire brigade explained he didn't have the right qualifications. At least he has that blister pack of Adderall in his bedside cabinet – what does it matter if everything goes tits up? He drives past the coffee shop where he's going to meet Kate and into Park Ave. There's a space in front of a camper van. He doesn't get out of the car right away but stares through the windscreen at the big bonnet stretching out in front of him.

He should not be here.

Meeting Kate is the worst thing he could do. She is out of his league anyway, and all he'll bring her is disappointment, and he could put her in danger too. What was he thinking? He nods as if he's made up his mind and turns the ignition. The engine turns over but doesn't catch. He waits ten seconds and tries again, the motor splutters and turns over but doesn't run. It's as if Ela does not want him to leave. He tries again. Perhaps he's flooded the engine. He might as well meet her.

On the corner of Park Ave there's a new café with wooden tables outside and a black sign. A few years ago, it was a hair salon but covid closed that down. An older couple sit outside in the morning sun with their coffee, and there's a pug dog on a lead next to the man. Gaz waits by the rails out the front. He's a little early, as usual. He would have been earlier if he hadn't tried to make a getaway, he's nervous and he takes out his phone to look like he has something to do. This is not a date, but it could be. Gaz is out of his comfort zone. Chanterlands Ave is mid-level busy for a morning, a woman passes with her baby in a red pushchair, the lady in the cat charity shop across the road is arranging the window display, again, a drugged out looking woman in her early fifties struggles by on a pink child's BMX. Gaz checks the time. It's eleven.

A few yards away is Kate. She gives Gaz a big smile and it shows the gap in her teeth. He finds himself smiling back.

"Have you been here long?" she asks when she gets there.
"Just got here."

They sit next to each other inside the window looking out onto Chants Ave. The seats are high metal stools. Kate wears jeans and a white t-shirt, she's got baseball shoes on without socks, Gaz can see her ankles. She ordered a black coffee and Gaz got an Americano – he doesn't want to have a kids drink in front of her so he will have to weather the way coffee makes him feel.

"Thanks for coming to meet me," she says. "How was the job?" Gaz forgot that he spoke to her as he drove to Leeds the night before.

"It got sorted," he says. He has a flashback to the fight with the bald man in the bomber jacket and sees the man's split face where he hit him with the wheels of the suitcase.

"You sounded worried about it."

"I was." Gaz blinks back at her and there's the silence between them again, she's giving him the space to talk. He takes a line from Wilkinson's playbook. It's a tell me about question. They work well usually.

"Tell me about what you're studying," he says. She smiles.

"At the moment it's all about working with kids. There's a lot of reading, some of it is quite heavy going, but the techniques are good. You can allow people to find out about themselves, that's how you help them." Kate turns the same question on him. It's like they are in a therapy session.

"How was the job last night?" Gaz is not good at lying or even telling versions of the truth, so that's why it's better not to say anything at all.

"It was for a client. I can't really say. I had to go to Leeds and pick them up and it wasn't as bad as I thought it would be."

"You didn't have to fight anyone then?" Kate says this in humour because she doesn't imagine that Gaz would get involved in that sort of thing. He swallows and she can see that there was trouble. She remembers his smashed-up knuckles that right now, he's hiding by his side. "Sorry," she adds.

"It wasn't that bad." There's the awkward silence between them, Kate is so good at giving people space that she's afraid to say what she wants. Gaz is much more straightforward. He comes out with it right away. "What is it you're after, Kate?" he asks. She likes how direct he is. It isn't cocky either.

"I'd like to interview you and do some counselling sessions with you for part of my course."

"Why me?"

"You work with violence. I'm interested in it. I want to know how it affects people."

"I'm just a normal lad," he says. "It affects me the same way as it would anyone else." This is not true at all. A body gets used to seeing people hit each other, it gets used to being hit as well, and dishing it out too. Gaz has been in so many scrapes that adrenaline doesn't always kick in. He would have a lot to tell Kate.

"That's why you would be perfect to work with." Gaz takes a sip of his coffee and it's bitter. Kate can see his bruised and red knuckles. He must have hit someone hard, but she doesn't feel frightened by him. Gaz doesn't have the arrogance that some men of his age carry around, he would rather disappear into the background than be noticed. "Would you help me? You might learn something about yourself too." Gaz puts his cup down.

If she didn't look like she did he might say no. He should say no anyhow. He shouldn't be here talking to her. He looks into her blue-grey eyes, she's not rushing him. That voice that he doesn't control at all answers her.

"I'd be happy to help," he says.

CHAPTER NINE
Lilly

It's started up with summer rain. Gaz won't be working today, he imagines. Lilly will be in no state to spread her legs for punters, but you never can tell, she is a tough lass, she has to be.

Gaz gets to the house at twelve. Lilly is in. She's on the phone in the kitchen with a cup of coffee and her make-up on. She's talking to a punter. When she sees Gaz is back she explains to the man on the other end that she'll be ready in half an hour. She is working again. She hangs up and puts her phone on the table.

"I didn't think you'd get back to it so quick."

"I talked to my mum last night," says Lilly.

"Oh yeah?"

"I'm giving it six months, Gaz. Six months and I'm gonna graft my arse off and not spend a thing. Then I'll pay my sister's mortgage off and go and live with her. Life's too short to keep doing this. I want out." Gaz nods. This is sense. He likes logical thinking, and he only hopes that this is true and not just a load of shite. She stands up and faces him.

"I want to thank you for last night, Gaz. I don't think I'd be here now if it wasn't for you."

"It's what I do," he says.

"I won't forget it. If there's anything you need from me, you only need to ask. I've got half an hour." She has a serious look on her face and her fake eyelashes blink back at him. Today, she's wearing a dark skirt and a shiny blouse – her secretary look, for some punter, probably. She is offering him sex.

"It's my job to look after you. I'm paid already." She reaches out and takes hold of his arm, her false nails are back on and they dig into his forearm.

"You'll be here today while I work, won't you?"

"Of course," he answers. She smiles and shows her bright white teeth.

It begins again. Gaz has made himself a cup of cocoa to take upstairs to the box room while Lilly checks her messages and bookings. Now she's turned on her green light, there are regular pings and noises from her phone.

Gaz had the locks fixed on the back door this morning, he made sure the back gate was closed solid and nailed a plank of wood across it to stop it opening again. He hopes the men who took her won't be back. Gaz scrolls through TikTok and watches daily stoic videos with the sound turned down and reads the subtitles. The man with black hair and wide eyes explains that a person has power over their own mind only and not outside events. One shouldn't affect the other. Gaz likes this. You have to take charge of yourself – it's all you've got. It makes sense.

The doorbell rings some half an hour later and the first of the punters comes up the stairs. This one has a deep voice and talks dirty to Lilly as he goes at her and the bed squeaks – he's a regular. More follow. Gaz plays Fortnite on his laptop with the sound turned off. There's the out-of-town doctor, a bouncer from one of the clubs in town, a lad fresh out of uni; Lilly deals with them all in thirty-minute chunks before a three-hour booking in the late afternoon with that older man who likes to talk to her. They have a cup of tea in the kitchen before getting down to it on the sofa in the living room. It's as good a day as it gets. At half five Lilly turns the green light off on the app meaning that she's not available.

Gaz comes back into the kitchen and puts the kettle on.

"I'll make us a drink," he says. She smiles up at him and looks tired. Two knocks sound from the front door and the smile falls from Lilly's face. There shouldn't be any more punters today.

Gaz goes to the door and opens up. Standing with his big

foot on the step is Rose. He's wearing a tight white shirt with an open collar to show his gold chain. Behind him in his customary dark suit with smart nondescript shoes, a laptop bag and a serious expression, is Saif.

"Can we come in and have a word?" says Rose. Gaz shrugs his shoulders.

"Sure," he answers.

Rose manages to sit on the couch like he owns the place. He has his legs splayed and his big arms stretched across the top as he leans back. Saif gets out the little laptop and sets it on his knee. Lilly stands at the backdoor and smokes a fag. She'll listen of course, but won't get involved.

"We got your message about what happened in Leeds," says Rose. "Very impressive." His tone makes it sound like he isn't very impressed. Gaz stands in front of these two men with the big black TV on the wall behind him.

"What can I do for you?" asks Gaz. Saif doesn't look up as he taps away at his little keyboard. "I'm surprised you came all this way."

"It's not far," says Rose. "We wanted to have a chat, face to face."

"Go on then."

"There's a big firm in Leeds," explains Rose. His beard is ratty and his bald head is creased on his forehead. "They're called the Northern Grid - perhaps you've heard of them, I know the name sounds like a power company or something, but they're legitimate." Rose's accent is cold and miserable, it makes his mouth snarl when he speaks. "They control most of the city, the drugs that come in and out, prostitution, some extortion, they also have affiliated gangs who sell their stuff for them, kids mostly from the estates. They keep them at war with each other too." Gaz shrugs his shoulders.

"So what?"

"You just pissed that firm right off."

"By getting Lilly back?" Rose leans forward and rests his elbows on his knees as he begins to explain.

"Yes, by getting Lilly back. Understand please, Gareth, that there's healthy competition between different companies. The Northern Grid is a rival to us, we provide security services to anyone who will pay us and they don't like that. They've kidnapped our people before, just to step on our toes, and it seems that's what this was. What usually happens is we get a phone call, and a figure of money to pay, and then we cough it up. They get to keep their status and we get put in our place and everyone walks away happy, except this time – you wade in with your heavy fists and hospitalize two of their lads." Gaz darkens.

"I'm not sorry about what I did."

"I am. This is bigger than you and Lilly. They were never going to hurt her. She's just a piece in a game, that's all. We're a security business, Gaz, not gangsters. We pay our taxes, we are legitimate even if the clients we work for might not always be."

"So what?" asks Gaz.

"Saif here wants to let you go. In my opinion you are trouble, Gareth, pure trouble, but you've got potential. You think on your own, you make decisions, you're resourceful and loyal too. That can't go unrewarded, son." Rose is complementing him but neither his tone nor his face have changed – he is simply stating facts as he sees them. "I've already smoothed things over back in Leeds with them, we're lucky, and they were impressed by you. How did you track her down?"

"Her phone," he answers. Rose nods. "What is it you want from me, then," asks Gaz, "if you're not going to sack me?"

"I'm sending you an email, Gareth," says Saif as he taps away at the laptop on his knee. "There are eleven locations such as this one with working girls. Most are right here in the city, some just outside in the leafier neighborhoods. They're all on our books and looked after by us. I also added a few names that owe Sandersons money that we haven't been able to contact – you'll visit them too and find out what happened to our cash." Gaz frowns as he begins to understand. "It'll be your job to visit and introduce yourself, I've already let them know you'll be dropping by in the next few days. They're aware that you're protecting them, and they'll need to provide you a sum of money – I've put the names and the fee next to each of the properties on the spreadsheet." Gaz swallows. He thinks back to what Our Dave told him that very morning, that this game didn't sound right at all.

"How can I protect all of them?" he asks and at once realises that he's not supposed to. This was the plan all along.

"It'll be mobile protection," says Saif, "you'll only be a phone call away if they need anything."

"You mean I'll be a pimp," says Gaz. Saif shakes his head as he closes up the laptop.

"That's not a word we use, Gareth. You're offering a service – it's protection and security. The girls can refuse any time they like, although we'd strongly suggest they didn't. You'll collect for your services, that's all. This isn't some gangster film. We are all professional people here."

"What if I say no?" asks Gaz.

"That wouldn't be a positive move," cuts in Rose. "I mean the firm in Leeds were desperate to know who you were. The men you injured are part of their organization. You know that one of them will never walk properly again? It wasn't in my interest to give them any of your details, but it could be, if you don't respect this company and the job we've asked you to do." Rose leans back into the cream white sofa where only an hour before Lilly was screwed by a man with a hairy back and ginger hair. "They're not nice people, Gareth, not nice at all and they'd find you no bother, and they'd find whoever you care about too."

"You'll be compensated for your efforts," says Saif. "I

mean that you'd receive a higher salary." It's good for him to use easier language when he's out in the field, especially here. "I've organised a significant bank transfer, and it'll go through by the end of the day."

"Was this your plan all along?" asks Gaz.

"What do you mean?" says Rose.

"I mean, you have me protect Lilly here for a few weeks before you set me up looking after a whole load of working lasses?"

"That is the model, Gareth. That is how it works. I thought we'd been clear with you on that."

"You weren't," says Gaz. "I was brought in as security. I'm not a pimp, I don't collect." Lilly has come through from the kitchen and stands in the arch between the front room and the dining room. Rose looks over at her and smiles to reveal little misshapen teeth. He is uglier for it.

"Why don't you explain to Gareth here, Lilly," says Rose. "Working girls don't have protection." Her face is impassive as she stands there – she knows these men, they gave her a job in the strip club, it's Rose who raped her in the dressing room of the Leeds Hippo Disco against a mirror, it's him who set her up as a working girl back here in Hull, and Saif who found the terraced house that they stand in right now. They are pimps in the real sense of the word. They wear aftershave and posh suits, speak in business terms, operate out of offices and eat at expensive restaurants but they are pimps, and they will make a pimp out of Gaz too. She is sorry that he is involved in all this, and she will be sorry that he will not stay with her anymore.

"That's just it, Gaz," she says. "I work alone. I have to. You'll be at the end of the phone if I need you." There's sadness there in her voice. Gaz looks across at her big brown eyes. He's been tricked, and he was too stupid to notice. He could rage at this situation; he could attack Rose where he sits and maybe he could take him - but what good would it do?

Gaz must take charge of himself – just like the man in the Tik Tok videos says, he cannot manage events in the world but he can manage his reactions to them. Saif has put the laptop back into its little briefcase and he stands up.

"Like I said, Gareth, it's all in the email I sent you," he says. Rose gets up too, and walks a few steps over to where Gaz stands opposite. The bald man is a few inches taller and a good deal wider than he is. Gaz knows fighting men, and Rose will have had more than his fair share of battles for his eyes are cruel and cold. He holds out his hand for Gaz to shake. He's trapped into this. They shake and Rose's grip is much stronger than his own.

"It's not just about being tough, Gareth, you have to be smart too." Despite the aftershave, Gaz can smell the man's rotten breath.

When they have gone, Lilly stands in the same place under the little archway between the kitchen and the dining room.

"I'm sorry," she says. "They have a way of sucking you in. They did it to me too and then you're too far gone to get out."

"Six months," says Gaz. "You said it was going to be six months before you got out."

"I wish it was true."

"I'll be out sooner than that," he says, "one way or another."

CHAPTER TEN
Kate

Kate wants Gaz to come tonight at half six. She can't do tomorrow because she's got work and one of her clients. Gaz follows the funny one-way system and finds the house halfway down Belvoir Street. These roads were never designed with cars in mind. It's 55. People call it Beaver Street round here. It's a good, terraced road to live on, there's usually a car parking space and the neighbours are bohemian types. The houses are bigger than they look with little gardens or extensions on the back.

Gaz knocks on the door. His mind whirrs about what happened this afternoon and talking to Kate will distract him, he hopes. It's six twenty-seven. He doesn't like to be late. Gaz has washed his hair, shaved, agonized over what shirt to put on and wears a little bit too much sweet aftershave.

Kate opens the door and gives him a smile to show the gap in her teeth. She is wearing jeans as before but is barefoot. His stomach churns. She invites him in.

"Thanks for coming," she says as he follows her down the hall to the dining room. There are two big, dark material sofas facing each other with fawn blankets over them. In the middle is a stout well-made coffee table where an incense stick burns sending perfume into the air. A modern art picture hangs on one wall and there's a cartoon print on the other, a black and white cat dashes from the room as Gaz enters. "I'll make you a drink," she calls as she walks into the long kitchen. "Is coffee, ok?"

"Have you got any chocolate?" he asks. "Coffee makes me jumpy."

"I'll see what I've got."

Kate sets down a mug of green tea on a coaster and sits opposite Gaz with a coffee cupped in her hands.

"Can I explain a little bit about the process?" He nods. This is not a situation Gaz has been in for quite some time. The room is designed to be calm without distractions. Kate's tone is smooth and even. "I'm in my second year of a master's with the university here. When I graduate I'll be a counselling psychologist. Part of the course is for me to interview and work with as wide a range of people as I can. I'm bound by a code of ethics and I'm a member of the BACP. That means I won't share anything we talk about unless I think that you are in danger, or a young or vulnerable person is." Gaz nods. That's fine. He isn't going to tell her anything anyway. She stops talking and sets her cup down on the table. Gaz notices the thumb ring and sees that her fingers are elegant and strong. It's his turn to speak although he doesn't want to. Perhaps it's what's happened to him today, perhaps he's tired of wearing a front, but truth comes out of Gaz even though he does not want it to.

"I don't think I'll tell you much," he says. He's not defensive, more apologetic.

"Why?" Gaz knows to leave questions unanswered that are too difficult.

"Did Our Dave put you up to this?" he asks.

"He said you'd be good to talk to. He said you had a troubled past. I'm sorry. Is that ok?" Gaz shrugs his shoulders.

"Sure," he says. It's been a long time since he's been that poor kid whose mother got murdered. Kate's blonde hair falls over her shoulders as she rests her elbows on her lap. It's the listening pose. He can see her collar bones under her vest, the line of her jaw and her even pale blue eyes blinking at him. It makes him feel like a letch and he looks away from her.

"You don't have to do this, Gaz, if you don't want to. There's nothing stopping you from walking out of here. It's your choice to be sitting on that sofa."

"I don't trust you," he says, "and I don't even know you. I don't know what you want."

"I explained. A patient like you would be really good for my studies, Gaz. I mean, I know you've been through trauma. One of the reasons I want to do this job is to help people through difficult situations because years ago when I was struggling, people helped me. It's my way of paying back. I'll get paid for it too, but it's not easy. As a therapist I have to go through the emotions that my patients do. I have to be truthful as well."

"How do you know what trauma I've been through?"

"Our Dave told me. He didn't say what."

"Is that why he had me drive you to the docks the other day?"

"I guess so. I approached him. I told him I needed patients." Kate asked him to find her another type of person as well, but she was joking, she thinks. "It would be part of my studies." Perhaps it's the light smell of incense in his nostrils or her bare feet on the floor, Gaz finds himself speaking the truth to her again.

"I'm not sure I'll be able to help you," he says.

"Why?"

"I won't be able to answer your questions. I won't tell you the truth."

"By telling me that, Gaz, you're already telling me the truth. Would you just humour me a minute, just until you've finished your tea, and then if you still feel the same way you can leave. Will you do that for me?" Gaz nods. This is easy enough.

"I'd like you to imagine something. Imagine that in front of you on the coffee table that there's a truth switch. When the switch is off - you're going to lie or avoid the question. With the truth switch off, being here is a total waste of your time, and mine. However, if you turn it on, everything changes, then you're here for you – and we can make progress. What do you think?" Kate has said these lines before, she heard them from her slim, half good-looking teacher up at the university with his thick black glasses and charismatic voice.

She's used the metaphor to good effect. She has put him in a difficult situation, for it's not in Gaz's nature to talk about himself, and he's got this far without having to do so. Gaz channels his rugby playing dad. He imagines the man running down the pitch with his muscly legs in his black shorts, a scrum cap tight over his sweaty short hair and the ball clutched to his chest as he powers to the line. There's a defender in front ready to bring him down and with smooth, effortless grace, he side steps:

"Would you turn that truth switch on too?" She's never been asked this before.

"Of course." This is a good gambit - to offer a bit of herself first will make him more willing to talk to her.

"How did Our Dave save your life?" asks Gaz. Kate pauses and blinks, she regrets that she told him this, most people wouldn't remember such a comment, or they'd just think it was flippant. Not so this serious man with his dark hair and his blue eyes blazing at her.

"This is your therapy session, Gaz."

"I thought you had to tell the truth as well, and you just told me the switch was on." Kate has shown her inexperience, she's shared too much of herself too early with this man and he has used it against her. She really will have to deliver something of herself.

"A couple of years ago I had a nervous breakdown. I had a drink problem. It was Our Dave that got me help. It was him who took me to the hospital. He checked up on me while I was there. I owe him." Her eyes have begun to water. She doesn't want to use the word alcoholic, it seems trite.

"How did he save your life?"

"He was my friend when nobody else was." They look at each other, these two, over the low coffee table with the summer sun shining into Kate's little garden out the back of her three bedroomed terrace on Belvoir Street.

"Why did you come here today, Gaz?"

"You wouldn't like my answer." Gaz isn't cocky when he says this.

"Try me."

"Dave asked me to get to know you as well. He said you needed someone to talk to." Kate picks up her cup and looks down into her black coffee. "You shouldn't have made me turn on that switch or I wouldn't have said anything," Gaz gives a smile out the side of his mouth.

"At least you're being honest with me. I think he meant I needed help with my course."

"He didn't mean that."

"Then what did he mean?"

"I don't know."

Our Dave said he would find her someone and he has. This is him. She couldn't see the wood for the trees. Our Dave has delivered what she asked for. Her face flushes red.

"We've made a really good start." They've talked for ten minutes. Gaz breathes a sigh of relief. Kate is not really finished.

"Am I ok to turn the truth switch off now?"

"Yes," she answers. "I'll turn mine off too."

They consider each other.

"I think Our Dave did set us up, Kate," says Gaz. "You know what he's like."

"Is that so bad?" she asks. Kate likes his calm presence. She likes that he smells good. His shoes are clean. Men usually get shoes wrong.

"It's not bad at all. I like you. I like the way you talk. I like the job you do at the library."

"Is that truth switch still on?" she asks.

"I'm not going to turn it off after all," says Gaz. "It's much easier if I don't."

"Do you lie to most people?"

"I just don't tell. I'm not a good liar. How about you?"

"I'm very good at it. You don't have problems like I did

without being an expert." She's vulnerable – that's why she will make a good therapist. She doesn't want this to be about her but that is what Gaz will make of it if she lets him.

"You came here because you wanted to, Gaz."

"I did." Gaz knows how it works.

"How do you feel about yourself?"

"Ok. I could be better."

"What do you mean by could be better?" This is where Gaz must tread carefully.

"I mean I could be a better person."

"How?"

"I could work harder. I could look after my friends more." He doesn't have any friends apart from Wilkinson, maybe Lilly too. You could count Our Dave.

"Why should you do that?"

"Look after them?"

"Yes."

"I guess because they deserve it."

"Why wouldn't you look after yourself first, then look after them? I mean, it's interesting that the first thing you say is you could be better, and you could look after other people better. Are they your family? Have you not looked after people well enough in the past?" Gaz's hands move to his lap, and he takes a deep breath through his nose. She has hit a nerve, and he must take steps to avoid her seeing that she has. Like a fight, Gaz must defend himself. He did not look after his mother all those years ago and the failure is in him with each breath.

"I look out for people," he says.

"Why?" Gaz does not have to take this, but he will look weaker if he stands up and leaves. He'd been doing so well just a few moments before.

"It makes me feel good, like I'm needed." Kate nods. "Is that wrong?"

"That's for you to decide. Do you feel like you have to?" He looks down at the coffee table and thinks about the truth switch. He's not going to lie after all.

"Yes."

"Why?"

"It makes me feel better."

"Is it self-validation?"

"Probably." The social media name for this could be people pleasing. It's a common response for those who feel they are worthless. Kate has read about it in core belief therapy books; she's watched videos on YouTube about it too and discussed it during tutorials. She feels it sometimes as well. Kate sits back on her sofa. She can sense that he is troubled. His nostrils are flared, and he sits up straight. She must be careful not to push him too far.

"I think we've done well today," she says. She wants to close this down.

"Don't you drink anymore, then?" he asks.

"No," she answers. "Life's easier for me if I don't." Gaz nods. He can see that she does not want to talk about this. "I'll tell you about it, sometime, the more I get to know you." This is a good line. She has offered a piece of her, in exchange for a piece of him even though it is not true. Kate will not tell him how her father taught her to drink, how she could get through a bottle of sherry a day before she went drinking properly or about all the men she doesn't recall being with. She was drunk at her old man's funeral too, and she doesn't want to remember that, but she does.

Gaz takes a deep breath in through his nose. He thinks of his rugby playing dad again as he catches the ball fired out from the back of the scrum somehow, the big man sees an opportunity, a gap between the defenders that he can exploit if he is brave enough.

"Why don't we just go out sometime?"

"We can chat here."

"I mean something else."

"Like a date?"

"Aye," answers Gaz. "Like a date." Gaz's rugby playing dad is powering over the pitch with the studs on his boots sending bits of mud into the air as he sprints. If Gaz pushes their relationship this way, there will be no more therapy, but a conflict of interests, it will be unprofessional for her to see him.

Kate considers the idea. Our Dave did have something else in mind when he suggested talking to Gaz. It would be utterly unethical for her to go out with a client, even for a coffee. She blinks her cool blue-grey eyes. He is not a client yet, she tells herself. He is the opposite of what she has experienced in men, he lacks arrogance, he's not afraid to be polite, he's guarded also. She likes him in the way that girls like boys. Perhaps that's why she asked him here.

"How did Our Dave save your life, Gaz?"

"He gave me a lift once, on a Friday night a long time ago. I was being chased by a gang of lads down Spring Bank and he stopped in his taxi and picked me up. I was going to get a kicking. That's the kind of answer I thought you'd give to be honest. I thought he might have fixed your gas fire or something." Kate swallows. He is not judging her, but she has shared too much with him for this to be a professional relationship.

"Are you really asking me out?" she says for clarity.

"Yes." Kate blinks. Why shouldn't she? It's been more than a year since she's been out with anyone, and she doesn't feel ready. Maybe she'll never be ready.

"Okay," she whispers.

CHAPTER ELEVEN
Wilkinson

Gaz looks out the window of Wilkinson's flat and down at Pearson Park. There are two drunks shouting at each other under the big tree there, one of them has a baseball cap and rotten teeth and the other has a beer can in his hand and a long green Parka coat like Liam Gallagher might have worn in the nineties. Gaz doesn't like men, but these drunks from the homeless shelter across the road are harmless enough. He's had run ins with them before when he was younger and gives them a wide birth these days.

He looks back to the kitchen where he has sat many times previous. There's the light smell of coffee as it brews in an eighties style percolator. He's back to visit too soon. Wilkinson will know something is wrong with him.

"Have you got a first name, Wilkinson?" calls Gaz. The woman is busy packing some pans into a big cardboard box.

"Are you taking the piss?" she answers. She does have a first name, of course, but nobody has called her that since she was a kid. She isn't going to tell Gaz. The woman hasn't really spoken to him since he knocked five minutes ago, and she invited him in and upstairs. She knows what he's like and that he'll speak when he's ready – that's how he is. She really is going away and there's a lot to pack – not to take, but to get rid of. She walks over to where he sits by the big window but doesn't sit down.

"Do you want a drink?" she asks. Wilkinson wants to ask him why he's here but won't – that's how you deal with these quiet kids, you wait for them to open up. She's had much rougher and more damaged ones than Gaz here through her doors, some of them work out fine, others become those drunks pushing each other around on the park outside, or in jail, or dead.

"Where will you stay out in Spain?" he asks.

"Like I said, I've got friends. There's a person I used to know. She asked me to go out there years ago. Now I'm going." Wilkinson can't help herself: "What are you here for?"

"Advice," he answers.

"You might as well get on with it then, Gaz. It's not like I've got all day." Though Wilkinson is bohemian enough, her father was still a trawlerman off Hessle Road and her mother worked in a patty factory, and there's that harsh humour for people she likes.

"I've been offered a better job at work."

"So?" Unless you explain the problem, Wilkinson won't understand it.

"I'm not sure if I can do it and I'm not sure if I want to."

"Do you get more money?"

"A lot more."

"What do you have to do?"

"Collect money," he answers.

"Like a debt collector?"

"Yeah. That kind of thing." Wilkinson breathes in through her nostrils. She doesn't like that Gaz is a bouncer. This sounds worse. If she knew what the job was really about, she would be more upset.

"Do you want me to make you feel better about it? Is that what you want me to do?"

"I just wanted to know what you thought."

"Come on, Gaz. It doesn't matter what I think, does it? I'm not here to massage your ego. Get your girlfriend to do that." He gives a half smile. Gaz understands it when people are cruel to him. It's what he's used to.

"I met a girl as well."

"Oh yeah?"

"I think she's out of my league." At this information, Wilkinson sits down. It's got interesting.

"What's her name?"

"Kate."

"What's her second name?"

"I don't know. She works at the library?"

"The one in town?"

"The one on Chants Ave." Wilkinson reaches for her tablet on the other seat and swipes open the screen. Her clever fingers begin across the smooth display to type the name. Gaz watches her work.

"What are you doing?"

"Stalking her." Gaz frowns.

"I don't know her second name, I told you." Wilkinson is good at stalking people, and it's easy. She's searched for someone called Kate who works at Chants Ave library on the council website. In twenty seconds, she has a second name that she pumps into Facebook to reveal a column of faces. She scrolls down and sees a blonde halfway down with a gap-toothed smile. Under her name it says Hull Council Library. She opens it up and looks at the profile pictures. There's a snap of her graduating with a gown and mortar, another against a starry foreign night sky with a summer dress, then laughing in a posh restaurant, then swimming in a perfect foreign blue sea. Gaz is right – she is way out of his league, perhaps even a few leagues above what he could hope for. She'll not say this. Wilkinson has had relationships with women out of her league as well. She turns the tablet and shows Gaz the pictures.

"Is this her?" she asks though she knows it is.

"Yes," he says.

"Nobody is out of your league, Gaz," she says as she shakes her head. He gives her a look with his eyebrow raised very slightly. Wilkinson sighs. "Well even if she is, that doesn't mean anything. People can be tricked. I should know."

"How should you know?" asks Gaz.

"All the girls I had were out of my league, that's why I was with them. I tricked them into believing I was better than I was. I tricked all the kids who ever stayed here as well. You know that. I told them they were smart when they weren't, I said they were special when they were normal. I tricked you too. It took a while, but it worked."

"You told me to pretend that I knew what I was doing. You told me to pretend that, and eventually I would."

"Do you know what you're doing?"

"Kind of."

"I always said you were a good driver."

"I am a good driver."

"There you go then," she says. "You get told you're an idiot and you'll be one. Get told you're a good lad and you'll be one too. I had to tell you to have some confidence in yourself, and now you have. It's a trick. It comes true as well. It worked on me first."

"I'm more about being honest with myself these days, Wilkinson. I have to know what I am."

"You're the same kid, Gaz. Coming here all quiet. You needed something. I'm giving it to you. Be confident with her, and the job as well. If you're not sure of yourself; pretend. The rest will come, you'll find it." Gaz looks out of the window again and the drunks have disappeared to leave the summer evening serene and calm with the last of the golden sun catching the leaves. He turns back to her.

"How come you know so much?" he asks.

"It's just pretend, Gaz." Wilkinson grins, she has a pretty smile. She has a nose ring and a thin, angular face. "You are what you pretend to be."

"I think you know a lot more than you let on, Wilkinson. Thank you." There's a lump in her throat at how earnest he is. She got into foster care for the right reasons, because she wanted to help, but Wilkinson soon realised that there was easy money to be made as well. A lot more than half of the kids she looked after were broken beyond her fixing, but every so often there were those that took to her and she to them. When Gaz says thank you, she knows he means it, and if she dwelt on the sentiment, it would make her cry. She's not built to show that level of emotion, not to anyone, not even herself.

"You just be careful though, Gaz."

"Aye," he answers. "If you need any help moving, or packing, then you'll let me know, won't you?"

"I will."

"Are you going to be alright, wherever it is you're going?"

"Of course. I'll be with my friend." Wilkinson does not like to tell Gaz the truth. There's no friend out there. On the coast just north of Valencia, where the sea is blue and clean and the mediterranean breeze is sweet, there's a place for her to go. It took a while to find. With the money from the house, she can afford to stay there for two years but the doctors have told her it will not even be six months. Nobody will see her go. That's the way she wants it.

"You will come and see me again, Gaz, before I leave." This is not a request.

"Aye, I will."

"And you'll bring this lass to meet me, if you get anywhere with her. I promise I can be good. I can be if I want to."

"You're good all the time," says Gaz. Wilkinson stands up after he says this and turns back to the kitchen. If she looks him in the face she will cry.

CHAPTER TWELVE
A visit from Rose

"I thought you'd like to meet somewhere busy," says Rose.

"Suits me," says Our Dave. He didn't want to meet at all. It's Sunday afternoon. The rugby game is over already, and the fans are on their way home from the stadium in big crowds along the wide paths, splitting off to go to the carpark or over the bridge back into town. Rugby supporters don't tend to cause nearly as much trouble as football fans even though it's a tougher game. Our Dave didn't watch, there have been too many disappointments inside the FC stadium for him to mention, so he doesn't bother anymore. Rose asked to meet at the café built in the side of the stadium, but it's closed so they've met outside after the game was over. Our Dave doesn't know this man and he doesn't know either quite how he got his number, he'll be friendly enough as he always is. They walk a little, slowly out into the official's carpark.

"Good game," says Rose. He's built like a rugby player who's gone to shite over the years with a reasonable sized fat gut, big hands and a thick knotty beard under a bald head. There's a mean twinkle in his eyes. Our Dave doesn't answer. "Your lads didn't show up," he continues. "I don't know which Hull team is the worst." There are two rugby clubs here in Hull, one in red on the East side and this one, Hull FC who dress in black and white and play here in the west. Our Dave doesn't care either way, the man is trying to belittle him. FC have just played against Leeds Rhinos and evidently lost. "It's all about preparation is the game of rugby," says Rose.

"Great," follows up Our Dave. "What is it you want, mate? You could have told me over the phone." Our Dave is not sure if the man is a dickhead or not. He's starting to form an opinion though.

"There's always someone listening. That's why I like to do some things old style." Our Dave sighs. He's taller than Rose and he's wearing one of his checked shirts with the sleeves rolled up to his elbows.

"I haven't got time for this, fella. Would you mind getting to the point?"

"You owe me money." Our Dave looks down at his shoes. Now he's certain the man is a dickhead.

"Really?" There's sarcasm on his voice.

"You do, a lot of it as well." Our Dave takes out his phone and checks the time. This conversation is over before it started.

"I'm a busy man, whatever your name is."

"Rose."

"I'm a busy lad, if I owe you anything you'll have to put it in writing, and we'll go down that route. You've got my address if you've got my number."

"I thought you'd rather me and you have a chat about it. I've been in this game a while, Dave. I know how it works and I know who you are, I know what you do as well." He won't know even a quarter of what Our Dave gets up to.

"Explain it to me then," he says.

"I don't know if you've heard of me. I work for a company called Sandersons, we're in debt collection and security. It's all legit of course."

"I haven't," says Our Dave. He has. After Rose called him, he called a friend of his out at Leeds and got a run down on this man and his aspirations. Our Dave sells spirits to all the bigger clubs in Leeds, including strip bars, pool halls, chain pubs and hotels, he has contacts there. They know Rose alright, he's small time at best, but nasty.

"I buy debt, you know, Dave. I have done for a while and the bigger I get, the more I buy. I collect on it too. I just bought a load of yours." Our Dave hasn't got any debt. He cut his teeth in the seventies when borrowing money wasn't a thing, back in his day, if you didn't have the cash to get something, you couldn't have it. It's a philosophy that's served him very well over the years. The two men have walked round the corner of the big stadium, and it towers high above them. Twenty yards in front is the pitch entrance, when they've had their wash, the rugby players will be out, dressed in suits once more to get on the bus and then be driven back. In the mid distance is their big vehicle, it's a luxury white coach with 'Leeds Rhinos' written on the side and a picture of a gruff rugby player running with the ball tucked into his chest.

"Like I said, put it in writing," says Our Dave.

"I thought you might like to know. It's pretty big. A few years ago, you borrowed a very large amount from a trader bank, two hundred thousand." Our Dave thinks back. He did borrow this for the big house he owns on Pearson Park, the one that's now flats. "Northern House Bank, I believe." Our Dave could tell him that he paid the loan back, but there's no need to give this gruff man any more information than he already has. If he wants to have a go, he will.

"At risk of sounding like a record player, mate. You'll have to put that in writing."

"I thought we could do a deal right here, me and you. I'll call off the dogs and it'll all be done."

"I paid it back." Rose screws up his face.

"You might have, but not according to the bank. You know how some people make mistakes, maybe they meant to put it in one account and it went into another – that kind of thing does happen, and it's nobody's fault, is it? It can come back years later and bite you on the arse."

"You're talking shite, mate," says Our Dave, his voice has a tired quality. Rose continues:

"I'll take the two hundred, as soon as you like, and then it might go away. Do you understand?"

It's like that then. This is extortion. Our Dave's shoulders drop and his big hand goes to his face to rub his eyes. He doesn't need this. When he looks back at Rose, the man is smiling and his teeth are ill formed, tiny and off white yellow.

"It's preparation, you see, Our Dave, like the rugby. Our lads worked a bit harder than yours, and when it came to it on the field, you just didn't show up." The arrogance is a little off putting, it leaves a bad taste in Our Dave's mouth. They've walked a little into the car park.

"Two hundred grand, you say?" asks Our Dave.

"That's what it'll take, or I'll start the interest rolling and you'll get visits, not from me of course, but from people who work for me. I've got lads in this city now."

"I'd heard."

"So, you do know me."

"Not you specifically, Rose, people like you." Our Dave is not sure how to play this. He prepared more than Rose here could credit him for. They have walked round to the big carpark at the back where the player buses park, not by accident. In the mid distance, there's the pointed tower of St Mathew's Church on Anlaby Road, it's halfway to being derelict already; just before covid, good sorts in this city were trying to bring it back to life as a community centre with a foodbank and a clothes swap – that never happened, but Our Dave still has the key. In the tower and looking down the scopes of an A115A3 British Army sniper rifle is Ryan, one of Our Dave's lads. He'll have Rose in his sites now. Our Dave checks the time again. There's a message. 'All lined up,' it reads. He looks up to Rose and takes a deep breath. The man from Leeds continues in his nasal voice, he rolls his r sounds:

"I've got computer gremlins who can fix and switch things round so what looks like it's been done hasn't." He means Saif, the nimble-fingered man in a dark suit who even now sits at his laptop in the passenger seat of Rose's silver Lexus in the carpark on Walton Street.

"Can I give you some advice?" asks Our Dave.

"No," he answers. There are always difficult decisions. The very best course of action would be for Our Dave to message Ryan right now, and for him to shoot Rose in his thick neck.

That would be the whole thing done. Our Dave wouldn't have to deal with him ever again, there'd be no more of these meetings, no more calls and nothing left of Rose but his fat, solid body laid on the tarmac pumping blood from his neck. However, there would be questions asked, the police would be involved, the bullet traced, Ryan would be found. The whole idea was just to see if Ryan could do it anyway – there was never any suggestion that he was going to pull the trigger. Our Dave knows the sharpshooter has troubles, and now he's with a Kurdish girl who drives one of his taxis, he's getting better, and smarter. Dave cannot endanger him at all, nor her. Ryan is only there in case this all goes terribly wrong anyway. Our Dave checks his phone again and pumps in a message, then puts it back into his pocket. He turns to the coach that has its doors open for the players, the driver has a cap and his having a cig at a respectful distance.

"They've done well this season, have your Rhinos," says Our Dave. It's obvious Rose worships them, and it's not uncommon. A bloke loves a sports team because it connects him to somewhere or someone.

"Three point ahead," answers Rose from behind. He likes to drop the s from words like those from West Yorkshire do. "We'll take the league again." Rose is pleased with himself. He feels like he's frightened the Hull man. Our Dave turns back to him, he has done his homework on this lad from Leeds, and he knows more about him than he lets on. He could threaten Rose's natty sister who lives in Harrogate, or his girlfriend who pulls pints in the East End Park Working Men's Club a few streets down from his terraced house, or anyone who works for him, even Saif, but Rose would not blink. He'll have to be stopped, and Our Dave won't bother threatening him, he'll just get it done. Those lads that have big gobs often haven't got any bollocks at all. "I'm a very nasty enemy to make, Dave."

"You were an enemy the moment you called me up, Rose."

"So, I'll start the ball rolling, shall I? Once it gets into the system, you'll have to pay one way or another. Once the courts get hold of it, I mean, and I'll screw you down all the way for the money you owe me." He grins, "Even though you don't owe me it." Our Dave thinks up to the tower of St Mathew's with its dirty yellow bricks from the traffic smoke; having Ryan up there was more of a game than anything real, like a practise run.

"I'm tired of telling you, mate. Put it in writing."

"There's something else," says Rose.

"Go on."

"A Hull lad who's working for us. His name's Lockwood." He means Gaz.

"What about him?"

"It's a small place this, not like Leeds. I can't imagine you wouldn't know him. He's a battler for sure, and when he gets older and a bit more full of himself, he'll be a force to be reckoned with."

"What about him?"

"It would be a real shame if anything were to go wrong for that lad. He's a nice kid. A real shame." Our Dave should have kept Gaz closer; he should have given him more to do, but he thought allowing the young man freedom would be good for him. Our Dave is angry with himself suddenly. It would only take a message and he could have Rose's thick bald head split open.

"I don't know him," he says.

"Little bird tells me you do. I know people, see Dave. I'm like the rugby team here, see, I've come here to this town to squash you flat." The two men stand looking at each other and there's the noise of the players leaving the stadium, these are the Rhinos who just beat Hull KR 23 – 15, they are overly big men with arms that look like they might rip their suits.

"Like I said to you right at the start of the conversation," says Our Dave, "put it in writing."

CHAPTER THIRTEEN
Humber Rescue

It's morning. Gaz sits in Ela and looks at the email that Saif sent on the black screen of his mobile. Last night he sat down with Lilly. It was her deception as much as it was theirs because Gaz was always going to do this, although he did not know it, just like Lilly was always going to be a working girl after she stepped into the Leeds Hippo Club to be a stripper. She levelled with him. She had been instructed to help, and it was her job to make Gaz feel like he was needed. Rose has nothing to do with that north Hull dickhead, Cod, and the kidnap was genuine as well. Gaz feels like he was the punter being played.

It's fitting that he has the classic car. Like the simple dark suit and the aviator style sunglasses, these will all explain that he's both not a punter and that he wants something. He told Lilly he would do this for a month, and once the salary clears, he'll be gone, and even though Lilly said the same thing when she first started, he believes it. He thinks about the bubble pack of Adderall in his bedside cabinet. He can get out of all this any time he wants.

Saif emailed Gaz a link to an excel spreadsheet just before he left. This is what he looks at now. It's a work of art. At the top, the headings detail the contents below: names, addresses, phone numbers, social media links and so on. There are notes in the column at the end. He reads along the first line, it's Jenny Single and the address is just off Calvert Lane, in the very last box it says, 'spoke to again and explained the situation. Paid in full – Rose'. This was filled in a month or so ago, in June. Gaz wrinkles his nose at the efficiency of the business and how the suggested violence sits so easily in the sleek modern display with temperate bright colours for the different columns.

Gaz begins at number two, since the first line appears to

be sorted. The name is Humber Boat Services, and the address is the Country Park, just below the mighty Humber Bridge. Gaz knows this place. He reads across the spreadsheet on his phone: amount borrowed: 4300, total to repay as of today 6455.90. Saif has got his excel spreadsheet to apply interest automatically. In the notes he reads that this is a debt owed. Gaz puts the phone down on the passenger seat and wipes his face with his hand. Now he's a debt collector as well.

He'll go and say hello, but he's not going to threaten anyone.

The drive out to the Humber Bridge does not take more than half an hour. He passes the busy traffic on Hessle Road and drives the fast A63 out of town on the way to Leeds. The bridge stretches out into the distance to the left over the water where the sunshine dances. He turns off at Hessle and takes the route along Livingstone Road past the car dealerships and then the rugby field. The river looms beside him.

Gaz parks on the gravel next to the kid's playground opposite the river with the grey bridge above. You can hear the cars rattling the concrete and steel blocks high up, and it's lonely here with the flat, dark water in front. It's been the same ever since he can remember, Wilkinson once brought him here to walk through the forest path behind. There's a red-bricked building with two huge garage doors and the words Humber Rescue written on a sign screwed to the wall. One of the big shutters has 'Emergency Lifeboat' stencilled on it. They are closed today, but behind the concertina doors are two boats that rescue folk from the Humber River in front. They go after vessels that have blown off course, rescue amateur sailors who get into trouble or the occasional swimmer, they pull out bodies too. The water in the Humber is so cold you can't last more than a few minutes in it, and some poor bastards jump off the bridge too.

There's a little door by the side of the shutters, and a man with glasses leans on the wall with the plastic cup top of a thermos flask in his hand. He's dressed in a long, dayglo orange coat and tight rubber boots to his knees. This man is Mike Dennis, a longtime Humber lifeboat volunteer. Years ago, Mike was a technician for the university and ran their research boats up and down this river. He gave it up to volunteer full time, he tinkers with the boats and pilots them as well. He's an academic, and his knowledge of engines and machinery is of a more refined and theoretical nature, he can tune up a carburettor just fine, and he can tell you how and why it works as well. Gaz wanders over and nods his head in greeting to the man in the rubber boots. He gets to business straight away, there's no need to mess about. Gaz is already embarrassed about doing this as it is.

"I'm here to see Harold," he says. This is the name he has read on the spreadsheet.

"You a friend of his?" asks Mike. He has to check before he says the next line.

"No."

"You'll have a job," says Mike. "He's been dead for three months." Gaz sighs.

"Sorry about that," he says. Mike examines the man in front of him with his midrange black suit, open collared white shirt and what look like smart but steel toed shoes.

"What did you want him for?"

"He owes money."

"That doesn't surprise me. He liked a drink and everything else."

"What happened to him?"

"He jumped off the bridge here," Mike nods up to the concrete and steel that stretch into the grey sky and across the river. "We fished him out, or what was left of him."

"I work for a company out at Leeds, he borrowed a few grand and put his address down as here." Mike grins.

"This is a volunteer lifeboat station, mate. We're a

registered charity. He was taking the piss." Gaz smiles because this means he can't possibly collect from here.

"Do you know where he lived?"

"I don't, mate." Even if he did, Mike is not going to say anything. Harold was an old timer, a Hessle Road lad who worked out on the trawlers in the seventies and eighties before it really took a nosedive. He knew the river and he loved boats as well, so he hung around the rescue station on weekends sometimes. Gaz looks out at the bridge above them in the grey sky and then back to Mike.

"Not much we can do," he says. He's relieved to tell the truth. If he'd found Harold, he's not sure how it would have gone, so it's easier this way.

"How long have you had the car?" Mike means Ela. He spotted her the minute Gaz pulled around the corner. He's had classic cars as well.

"A couple of days," answers Gaz.

"She looks pretty good, sounds like she's running on form as well. Did you tune her up?" Gaz shakes his head.

"She just likes me, I guess."

"You look familiar."

"I've been around."

"Do you know Our Dave?" he asks. Gaz nods. "That'll be where, then."

"Do you work for him?" asks Gaz. Mike shakes his head and takes a delicate sip on his plastic cup. He does work for Our Dave because when something gets dropped into the Humber on purpose, Mike here will fish it out; that means crates of booze that have come off boats in the past, wooden boxes, bags of things, some of them heavy – Mike doesn't ask any questions because Our Dave makes sure he is well looked after. Mike tells everyone that he sold his collection of classic cars so he could buy the big house he has over in Barton, but this is stretching the truth. They did help though, and it made his wife less suspicious.

"Sorry about your mate," says Gaz. Mike nods.

"He wasn't a well man. He had all sorts wrong with him in the end." Gaz looks up at the bridge again and thinks about what it would be like to jump off it. It makes his legs go funny. "You look after that car, won't you?" adds Mike.

"I kind of get the feeling she's looking after me," says Gaz. He doesn't say this sort of thing usually.

"That's what old cars do, that's why they've been around so long." Gaz is not sure what he means. He walks back to the Capri with his shoes crunching on the gravel and gets in.

As he drives away, Gaz sees the lifeboat volunteer watching. His presence there will be noted.

CHAPTER FOURTEEN
A working girl, a massage parlour, and a brothel

Gaz follows the sat nav on his phone along the bypass all the way to Beverley. He goes through the market town along the one-way system and past the imposing, medieval church on the corner. As he drives, kids and petrol heads turn to look at the Capri, they marvel at the roar of the engine. At the lights near the North Bar, and old man taps on Gaz's windscreen, and he winds it down.

"I used to have one of those," says the man with a white moustache and a big smile.

It doesn't take long to get to Molescroft, it's a five-minute drive from the centre of the little town and quiet. He parks on the street in front of a semi with a red front door and a white garage down the drive. This is job number three. He gets out and walks along the path. The door opens as soon as he gets there, and he steps inside. A red headed woman in her fifties leads him through to the kitchen. She turns to face him. Her name is Violet according to the details. She's to pay three hundred quid.

"Are you Gaz?" she asks.

"Aye."

"You're better looking than the last fella."

"Really?"

"He was a bald bloke with a beard and horrible teeth." This would have been Rose. "He told me to set up a direct debit, and then he stopped coming so I stopped paying. Are you his replacement?" Violet's dark red hair could do with a re-colour, there are grey whisps around her ears. Her face is wrinkled, possibly from using sunbeds too much. She would have been a looker back in the day. Gaz is nervous to speak:

"I'm here to collect," he says. "You can do a bank transfer on the website or give me the cash." Violet nods.

"How much is it?"

"Three hundred," he says. She sighs.

"Do you want to do me a discount? If you've got time?" Gaz can see that the kitchen is tatty, the carpet in the little corridor is threadbare, there's the smell of damp too and Violet's eyes have bags under them, covered by the make-up. She reminds him of his mum in many ways. She smiles and her teeth are straight but off white.

"I'm just here to get the money," he says.

"Well, I haven't got it. Not at such short notice anyway." her hands are wrinkled with long pointed red nails on the end of her fingers.

"I see," says Gaz. "I'll have to come back for it another time, then." He delivers the line in a monotone voice.

"Is this your first job?" she asks. Gaz kind of nods his head.

"I've done a lot of bouncing work, but never collections."

"I can see your heart's not in it." She's got wise eyes. "That other fella with a bald head would have threatened me already. Are you going to threaten me?"

Gaz shakes his head.

"You're gonna have to come back next week then, son. I've got nothing at the moment." It's like that. She goes back down to the front door and opens it up to let him out. Gaz walks down the hall, and she fixes him with a stare as he goes past. "If you want some advice, son," she whispers. "Get out this game while you've still got the chance."

Gaz drives down Freetown Way in Hull. He goes over the blue iron of North Bridge and Ela rumbles on the tarmac. This is the spot where rugby allegiance turns from red and white to black and white or the other way round depending on which way you're going.

Holderness Road is settling into mid-morning. The rush hour is long gone and the traffic is light, an old man is out for a stroll in the sunshine, a little trio of skag heads move with purposeful steps, they are deep in earnest conversation, two big policemen queue at the Cozy Café sandwich shop with their big armoured vests and the pockets stuffed with equipment. This is the longest shopping street in Hull and stretches more than two and a half miles. The businesses are takeaways or nail bars, closed down newsagents, charity shops and hair salons, like the whole of this town, Holderness Road suffers from poverty, neglect, and crime. Gaz pulls off into a side street and parks up behind a white van. He checks his phone and the address before getting out and walking onto Holderness Road proper. Between Heavenly Nails and an undertaker there's a white door with a colourful sign over the top that reads 'Happy Yu Thai Massage'. Gaz taps on the glass with his knuckles. He doesn't want to do this. He wonders what it would be like to be a firefighter or to work for the police. He wonders if he'd get the sense that he is doing something wrong, this is the feeling he has now.

A little woman opens the door. She could be Vietnamese or Thai. She wears a white tabard like she's a nurse and has black hair and dark olive skin.

"You have appointment?" she asks. The company he works for, Sandersons, have emailed her already and they will have called as well to let them know Gaz would turn up this week. They will probably fob him off like the redhead did in Beverley.

"I've got an appointment," says Gaz. She beckons him in and he follows her up some stairs with a mucky light green carpet. There's the smell of floral massage oil that is just going off mixed with the cheap chemical stink of air freshener. When they get to the top, she points to a row of plastic chairs in front of three doors. He doesn't sit down.

"Which girl you order?" she asks.

"I'm here to see the manager," says Gaz. She looks at him for the first time and her expression is off. Lilly has explained the sex industry to Gaz, he knew something about it of course, but not how huge it is. There are titty bars in the cities, brothels, saunas, escorts, online dancers, trans cam girls, sugar daddies, gay telephone sex lines, and massage places like this one. This lass, who could be from Cambodia or Malasia, will give a fella a massage and then toss him off for an extra tenner - with her tits out for another fiver.

"No manager here," she snaps. "You got an appointment or not?"

"Your manager knows I'm coming," says Gaz. He's calm as he stands there next to the three closed doors which will have massage beds and clean towels in them. The woman goes into one of the rooms and speaks to someone in a foreign language. Another Asian woman who is much bigger comes out. This one has big fat arms and blonde streaks in her short dark hair.

"Not manager here," she shouts at Gaz.

"I'm here to collect money," he explains. The bigger woman flares her nostrils. Rose would have been here before to hassle them. That's why she's reacting like this.

"Not manager here, and no money. You understand. No money here." She's frowning and her voice is confrontational. Gaz narrows his eyes down at her. The smaller girl stands behind and her face is frightened and defiant at the same time. These woman are both a long way from where they once called home, and the story of how they got here will be a complex one. They could have been brides, tricked or trafficked, or their family might have scrabbled together to find enough money to get them here with smugglers – who they would owe. Gaz has an understanding of this. He steps back.

"You not get money, no manager here," says the big woman again. She's aggressive already, and this comes from fear. Gaz is probably meant to turn nasty. He steps further back, but his face remains steady and serious. He knows from his days as a bouncer that people attack when they think you are weak, although he will not hurt these two, he doesn't want any sort of hassle from them.

"I'll come back another day," he says. The big woman's teeth grit in anger.

"You not come back. No money. Not manager here." Gaz shrugs his shoulders. There will be someone in charge. These girls will pay someone, maybe that's what the bigger woman does. Gaz holds his hands up with his palms facing them to show that he's not a threat. He's not Rose, he isn't going to hurt them.

"Someone will come to get the money," he says. "It might not be me. You can wait for them."

"You no come back," says the bigger one. Gaz shrugs again. He walks down the stairs and lets himself out the front door.

Back in Ela, Gaz sits at the wheel and rubs his face. He is not cut out for this. He's got one more place to visit and then he'll call it a day. He starts the engine, turns the car, and then drives off into the traffic of Holderness Road.

Lilly has explained the game to Gaz. Brothels are illegal under UK law. That means that two girls working together in a flat or house is a brothel. Like the Thai place they pretend to be massage parlours with the stipulation on the website clear that any money exchanged between the woman and the punter is between them. That's not what really happens. The girls will pay the house something like fifty percent of what they earn and then there'll be a charge for the rent of the room and the bedding, the cleaning too. Gaz has driven twenty minutes back through town past the big hospital where tower blocks loom over the streets. At the top of Boothferry Road there's one of these parlours. Gaz was offered a job here, standing at the back door, a few years ago but he turned it down because he didn't want to get into this business. Here he is, into the same business, but deeper.

It's just after twelve and the street isn't so busy. He finds a parking space on the main street outside the Polish butcher. On the left is the massage place. The shop front and the windows have been painted completely white like the door, there's no sign, and yet everyone knows what this place is. You don't go in through the front, you go down the little street on the left and past the back of the shops and houses. Gaz walks down there. At the back, there's a big white door, Gaz taps on the frosted glass and it opens to a tall man with shaved ginger hair and a fat, dumb looking face.

"It's ten quid to get in," he says. Gaz narrows his eyes at the man.

"I'm here to see Maryanne," he says.

"It's ten quid to get in," repeats the ginger lad. He must be six foot two, Gaz can't see the rest of his body because it's hidden behind the door. This is what Gaz would have been doing if he'd taken the job. He examines the man's piggy eyes and the bad skin, his faint stubble and flabby neck. He knows him.

"It's Cliff, isn't it?" he asks.

"Yeah," says the ginger man as if this was common knowledge. "Who are you?"

"Gaz. We bounced at the Admiral a few years back." This is where he knows him from. He's older than Gaz by a few years and they both worked the door at the big pub in town where the drinks are cheap and there can be a lot of trouble. They fought a few times side by side. The piggy ginger lad is called Cliff because his second name is Clifford. He's as dull as a muddy puddle. He frowns as he looks at the visitor.

"Gaz?" he asks as he opens the door fully. He's a lot bigger since they last met.

"Alright Cliff," says Gaz. If they'd had a better relationship when they worked together, he might mention that the big man has put on a load of weight. There were fights where Cliff was more heavy-handed than he needed to be, and punters returned to sort him out when he was off work. Gaz heard too that he was in trouble for some underage lass he got caught with.

"It's still a tenner if you wanna come in, Gaz," he says.

"I'm not here as a punter, I'm here to see Maryanne." This is the name of the madam according to Saif's notes, he keeps detailed information about bigger establishments like this.

"It's still ten quid," repeats Cliff. He's got a breathless quality in the way he speaks from his fat neck. Gaz fishes out his wallet and passes over a ten-pound note. Cliff takes it and beckons him to come in. "Where are you working now then, Gaz?" he asks as he leads him down the corridor.

"I'm kind of in protection," he answers. "People aren't nearly as friendly as they are in pubs." This is true. Gaz goes through a fire door, leaving Cliff behind him, and there's a chest level reception desk opposite a ratty looking sofa and a coffee table. The receptionist is well into her sixties with a cracked and wrinkled face under heavy make-up and smoker's black lines between her teeth when she smiles. She's blonde with a big quiff held tight by hairspray.

"Hiya love," she says. Her voice is husky from the cigs. "Is this your first time or have you been with us before?"

"I'm looking for Maryanne," says Gaz. He's businesslike and straight to the point. The woman's face changes.

"Who's asking?"

"I work for a company called Sandersons. You have an agreement with them, I believe. I'm here on business. Did you get an email?" Gaz surprises himself with his clarity. This is not the kind of thing he expects himself to say, he sounds all calm like a salesman.

"I'm Maryanne," she says. A scowl forms across her wrinkled top lip. She motions her head for him to follow and he steps through the hatch in the reception bar into another room behind. She smells of cigs that have been sprayed with cheap perfume and he winces as he walks through the cloud of it. In the back room, there's an old filing cabinet, a desk with a laptop against the wall and no windows. A single bulb hangs down from the ceiling. She turns to face him.

"Where's the big ugly fella who came round last time?" She means Rose.

"I'm his replacement."

"Haven't you done well?" Her tone is sarcastic.

"I assume he explained everything to you."

"He did. I told him he'll get nothing. I also emailed your company and I told you straight." Gaz does not say anything. He can see she is instantly rattled. "I was very clear. This is a legitimate business, I pay my tax and I'm all above board. So, you see, Love, I'll not be paying protection money to you, or anyone, that's not how the game works, and if you don't like it, I'll have Cliff come in. Now, I've explained where I am by email, and I'm explaining it to you to your face – that should be clear enough to you people. You're not getting any money." Gaz stands looking at her lightly froth with her blonde hair wobbling where it's been fixed with spray.

"On the account it says you owe two grand," he says. She steps closer to him so the scent of fags is raw.

"I'm not going to pay. What are you going to do about it?"

"Nothing," says Gaz. This is not the answer she was expecting. Maryanne was once a working girl herself so she knows the tricks. Behind her, on the table next to the laptop is a police style hardened baton that she bought off eBay for personal protection. Her left hand is ready to grab it if he makes a move to hit her. "I'm not here to do anything to you at all," explains Gaz. He feels like he's Rose as he's talking. "The first thing they'll do is shut down your website for the business, then they'll close any social media accounts for it, then your personal social media, and those of the lasses working here. They'll go for your bank account next, and they'll empty that. The computer guys they have at Sandersons are out of this world." He means Saif. "I've also heard they've hacked the land registry, so they can transfer the deeds of properties into different names, if you own a house or a flat or anything, that could be you. They'll have that as well." Gaz is just stating facts and his voice is monotone. He watches her nostrils flare. Gaz does not like doing this. This woman will no doubt be a horror to the girls who work for her, but what kind of horror has been inflicted on her to make her so? The words coming out of Gaz's mouth feel worse than corporate poison but he can't stop now he is this far in.

"I'll have Cliff come through, shall I?" she asks.

"You can do," says Gaz. "He knows me. We bounced together. He's seen me at work before." This is the first threat of violence he's made.

"It's taken me years to make this business work," she whispers. "Years of graft and struggle. Do you know how hard it is to make a living doing this?" As they speak, there's a working girl somewhere upstairs, looking up at the ceiling with her legs splayed and her hands on the hairy back of a fat man in his fifties as he rides her. Like lots of bosses, Maryanne here thinks she does all the work.

"I'm sorry," says Gaz genuinely. "I'm just a messenger. You can pay me in cash."

"We're just honest working people, why can't you leave us alone?" Gaz feels remorse. "You seem like a nice lad. How have you got mixed up in all this?"

"Who says I'm mixed up in it?"

"That's what happens to us all, kid. You do it for a day and then it's a week. Next it's a month and then one day you wake up and you've been at it for ten years. Is that what you want?"

"I'm just doing what I have to do. You just have to pay. They're horrible people, even to their own, even to themselves." Gaz thinks about Rose and his dull grey humorless face and ratty beard.

"How long have I got?" she asks.

"Today," he says.

"You know in the eighties men like you used to come

round with cricket bats and bike chains. They'd fight the bouncers and if they won, then the misses would pay. Times have changed. We used to get robbed fair and square. We'd be protected too from the others." Of course, Maryanne could go to the police and say this is extortion. She doesn't want them involved or she'd probably have to pay them as well.

"We're all getting robbed one way or another," says Gaz. Maryanne seems to relax. She goes to the desk with the laptop, just behind the screen is an open packet of cigs, she pulls one out and holds it in her hand before she puts it in her mouth.

"What kind of protection do I get from you?" she asks.

"You can call me for anything you need. Sandersons will also handle any internet nasties you get, that includes the tax man." Maryanne will know all this. She paid Rose last time of course. She's just testing him. She lights the cigarette. She was probably going to pay him all along.

"I'll let you have a grand now in cash, and I'll transfer the rest over later on today. Just to be clear, I will call on you. I'll get my money's worth, kid. What's your name?"

"Gaz."

"And you say your harder than Cliff?"

"He'll tell you." She nods. Maryanne knows people who can actually handle themselves don't need to prove it. She employs Cliff outside because he's all bravado and bluster and he's big with a booming voice, that's all good for scaring people. Maryanne takes a brown envelope out of the drawer. This will be the money. She walks over to Gaz and hands it to him.

"I'll be calling on you, kid, mark my words."

"See that you do," he answers. Maryanne thinks she can see him swallow.

She knows a nice lad when she sees one.

CHAPTER FIFTEEN
Kate

The thousand quid in the envelope is in Ela's glovebox. Gaz doesn't actually want it. Now he's a pimp, he can decide when he works. He's had enough of seedy brothels or massage spas already and he wants to see Kate. It's Sunday. Lilly is off at her mother's. He asked Kate to meet him late afternoon. Gaz hates coffee and doesn't drink beer, so he suggested taking her to the Marina. They could walk along past the boats and get an ice-cream from the little shop that overlooks the big river. Gaz did this with his mum once, years ago. He tried to channel his airline pilot dad to think of somewhere better to go, but all he could come up with were expensive restaurants and posh boozers. Gaz has to rely on himself most of the time. Years ago, his imaginary fathers helped him out a lot more than they do now.

Kate said she finishes at the library at four, so he offered to pick her up from Belvoir Street. Gaz is early and has managed to find a parking space for Ela not too far away. He gets out and walks towards her front door, his mouth is dry, and he can feel his heartbeat shallow in his chest. Part of him - the thinking part, knows that this is the wrong thing to do, but there's a deeper element that keeps his feet walking.

At the red front door, he knocks and steps back. His hands go to smooth down his hair and he checks that his shirt is tucked in. Before he can finish, the door opens, and she is there with her straight blonde hair over her shoulders and a big white smile that shows a gap in her teeth. She wears a long dress and no shoes or socks.

"Do you want to come in for a minute?" she asks. "I've just got to send this email to someone at the uni." Gaz nods and steps in.

He follows her down the hall and to the room with the two sofas where he spoke to her before, and where she unpicked him so effortlessly. His throat is sore. There's a laptop open on the coffee table, and she sits down at it, her fingers are a blur of movement over the keyboard. He can see her smooth shoulders and the curve of the muscles on her forearm. She closes the laptop and stands facing him with that smile. It falls as she sees him looking at her.

There's something between them, something that Gaz can't put his finger on. He's been with girls before but more because he thought he should than he wanted to – the deed of sex itself is something he is not comfortable with even if it's something he needs. He knows this is screwed up, but Gaz has given up trying to change the way he feels. When he looks into Kate's eyes here, he feels that this is different, clean somehow because they are not drunk and nobody has paid money, there's been no threat of violence – he holds nothing over her, and she has nothing over him. They are in the same room he thinks, because they want to be.

Gaz does not have anything to say. Where there should be a cheeky smile and smooth chat, he has nothing but his earnest stare and his sharp, blue eyes. His intelligence tells him, like Wilkinson explained, that she is too good for him. She does not stop staring up into his eyes.

Kate has been chatted up too many times to be won over by clever talk, she has fallen for smart dressers, and suave movers who charm with their confidence and guile. It has to be something real for her or she would rather not bother. This is what Gaz has, she can see it in his eyes and his flared nostrils. She swore she would not do this kind of thing again. Gaz's stomach gurgles and his legs wobble. He is moving towards her and she to him. He leans down and they exchange a single tender kiss, the electricity of it rattles down Gaz's spine and across his back. He steps away.

"What is it?" she asks.

"This is moving too quickly for me," he says. "I really like you." She nods. Gaz means it, but if he channelled his airline pilot dad, this would be the perfect line for the situation. She smiles up at him and he can see the wide gap between her front teeth. Without knowing how, Gaz is moving towards her again, and their arms go around each other.

It's not like Gaz has had before.

Not at all.

They kiss, tongues and lips, but there is no error here, no slip or mistake on either part. Gaz's hand goes up to hold the back of her head through her smooth blonde hair, and he can feel the curve of her neck. She grips his back; her fingers claw at the thin material of his shirt as he kisses her. The angle their heads bend is the right way for the other, for this is a movement they make together. Gaz is gentle and he finds that he is good at this, as good as she is even.

There's no sleaze to it as she sits on top of him on the dark couch where they chatted a few days before. Gaz doesn't manage to take his trousers off one leg and though she takes off her dress over her head, she keeps on the bra. It's deep and warm in parts, desperate and tender too. The light smell of her gets into Gaz's eyes and he is lost in her long hair. He is sure of himself, that's the way she makes him feel, these movements are unrehearsed but work almost like he was meant to be here with her, and she him. Gaz holds her tight as her bones shake inside her, he sees her teeth grit as she moans, he feels her stomach tighten. For a minute or more they hold each other, sweating lightly and stuck together with her hot breath in his ear and his face in her shoulder. Her pleasure gives him power – like he's worth something, like he's done something right.

Upstairs in the bathroom, Gaz washes his face because his eyes are watering, perhaps it's relief. He wipes them away with the back of his hand. He spent years in children's homes, so he knows how to do this without making a sound, but he is conscious that he has left her downstairs.

In the kitchen, she's drinking a glass of water, and her

blonde hair is messed up. She smiles at him when her returns.

"I didn't expect that to happen," she says.

"Me neither."

"I'm glad it did." Her tone is not at all playful. In her experience, men take the piss ultimately because they only have one thing on their mind. It feels different with him.

"Me too." Gaz is tongue tied. He has to rely on the truth, it's the only thing that he's got. He searches for something to say, but the deep part of him, the one who brought him here against his common sense speaks before he can come up with anything. "How about that walk around the Marina?" he asks. She smiles and it makes her face light up.

"Yes. You said we could have ice-cream." Gaz smiles too. He goes to the dark sofa and puts his shirt on while Kate watches him from behind. "You know I've had my problems too, Gaz," she says. He turns. Her face is serious. She is not sure why. "You're the first since I got sober. It's been more than a year."

"You don't need to tell me," he says.

"I want to. You told me about yourself. I need to tell you about me. It's only fair." Gaz does the buttons up on his shirt. He didn't expect this. Kate seems so perfect and together, with a future and plans and education, with a wide and bright smile that does not look like it could ever be in trouble.

"You could tell me when we walk around the Marina, if you want," he answers. Gaz is surprised at how well he can reply sometimes, almost without trying. Kate smiles again when he says this, and nods. Gaz slips on his jacket and fiddles for the keys to Ela. His phone buzzes in the inside pocket. He looks down at it and then to Kate. Whoever it is can go away.

"Aren't you going to answer?" asks Kate.

"It'll be work," he says. "I don't want to." The buzzing stops and then begins again, like an angry bee at his chest. He fishes it out only to turn it off. There are missed calls from Lilly and many texts, he reads the latest:

'HELP,' it says. He swallows. Kate sees his face go pale.

"What is it?"

"Trouble," he whispers.

"Work trouble?"

"Yes. Someone's in danger." She blinks at him with her clear blue-grey eyes.

"I see," she says.

"I have to go. I'm needed." She does not look the same without her smile. "If it were anyone else… this is someone I look after." She nods. This doesn't feel right to Gaz. He wants to take her for a walk on a sunny day like today. They could look out over the water at the south bank in the distance. He could pretend to see a dolphin like he used to do with his mother.

"Will I see you again?" she asks. She knows she will.

"Of course."

"When?"

"Tomorrow, in the evening. I'll message you." She comes forward to him and they kiss as before with lips and tongues. Gaz holds her face in his hands and looks down into her blue-grey eyes, he holds the stare and feels her looking back at him.

"Please don't play with me, Gaz," she whispers. "I'm only just getting better. I've only just come back to myself."

"I wouldn't," he says. Kate wants to believe him, but she knows men; they aren't complex creatures and whatever Gaz is, he'll be a man first.

Ela does not start first time round. He turns the key and her engine splutters and coughs. He is patient and takes a moment to get out his phone, he dials the answer machine and puts it on the speaker so he can hear the message again. Ela starts and he edges out of the car parking space and moves off down Belvoir Street, the message from Lilly kicks in.

"Are you there, Gaz?" at once, he can hear that she is drunk. He breathes a sigh of relief as he gets to the end of the street. "I'm coming back from my mum's at six and I just wondered if you'd be at home?" She has cried wolf. The message clicks off and another clicks in straight away, this will be Lilly again. Her words are slurred and stupid. "I need you to help me with something." Gaz drives along Princes Avenue past Pearson Park and he darkens. He could be with Kate. He's been tricked, and not for the first time. He turns off past the Queens and at the lights on Beverley Road, he taps his fingers on the big wheel in front of him and looks down at the round eighties style dials and the petrol gauge. He has to wash his hands of Lilly, if he's going to get anything sorted.

It has to be sooner rather than later as well.

Lilly comes back from her mum's at just after six. Gaz let himself in and waited. She says she's more full than drunk, but she is drunk all the same. She carries in all her washed clothes in two bin liners from the taxi, and Gaz helps her take them upstairs. Back in the kitchen, she drinks a black coffee and eats biscuits. It sobers her up, but only so she can have a bottle of wine in the bath. Gaz sits down in the chair in front of her.

"What did you text me for? You said you needed help." Lilly looks at him and her eyebrows have been drawn on wonky. She will have forgotten she did.

"It was just a laugh," she says back.

"I was busy," says Gaz. There's a ping on Lilly's white phone and she digs it out of her handbag to look at the black screen.

"You could have told me to piss off?" she says as she scrolls the phone with her thumb.

"I'm meant to look after you." She looks up.

"I can look after myself, Gaz. What do you think I've been doing all these years?"

"Do you remember what you said the other morning?"

"I don't remember what I said this morning," Lilly has a cruel streak. She wants him here, but only so she isn't alone.

"You talked about getting out of the game." She scoffs when he says this, as if she was a child to even thinks so. With the aid of drink and the warmth of her family that afternoon, Lilly will have forgotten the rigours of having sex for money and also, the stone-cold face of Rose and his nasty ways.

"You should loosen up you know, Gaz," she says. "Have a drink for once. Spend some of your money. How much did you collect today?"

He shrugs.

"Are you gonna at least try to get out?" he asks.

"I wasn't thinking what I was saying, Gaz. I'm gonna ride this out till I get enough money to pay off my sister's mortgage. It's not like I can just walk into a job, is it now? I'm not qualified to work anywhere."

"You could be," says Gaz.

"Me? I'm a working girl. That's all I am, that's what I'll always be." It's easy to say a thing like this when drunk, because you can't feel what it means. Rose trained her to believe this too.

"I think you're talking shite. I'll be out of this as soon as."

"So, you're just going to run off, are you? Like Rose will let you. You're as trapped as I am, only more so. You'll not be worth anything to him at all. At least I make him money. What do you do?" When she explains it in these terms, he feels foolish having confided in her.

Gaz stands up. This is his reaction to conversations that he does not like or cannot handle. He usually removes himself from them. Lilly continues:

"You're swimming with the sharks already, kid. If I were you, I'd just do exactly what I was supposed to. Rose can get to you, Saif will already have tracked everything you've ever done online, he'll know everything about you, where you've been, who you talk to and what you say. They'll hurt someone if they don't hurt you." Gaz thinks about Kate. He must not get close to her.

"I don't have anyone," he says. She scoffs once more.

"You're not a hard man, Gaz. You might have the moves, but you're not cruel enough. You're wide open and someone like Rose will just rip right through you."

"Should I have left you with those lads in Leeds?"

"Maybe you should, for you, not for me. That's what you don't understand, Gaz. You have to put yourself first. I've known blokes like you before, they do everything for everyone else and they think it makes them a better person. It's needy that's what it is. Nobody likes the tit who wants to hold your shopping bags." She is cruel to him. Lilly drank a bottle of white wine with her dinner, and she is starting to sober up now – the creeping headache forces the truth from her in the worst way. "Have we got any vodka?" she asks as she gets up and goes to the cupboard. There's a three-quarter full bottle with a fancy label that a punter bought her a while back. She grabs it down and unscrews the top then brings it back to the table and pours a good measure into her empty water glass. She'll drink it neat. Gaz can sense her pain.

"I think it's best if I don't stay here anymore," he says. Lilly has had this information in the back of her mind all along. She takes a sip on the vodka. She likes having Gaz around. He's quiet and steady, but he does not need her, and this is why he is not weak like the men she has just described. Unlike the punters who visit Lilly, Gaz is there to look after her, and she believes it is because he is paid to do so. It's not that at all, he said that he would, and Gaz will not break his word. He would carry her shopping bags if she asked him, not because he is under her control but because he looks after her. Lilly has already planned to have another working girl come and stay with her when he goes, for there is safety in company. She didn't think he'd go so soon. She looks up at him with her dark eyes and they are crooked and pissed up.

"You could stay one more night."

"Why? You can look after yourself."

"I was talking rubbish." She looks up at him again. He is professional in all this and still remains calm and polite. "You have to be real about the situation you've got into, Gaz. If you don't want to do the job, go and see Rose, give him back the money you earned and say no thanks, then walk away. He'll not be happy, but for every day you spend doing his business it'll be harder for you to get out. I know. It happened to me." She takes a glug on her vodka and her face has no emotion as it goes down her throat. "If I got out, Gaz, he'd go straight to my mum. He knows where she is. He's told me what he'd do to her, and I should know. He's done it to me." Gaz looks down at the lino floor and breathes in through his nose.

"I won't involve you and you don't know anything," says Gaz. "You're right, I do too much for some people and I know why. I do it because it makes me feel like I'm worth something." He can see the snarl form on Lilly's face.

"Will you stay one more night? You can leave before I wake up if you want."

"I've got to see a man about a dog," says Gaz.

"What about me?"

"You've looked after yourself this far, Lilly. Another night isn't going to hurt."

"I'm just a whore to you, Gaz, is that it?"

"My mother was a whore," he answers.

"You never told me."

"You never asked."

"You're lying." She can see that he isn't. "She still in the game, is she? Have I got competition?" It's so easy to be cruel to Gaz.

"Not anymore," he answers.

"Did you help her get out? I bet she was so proud of you. I bet she was so happy to have a son like you." Lilly can see that she is close to crossing a line with him, his eyes blaze in anger.

"She's dead," he says. At once Gaz wishes he hadn't said

this. It gives Lilly too much information about him. This is a job. She is a client. He is not involved, but his anger has caused him to reveal too much of himself. He steps into the living room towards the front door. Lilly stands.

"I'm sorry, Gaz," she calls. She really is. She's too drunk to go after him.

On Hessle Road, next to the trawlerman's charity shop, there's a motorbike place. It wraps around the corner onto Subway Street with a little workshop on the side. This is Clarendon Bikes, and Gaz rents the tiny flat above it. The owner is a metal head called Alan who lives just out of town. Hessle Road is a tough street so he would rather have someone there in the little flat at night and when he's not open. Gaz once did a weekend shift at the Silver Cod on Anlaby Road, it's got a fierce reputation, and he stopped Alan from near killing a skag head who'd glassed his mate. Retribution is one thing, but serving time is quite another. It's hard to see sense through drink sometimes. Alan charges Gaz enough to cover any bills he might run up and a bit more to save face, just by being there he's probably stopped a burglary. Gaz unlocks the gates at the back and drives Ela into the car parking space. It's the first time he's brought the car here. He wonders what Alan will make of it.

Upstairs the kitchen is clean but outdated. One of the cupboards is full of mugs for the mechanics and shop staff. They've left their dirty spoons and an open sugar packet next to the kettle. The fridge has long life milk and a left-over lunch box but nothing else.

In the single bedroom there's a bed, the glass in the window that faces the street has been painted black, it feels cold even on a warm night like this. In the thin wardrobe are Gaz's shirts and the two Top-man suits. The wallpaper is brown and there's no lampshade on the light, so the low watt bulb hangs lonely.

Gaz's brain buzzes. He hears Lilly's sharp words in his ears. A lot of what she said is true. He is needy and that's why he does what he does, that's why he went all the way to Leeds, not to save her, but so that he did not get it wrong. He thinks back to Kate and the way she got inside his head to discover what he thought was hidden, and how she did so effortlessly. Gaz opens the drawer in the bedside cabinet and sees the blister pack of Adderall that he found on the floor of a nightclub toilet. He knows that five or six of the little ADHD tablets will kill him. He does think he's worthless. Maybe that's why he rents a flat like this one, without warmth or comfort. Maybe this is all he deserves.

In his younger days, Gaz daydreamed that one of his fathers would find him somehow, and they'd drive away into the world together. His rugby player dad drives a rugged Land Rover, his pilot father has a vivid red sports car with the top down, and his professor dad sits in the back of a black cab with a cigar and round glasses above a wise grin. It's beginning to fade. His father was more likely one of the men who he has seen visit Lilly, men whose hairs clog up the shower drain and who cannot hang towels back on a radiator, men who think that Lilly likes them even though they pay her to do so. Gaz does not judge them as harshly as he judges himself.

He remembers Kate's lips on his, the smell of her neck and shoulders and her educated hands on his bare back. That cannot be allowed to carry on, not with what Lilly told him about Rose. The man will find her and hurt her. Gaz will not let that happen.

Maybe when he's ended it with Kate, he'll come back for the Adderall after all.

CHAPTER SIXTEEN
Gaz and Kate

It is the next day. Kate has invited him to her house for coffee but Gaz asked to meet her in the café opposite Sainsbury's on Princes Avenue instead. In light of what Lilly explained to him, it's best for him to stop this going any further. He could do this over the phone, and then he would never have to see her again, but... he does want to see her again.

She's late, and so he stands outside checking his emails. He's only concerned about anything from Sandersons. Gaz doesn't do social media really, he'll have a look, but he hasn't got anything to say and even if he did, he's not sure anyone would be interested.

She appears next to him with a hello and takes hold of the top of his arm to pull him down for a kiss. It's warmth that he's not used to. She smiles and shows the white teeth with the gap in them and her grey-blue eyes. Gaz's stomach rumbles. She's got her blonde hair in a ponytail and it shows the curve of her neck and her ears. Any sense or intelligence that Gaz possessed a few moments previous is gone. She smells sharp and sweet at the same time and takes him through the doors of the café then finds a table inside where she sits next to him against the wall. It has happened so quickly and Gaz finds himself smiling at her.

"I've been thinking about you," she whispers, and before he can stop himself he repeats:

"I've been thinking about you too." He has. It's been like a CD stuck on repeat, he gets flashbacks of kissing her, feels the pressure of her lips on his and her hands clawing at his back with her breath hot on his face. The Polish waitress takes their orders, Gaz has a green tea and hopes it doesn't make him look like a bohemian type tosser, Kate has an Americano. When the waitress has gone, they are alone again, she's sitting close to him. Gaz remembers why he's here. However much he likes her, he is involved in something that's dangerous and if she's seen with him, she'll get dragged into it as well. This line of thinking is convenient for Gaz, too, because he is already uncomfortable with how he feels about her. He's not felt like this for anyone before. It makes him vulnerable.

"We need to talk," in Gaz's experience this is how people begin difficult conversations. "I don't think we should see each other anymore." She takes her hand off his leg.

"We're not seeing each other," she says.

"I know. I mean I don't think we should carry on."

"We've had a kiss and a cuddle. Does that mean we're in a relationship? Is that why you wanted to meet here?"

"Yes." Gaz looks at his green tea.

"What have I done?" she asks. She has a slight frown. She likes him. Gaz doesn't have the wit or the experience to give her anything but a version of the truth. He is concerned about Rose finding out about her, but he is also worried for himself. She will hurt him. Like Wilkinson jokes, Kate is out of his league. It's best to end this now before he starts to get involved. He already is involved.

"I don't want anything serious."

"We've met a few times and had a fumble," she says back. "Nothing's had time to develop." He looks up at her, right in the eyes. Desire does not need time, like hope. It happens in a flat second. She can see that things have already developed for Gaz. Both of these two are lying.

Gaz looks out the big window at the midday Princes Avenue traffic in the sunshine.

"What are you afraid of?" she asks.

"Messing up. People getting hurt. You getting hurt." Kate understands this as emotional damage but that's not what Gaz means at all. He means thugs from Leeds booting down her door and smashing up her house, possibly doing worse to her.

"You could just take a chance."

"I can't." Kate drinks the rest of her coffee in two gulps. She's out of options. There have been men recently, of course: the junior doctor from down south, the lad who played the bass in the indie band, the mild-mannered college lecturer – all good types but with nothing of the danger and raw emotion that Gaz here has. The car salesman she lived with told her he loved her, but she could see that it was not true, unlike this man who sits next to her who has the way he feels etched all over his face. He's earnest and vulnerable – she wouldn't hurt him. This is not over at all.

"You'll walk me back to mine then," she says. There's no need for him to.

"Ok." He doesn't think it's a good idea, that was why he wanted to meet her here and not at her house. Things may develop. If she invites him inside he'll go. He will not be able to help himself at all.

They go over the zebra crossing and walk back towards Belvoir Street. Gaz's mouth is dry like his throat. They don't say anything as they go along past the big bay windows and parked up cars, past the blue and black wheelie bins and the tabby cat peering down at them from a bedroom window. He knows he should not be doing this, but he cannot help it. Halfway down she stops at her door and opens the yale lock with her key. She goes inside and looks at him over her shoulder as she holds it open for him.

"It's just a fumble," she says. He steps inside.

That's not what it is at all.

Gaz sits in Ela when it's done. He puts his hands on the steering wheel but doesn't start the engine as he stares blank ahead through the windscreen. He gets flashbacks of the event like he used to when he'd been in a fight, only there's nothing negative about his time with Kate. His head is dizzy with her smell still in his nose. When it was over, they laid next to each other and she talked to him, sweet and open about her work and the gossip from the library, she talked about cooking and her sister, where she wants to go on holiday and the cat. There was no talk about what Gaz had said to her in the café, as if they'd never been there at all. She didn't ask, but somehow Gaz told her he was brought up in care after his mother died, and of the various places he stayed before he met Wilkinson, and she took him under her wing. He felt he could talk to her, and this is the most dangerous part, he thinks, as he looks over the long bonnet of the 2.6 Lazer Capri to the car parked in front. Understand that Gaz does not speak to anyone about himself in any depth but he could tell her anything, and he does not care if she hurts him even.

Gaz rests his head on the steering wheel as he worries – the business with Sandersons is dangerous. They cannot know he has been seeing her, and it has to stop, right now, for her own good. He's already said that to himself, and he already couldn't do it once. How will he do if he tries to end it again? At least the punters pay Lilly and then walk away. Gaz is going to end up just walking away from Kate without even a goodbye.

There's a tap on the passenger side window. Gaz looks up. A tall figure with a bald head and a grey beard looks back at him. It's Our Dave. The man opens the door just enough so he can put his head in.

"You ok there, Gaz?" he asks. He's genuine. It's not unusual to find Our Dave walking these streets from an odd job he's been doing for someone.

"I am," Gaz has to remember that although he doesn't like men, he has greatly wronged a good fella like Our Dave by stealing and effectively writing off his posh van. "Can I give you a lift anywhere?" asks Gaz. He wants to make amends.

"Go on then," says Our Dave as he gets in. He sets his tool bag in the footwell with a clink and then sits down. "This is something special, isn't it?" He means the car. Our Dave looks over the long bonnet and behind him at the seats and then to the dashboard. There is something familiar about Ela, as if he's sat in this seat before. "Takes me back to the eighties. Where'd you get it?"

"Richmond Street garage." Gaz is beginning to realise that the car is something much more special than he thought when he bought her from Barry for three and a half thousand pounds. You can sometimes learn the value of things through how other people see them. "You can have her if you want, Our Dave," says Gaz. He wants to make it right between him and the old man, for his own conscience as much as anything else.

"It's too nice for me, Gaz, and I bet she drives like shite."

"Sometimes she does," says Gaz. "Other times she kind of does it herself." He doesn't really know what he means, again.

"They've got minds of their own have these cars, Gaz. You have to treat them right. I had a mate back in the day who had one, the same colour as this, could even be the same car." Gaz starts the engine and it roars into life as he moves off down Belvoir Street to Princes Ave. Two young lads stop and stare at the beast as they drive past. Gaz will take Our Dave up Westbourne Ave to Chants and then on to his taxi office. It's a five-minute ride depending on traffic.

"I'm sorry about what happened, Our Dave. I really am, and if there's anything I can do to make up for it, I'd do it."

"You've said that already, Gaz. You know I've been hearing things here and there. People tell you all sorts of stories when you work in a taxi office, and this car isn't exactly inconspicuous."

"What have you heard?"

"I heard that you've been out and about, to certain places that aren't very nice, if you know what I mean." They've turned off the main road and are going slowly up Westbourne Ave - even slower up the speed bumps. On either side are huge, terraced houses with three storeys and vast backyards. Gaz senses that Our Dave bumped into him on purpose.

"I've been working for that company in Leeds, they're called Sandersons. It's a protection thing," he realises this sounds dodgy although he doesn't mean it to. "I'm not going to cause any trouble, and I'll help the punters out if I can. It's just temporary as well."

"I've told you already about those fellas in Leeds, Gaz. I warned you. They're not the kind of people you can do business with, you can't trust them."

"I'm just looking after people, that's all. It's security. I'm not gonna hurt anyone."

"You'll be expected to, in the end," says Our Dave. "That's how it'll have to be."

"How'd you know?"

"You see patterns, Gaz, you learn how the world works."

"What if this is different?"

"It isn't, is it?" Gaz nods. "Get out while you still can," says Our Dave.

"I will. I'm going to."

"Where?"

"I don't know, out of this city."

"I'd offer you something, Gaz, but you need to get your head straight first. Go back to bouncing doors, or take some time off, you must have money. And if you're going to leave town, now's as good a time as any, before it gets really nasty."

"I can handle myself," says Gaz.

"I know that. It's just the longer you work with them, the more chance they'll have to get under your skin. I'm not worried about what folk will do to you, Gaz, it's more what you will do to folk." This is something he hasn't thought of before. In the massage place the other day he felt himself getting angry with the misses. It might only take a few more steps for him to become as nasty as Rose. Dave's advice is hard won. They have stopped at the end of Westbourne Ave and Gaz has parked up opposite the little supermarket.

"I'm already in over my head, Our Dave," he says.

"You're never trapped. There's always a way out, it will make you a better man as well." Our Dave opens the car door and gets out, he leans back in to grab his tool bag from the footwell.

"Who was it that had this car?" asks Gaz. "I mean the lad you knew back in the eighties?"

"He was a skipper off the docks, as I recall, older than me and tall with black hair. A good bloke. He helped me out once upon a time. Had an animal second name, Lamb or Fox or something." Our Dave closes the door and Gaz looks at him through the clean glass of the passenger window. The eyes are worried and the old man wears a slight frown. He watches Gaz drive off in the black Capri into the late afternoon.

Our Dave is right, Gaz is getting sucked into many things. He has to get himself out.

Gaz drives along Chants and takes a left, he goes down Spring Bank West, past the big cemetery and then onto Spring Bank proper. It's Sunday night and just turning dark, the traffic is thin and the streets are empty of people. He parks up just after Morpeth Street on the left in front of Zam Zam, it's a Kurdish restaurant with big glass windows and faded pictures of shawarma and kufta next to the menu and special offers. Gaz has been here a few times. Kurds arrived a bit more than twenty years ago, originally there was just the one restaurant, then came the takeaway across the street, then there was a barber on the corner, and then the international supermarket. Now there are two Islamic butchers, numerous Arabic shops, a couple more barbers and a bakery. Gaz waits in the queue and orders a chicken shawarma with everything to go, and the chef with huge forearms wraps it up for him.

Gaz would never eat in his car. It would go all over the seats so he stands outside on the street and takes bites from the rolled-up flatbread. A guy from inside steps out and lights up a cigarette. He's got a black beard and wavy, well-styled short dark hair. The sun is going down and it sends long shadows across the road. The man who stands next to Gaz looking at his car is actually Kurdish Syrian, from Afrin in the north.

"It's a nice car," he says.

"Thanks."

"You can sit down inside and eat," he says. "You don't have to stand out here."

"I'm busy," says Gaz. This is another way of saying he has nowhere else to go. For, when he's eaten this, he will drive back to Hessle Road and the cold flat.

"How much did you pay for the car?" asks the man.

"Enough," says Gaz.

"If it was for sale, how much do you want?" This is a good sales technique. Gaz has heard it before.

"She's not for sale," he says.

"You know there's someone looking for you?" Gaz frowns. "A blue Mercedes drove three times now past here. It came slow the last time."

"Did you see the driver?"

"He was fat with a woman in the back seat. She was dirty looking." The man has a strange Hull accent mixed with his native Kurdish.

"Thanks," says Gaz.

"You are welcome, bring your friends next time and eat inside." Gaz gives him an uncharacteristic grin, the man isn't just being kind because he's nice. He's giving Gaz some advice because he wants him back in his shop to buy more shawarma, and because he knows how men act when they're lonely.

In the car, Gaz waits looking in the rear-view mirror, and sure enough, along the wide and half deserted street behind him, stopping at the red light of the pedestrian crossing is the blue Mercedes that the Kurdish guy told him about. This is the same rusty muscle car from a few days before. He sees the flabby face at the wheel with piggy eyes. He remembers, this is the guy who said his name was Cod, and it was his associate who threatened Lilly with a machete and who Gaz clobbered so hard that his head smashed into a mirror on the bedroom wardrobe. Gaz starts the engine and she purrs. He eases off into the light traffic two vehicles in front of the blue Merc. He'll lead them somewhere and lose them - if they're even following him.

It's night proper as Gaz drives back down past the old graveyard on Spring Bank West. He goes over the railway lines then takes a right into one of the smaller streets. He drives slowly and Ela rumbles beneath him. In his rear-view mirror, he can see the blue Merc creeping along behind – they're not very good at this, if it was a mission on Grand Theft Auto they'd have already been spotted. Gaz leads them slow through the mid-range terraced houses with cars squeezed in on one side. He turns right again, parks up on a bigger street, gets out and walks away from the car. With any luck, they'll stop behind him and follow. There's a track here at the back of the houses that leads to a bridge over the railway line. It's lonely, even in the daytime and scrawled with graffiti, the kind of place where teenagers would go to try their first spliff, or an edgy indie band might think to do a photo shoot. Gaz has crossed this bridge many times, and he likes the darkness of it. Wilkinson used to tell him, if he was walking home late, to make sure he went under the streetlights, but that just makes you easy to spot. Gaz walks down the track towards the footbridge, he goes past the two houses on either side in the darkness and gives a light cough so they will know where he is. Then, with a quick sidestep, he moves off the track and into the bushes and is hidden there in the darkness leaning against a wall.

Sure enough, they follow. They're rude and noisy as they move. He can hear the clump of the fat one's big feet on the gravel. There's a whisper in the darkness nearby:

"He came down here." Gaz will wait for them to cross the bridge and then calmly walk back to his car and leave. No doubt this lad will want his revenge. Gaz wonders if the voice was the man who threatened Lilly with a machete. He heard on a TikTok video that a battle avoided is as good as a battle won. He waits a little longer until he can hear the clang of their feet on the middle of the railway bridge before he moves out of the bushes. He takes a few steps back down the track and there's a figure standing in front of him in the darkness. He can see her rounded shoulders and a topknot on her head silhouetted by the streetlight behind, Gaz can almost sense her grin at him as he hears the drawing back of the hammer on the pistol in her hand. She levels it at him.

"Cod!," she bellows into the darkness of the track at her brother on the iron footbridge some way away. She's got a low guttural voice that carries. "Here!"

A person is not designed to do things alone. Many hands will make light work of a heavy job, it's better to cook for more than just yourself, you feel safer in a group, you hunt in packs. This is why street gangs work so well. This is why Cod and his ratty sister, Shell, get things sorted on Bransholme Estate. The world has trained Gaz to look after himself, and to do it without a heavy heart. He didn't fight back too much when they dragged him towards the footbridge, he'll save his energy for an opening, that's how fighting is, you look for a chance when you can get it. There are three of them as well as the girl, he can't quite see who they are but once he gets the opportunity, Gaz will throw a punch or two. He's been in worse situations. There's a twist. Cod's sister Shell likes a bit of S and M as well as the skag, and so she's got a pair of police grade handcuffs – she bought them off eBay. Cod uses these to clamp Gaz's left wrist to the railing behind him, and Gaz pulls against it as the three men move back leaving him in the orange glow from the streetlight. Gaz would have fought harder if he'd reckoned on being handcuffed to something.

"Do you remember me?" says a black-haired man. This is the lad who Gaz battered a few days earlier. His face is a mess and his eyes are black and puffed up.

"No," says Gaz. They are going to hurt him, so he won't be polite. Shell steps through the men, her face is drawn and ugly, she's on heroin like her boyfriend with the chain, but she's not a monster on it which is why she's survived so long. If not for the drugs she'd be a hairdresser or own a nail bar or a sandwich shop, she might have a cleaning business – she gets things done and sorted does Shell, like her mum used to. If she'd had the education or opportunity, she'd be a headmistress or a business CEO because she has vision, and aggression as well. She holds the gun level at Gaz again, like she did before. Gaz considers the taser that he knows is still in the inside pocket of his jacket, the one he found in Lilly's bedside table drawer. He might be better off just using his fists, it's probably knackered anyhow.

"I might just pop him right in the head," she says. She won't mean this. If she was going to she would have already thinks Gaz. Then again, these four are thugs and amateurs to say the very least. Who knows what they'll do.

"This is what you get for messing with Dalwood Close," calls Cod as if his home street is a football team. Gaz doesn't know the street but guesses that it's up on the estate there.

"I'm having him," says the man with the black hair and smashed up face. His fists clench at his side, and his nostrils flare as he gears himself up. Gaz notices the fake Gucci belt and the heavy watch. The man starts towards him with a roar.

If they'd thought on, they would have handcuffed Gaz by his right hand so he couldn't use that to belt them. They might also have taken the time to talk before they got straight to the fighting, they could have learned more about him – fights like this, that just explode, are usually won by the person who connects in the right place first, regardless of skill. The man thunders at him with the right hand pulled back behind his head. Gaz can see the white powder around one of his nostrils, he's operating on aggression alone, which is fine if you're fighting someone who doesn't know what they're doing. Gaz has been in so many scuffles that he couldn't possibly remember them all. He waits for the ill-timed punch to fly, then bobs down and to the side so that it misses, the man's body crashes into him and Gaz swings his fist up in rapid strikes to the back of his head. In boxing or MMA, you aren't allowed to hit people here because it's too close to the spinal cord and brainstem. Gaz is handcuffed to a rail down a ten-foot next to a deserted railway track so he figures the punch is in order, especially since this man thought it was ok to threaten someone with a machete a few days before. The first blow to the back of the head staggers him and his face crashes into the railings. Gaz manoeuvres his body so he's almost hugging him and delivers more of the punches at speed to the back of the man's head – he feels the body shiver with pain as he does. This bloke took a substantial beating a few days before. Gaz does not stop. He keeps on at him until he notices the big man stepping into the fight.

Cod grabs Gaz by his black hair and then clobbers him so hard that his skull smacks against the railings behind with a clang. He pulls his hand back to do the same again. Of course, the four of them are going to win, Gaz is handcuffed. His second blow hits Gaz in the cheek and splits it. The third finds his eyes. His head spins and shudders in his skull, in this sort of situation, he has to operate on instinct alone, he returns fire with a punch to Cod's chin. It snaps the fat man's head backward and shocks him. Cod is not a great fighter because he's so big and slow, couple this with no fighting training or any sort of exercise for many years, and the recipe is not perfect. He's always used his size to intimidate and it usually works. The people he frightens ordinarily are heroin addicts who want to borrow money, alcoholics, and those who have nowhere else to turn. Gaz's blow staggers him and he steps backwards with his eyes reeling.

Shell sees what's happening because she's not stupid. She understands already that Gaz is actually dangerous, she understood as soon as she saw him move his head to avoid the first punch. Shell gets things done, like her mum; that's why she took some of the money that her brother made and started up a cannabis factory in the old woman's flat opposite. The old dear complained, but as Shell pointed out, the heating was always on through the winter. She's got three other locations now, two more flats on Bransholme and a rented out place in a posher suburb. Shell has her eyes on the future. She knows what will happen. Just like now. She knows that her brother will attack Gaz once more and maybe he will win in the end, but he'll be hurt – she's had enough men whinging about their wounds for one week. Shell knows a Vietnamese bloke off Spring Bank West who's a whiz on computers – he managed to 3D print the gun she holds between her nail bitten fingers. She got the bullets from another lad she knows.

She has to stop this right now.

Shell aims the gun at Gaz, and does not consider that she may kill a man by doing this, or that it could land her in jail where there will be no heroin or Saturday night sessions where her man chains her to the bed. She hasn't fired the gun before, so she's not sure if it will even work. Let's see. She pulls the trigger and the pistol gives a sharp clack as the bullet erupts from the barrel. Gaz looks up, he does not have time to realise that the fight they were having has taken a dangerous turn. He feels himself slam against the railings as something hits him. There's no pain, but the contorted, worried face of the woman holding the gun at him makes him realise something terrible has happened.

He's been shot.

The gang give it legs.

CHAPTER SEVENTEEN
Kate

There are places in the world where you might hear a gunshot in the evening from near the deserted railway track. Just north of Spring Bank West in Hull is not one of them. It's a tough place to live in many ways, you would definitely get a fight if you wanted in the Halfway House pub five minutes' walk away, and you will get bullied at school if you can't stand up for yourself, but gunshots – not here. That's why nobody noticed either the scuffle or the sound of the pistol being fired.

Gaz comes to his senses. His left arm is numb from being handcuffed to the railing for however long he's been there and his face stings from being belted. He appraises his situation. There's blood all down him from his shoulder, it's sticky on his jeans and on his black shoes. The woman shot him somewhere in his left shoulder, the pain is fierce across his collar bone and down his arm but he can still move them. He has to get some sort of medical attention and yet he's handcuffed to a railing. He shuffles closer to where he's shackled and works the handcuff down to the bottom of the rail. These are steel palisades with a spike on the top to stop people getting onto the track but they're like most fences in Hull. In the summer holidays, his mum used to work a house off Hessle Road and took him with her to save on childcare, Gaz played on the railway line with other kids, they showed him how to pop these fences – you put a load of pressure on the bottom bolt – it's better if you can use a plank or a big stick as a lever. Gaz doesn't have these to hand. He grabs the bottom of the rail with both hands and pulls. It doesn't budge. He tries again. It holds fast. He grins. Sometimes, when things are very bad, Gaz feels at home, like this is where he belongs after all. He tries again. There are footsteps behind him. Then a voice:

"Are you alright, mate?" It's a middle-aged bloke with a

little white poodle on a lead and a sensible jacket. It's the kind of thing people say around here, as if he expects Gaz who's covered in blood squatting next to a fence to be ok. Gaz turns his head to reveal a bloody grin.

"I'm fine, mate," he says back. This is the standard response. "I've been shot and I'm handcuffed to the railings." There's no sarcasm in his voice although some folk would add it.

"Shall I call the police?" asks the man.

"I'll be alright, mate," says Gaz as he gives a final big pull and the bolt at the bottom of the rail pops out. He slides the handcuffs off the palisade and stands up with them still attached to his left hand. The man with his dog winces at the sight of him.

"What you been doing?" asks the man, as if it's Gaz's fault that he's in this state.

"It's a stag do gone wrong," says Gaz. "They left me here for a laugh." He's surprised how quickly he lies.

"With all that blood?"

"It's not real," adds Gaz. The man tuts.

"It's getting worse and worse round here," says the man. "Used to be safe these streets did. You should take your bloody games back to your own end."

"Sorry," says Gaz. The man and his poodle walk into the darkness towards the footbridge, he tuts again as he shakes his head.

Gaz walks in a staggered, zig zag line to Ela. There's a part of him that doesn't want to bloody up the seats. He gets in. Ela's engine fires up first time and Gaz raises his eyebrows, it's as if she knows he's in trouble.

He drives back along the street and struggles to change gear. The traffic is lighter than it was earlier. Gaz does not know where to go. He cannot go to the hospital because there will be too many questions and the police will be involved, he cannot go to Our Dave because of how much trouble he's caused the man, he can't go to Wilkinson because she's got enough on her plate and Lilly would just go to pieces if she saw him. The railway barriers are down and he waits with his sight blurring in and out at the red lights until the train rattles past. He stops again at the pedestrian crossing just after Perth Street. A couple pass, they are arm in arm, the man wears thick black glasses and she has long blonde hair, she smiles at him. Gaz has only one place left to get help, he wants to see Kate so hard, but he does not want her to see him like this. He can feel the energy draining from him, if he does not get help soon there's a chance he won't see tomorrow after all. She may be his last hope. It has to be Kate.

He drives down Marlborough Ave and then turns left into the one-way system and then onto Belvoir Street. Halfway down the road there's a space for his car. He parks up and then turns off the engine. Maybe he should just let this happen. Maybe he should just sit and let the life blood flow out of him so he won't bother anyone again, so he can't hurt punters like Our Dave thinks he's going to, so he can't break Kate's heart like he knows he will. There are too many loose ends for him to leave it all like this. He gets out the car as best he can. Gaz must keep this together. He staggers like a drunk the ten yards to her house, goes up the tiny path and leaves blood on her door knocker as he bangs it against the wood. He can't stand up straight and the handcuff hangs loose from his left hand. She takes a minute to answer and opens up. When she does, there's at first a great big smile and then it falls from her face as she thinks he's drunk, then she sees the blood.

"I need your help," whispers Gaz. "I've been shot."

Kate is good in a crisis. Gaz doesn't know, but she has been through a good deal more than she lets on. Her father was a drinker, that's how she became one, and after her mother ran off, more so. She knows what to do with a drunk, and guesses that a man who's been shot must be mostly the same. In the bathroom in the extension downstairs, she puts him in the bath, takes off his jacket and pulls off his shirt that's sticky with his red blood. The police grade handcuffs that Shell bought off eBay are not quite that, Kate doesn't ask any questions as she examines the mechanism that is clamped around his left hand, she wiggles and turns at the catch and it falls off. They are designed to withstand force if pulled but twisted the right way, the cheap design will come apart. You don't always have to try hard to get something sorted, intelligence and luck have just as much to do with it. Kate's great grandmother was an ambulance driver during the blitz of Hull in World War II, she told Kate of the horrors many times, and how she had to keep calm in the face of it all. Kate also did a first aid course with the council as part of her library training. There's a bullet hole just above his collar bone and it goes out of his back where there's a much bigger exit wound. Gaz does not make a noise as she inspects it.

"It's gone right through," she says.

"Can you stop the bleeding?" he asks.

"I'll try." Kate uses all of the gauze pads from her first aid kit and her two cat towels to wrap his shoulder up. She keeps the pressure on tight and gets Gaz to hold it in place with his free hand. Now she's not so worried about him bleeding to death she marvels at the amount of blood over the eighties style green bathroom. Gaz looks at her as she stands up from kneeling next to him, he's shirtless with his trousers and shoes on in the bath, she has his blood on her face. Normal folk would be worried by all this. Kate is, of course, but she is level-headed. Her father was a fighter too and he came home bloodied more than a few times so that it seemed normal. That's why Kate thought it was okay to drink the way she did.

"I'll fix us a drink," she says. In the kitchen she pours a large glass of her Christmas cake brandy into a tumbler and apple juice into another. Kate does not drink anymore. She brings them through to the bathroom and passes the brandy to Gaz. His bloody hands smear the tumbler. Kate sits down on the toilet with the lid down. "It's brandy," she says.

"I don't drink," he answers.

"You'll have to go to hospital, Gaz. You need proper attention. If it gets infected, you'll die."

"I can't drink this," he says. "I think I'll be ok now you've stopped it bleeding."

"It might make you feel better." Gaz takes a sip. It's horrible. The smell in his nostrils makes his eyes smart.

"You make me feel better," he says. He doesn't need drink to tell her the truth, he's already lost too much blood and his resolve is weak.

Kate has changed the dressing once more. She's taken off his shoes and trousers and his underpants too, the only thing she has for him to wear is a purple and tatty towelling robe she puts on in the winter. He looks odd there, sitting on one of the dark sofas, embarrassed almost. He didn't touch the brandy she poured him. It's nice that he is sober. Even though he's been shot he doesn't babble on and on. It's refreshing. She likes that he needs her. Kate has got changed into her pyjamas too, she was covered in his blood.

"You'll have to stay here tonight," she says.

"Thank you," he answers.

"Do you want to tell me what happened?" This is a genuine question, it's not part of her university training.

"It was just some idiots who wanted to beat me up, it went wrong. I don't think they meant to kill me."

"They shot you. They had you in handcuffs."

"They wanted to scare me, that's all."

"Is that what kind of business you're in?" Kate is lightly taking the piss. She is good at it.

"Not really. It was someone I had to deal with. They followed me to teach me a lesson. They'll think I'm dead.

They'll be shitting bricks now."

"You'll have to get it looked at professionally tomorrow," she says. "They won't ask any questions at A and E."

"They will," says Gaz. "I'm sorry I had to come here. I didn't have anywhere else to go. I'll make sure I'm gone early. I know you're busy, and nobody will know."

"I'll be online, you don't have to rush." Gaz feels out of place in her purple bathrobe on her comfortable couch with his bare feet on her laminate floor and the smell of brandy in his nostrils. "Don't you want your drink?" she asks.

"I'm not a drinker." Gaz has been drunk before. He's a dickhead with it. He's seen so many people change once the booze gets into them, and he doesn't want to be like that. Drink makes him say things he wouldn't say, if he downed the brandy he would think about his mother. He would probably think about Kate if she wasn't here. She has already explained that she doesn't drink anymore, Gaz likes this.

"I think we can help each other," she says.

"How can I help you?" he asks. It's rhetorical. There's no malice in it. Gaz has lost a lot of blood. He hasn't had enough liquid to drink. She is perfect; smart and intelligent, brave too, independent, and not flustered by disaster. It's not just her physicality that he desires.

"You'll just have to listen, and not say anything," she says. "You'll have to do that. Do you understand?" Gaz nods. She finishes her apple juice. She is going to have to give up part of herself, not because she needs him, but because there might be a chance of something special here. She thinks about him when she wakes up and goes to bed, agonizes over the texts she sends, looks to see if he's online, wonders how he feels about her all the time. Kate has known all those boys before, but not like this, not like him, there is electricity when they touch and when they look into each other's eyes. She cannot contain it.

"I'm an alcoholic, Gaz. I was addicted to sleeping pills as

well. I had sex with almost anyone who was nice to me. I was lost and drunk and out of control, but I'm not like that now. I've been clean for nearly a year. I don't take the pills anymore and you are the first man I've kissed in a long time. I'm coming back to myself. I want a man like you. I want someone who doesn't get pissed up or off their head, I want someone who I can depend on, and someone who can depend on me. He has to look after himself, have a nice smile and he has to be kind. That's you, Gaz. I want you. I'm sorry to be so blunt, there's just no point in me messing about. I need to settle down. I want a person to share my life with. Does that make sense to you?" She is aware just how foolish this sounds. Perhaps her emotions have got the better of her. If she was thinking straight she'd see that Gaz is trouble. Any man who turns up and has been shot and wearing handcuffs is probably going to be a handful, regardless of if he drinks or not. Gaz looks troubled and pale.

"I'm mixed up in something. If I'm with you, then there's a chance that you could get hurt as well. There's something I have to fix and it will be impossible for me to do without getting hurt." Gaz is weak. He shouldn't have told her anything, the less she knows the less danger she is in.

"What are you involved in?"

"Protection stuff. I'm working for a man I shouldn't be working for."

"Is that why you got shot?"

"No," he smiles. "That was someone else altogether. I'm sorry I came here, I didn't have anywhere else to go."

"That's not true at all," she says. "You could have gone to A and E, you could have gone to Our Dave, there's a walk-in medical centre up at Orchard Park. You came here because you wanted to, Gaz. I've helped you and so you owe me the truth." Kate is self-aware, she knows herself, that's why she's got this far. She learned to drink by watching her dad, and it numbed her enough to do things she wouldn't ordinarily do.

Counselling helped her through but she had to face demons first, she still does, she can see that there is something wrong with Gaz.

"You're right," he says. "I wanted to see you. All I do is think about you." It sounds so trite, like something that a soap opera character would say or you'd hear in a love song. His head is weak and his eyes swim. He feels words coming up from deep within him, like bubbles from the bottom of the dark ocean, he cannot help himself, he is powerless to stop them rising up through his chest, forming in his throat and breaking the surface of his mouth into the air. He's never said it before and he thinks it might be true, even though he's not sure.

"I love you," he says. It has happened so quickly. Lots of men have said this to Kate. Lots. Usually because they want her to spread her legs or because they're drunk, or just because they like to lie. She can see the words have cost him, and it is sweeter that he could not help it. She believes him. Kate stands up and moves over to stand in front of him. Her eyes are bright:

"No more words, tonight, Gaz," she says. "Not a single one."

Wilkinson looks down at her phone. These days she has to wear glasses to see anything up close. She's navigated to Gaz's contact details and there's his number on the screen. All she has to do is press the button and she'll call him.

She hesitates. She's left it too late. At this time of night, he'll be busy with something, maybe he'll be with that girl. Wilkinson has packed up the flat, she had a man come round from a removals firm and he bought all the stuff she doesn't need any more like the kettle and the oven, he took lots of the furniture too. She donated all her clothes to the Red Cross charity shop, two women came round with a white van and took everything that she'd put in black plastic bags.

She looks up from the phone at the kitchen around her. It's bare and empty. She's managed to get everything she needs into a red suitcase; she knows she promised Gaz she would let him take her to the airport, but it's too late for that. The taxi is already on its way. She doesn't want to bother him. He'll have better things to do.

In the bathroom Wilkinson turns off the boiler. She won't need any more hot water. She opens the cabinet to check that she hasn't left anything, she doesn't want to bother the next person who moves in with her tat. Like all the cupboards in this big flat, it's empty.

In the kitchen again, she looks out of the big window to the darkness of Pearson Park below. She was happy here. Looking after kids was what she was good at, she is pleased she gave her time to it. There have been many who have passed through here, some she still knows and they are friends on Facebook, some are dead or in jail, most have disappeared into the world. That is just what Wilkinson is going to do. When the taxi arrives, she will carry the red suitcase down the stairs, and be off to the airport outside Leeds. Tomorrow afternoon she will be in the hospice in Valencia and she will never see Hull or these streets again. There's a part of her that wishes she could have said goodbye a bit better, she has friends on the Avenues, she knows Our Dave from the taxi office, she could have let Gaz know in better time. That's not what Wilkinson is like, she doesn't need the fuss or the tears – you get on with things, that's how it's done. Everyone has their time to go, and this is hers. No regrets and all that.

There's a beep from her phone and she looks at the screen. Her taxi is outside. She takes one more look around the big kitchen where she lived for so long, then walks to the door picks up her suitcase and makes her way down the stairs.

CHAPTER EIGHTEEN
Kasia and a visit from Rose

Even though Kasia has a lot to do at the Dairycoates Inn, she likes to ride out on her bike in the summer when she gets the chance, especially on a fine morning like today. She still has her shopper bike with the basket on the front, she doesn't think she goes fast enough to need a helmet, and her rides are not about fitness or getting anywhere quickly. It's time for her to slow down and look at the city as it is. She likes the wind in her hair and it reminds her of riding to school when she was little back in Poland. The shopper bike she has is traditional and sturdy, with a steel frame and fake flowers around the basket on the front, she bought it from Steve's Cycles and she has him service it every year as well, even though it doesn't do as many miles as Kasia would like.

It's taken her half an hour to ride up Sutton Road on the path and then onto Bransholme Estate, the journey has been peaceful and these roads are not busy. It's just after eight o'clock. She thought about what Our Dave said when he visited the other day. She's heard things too about the teenage delivery drivers on mopeds that cris-cross the city selling weed on demand. Her own people have explained that the kid riders think they're untouchable somehow. The whole operation may be getting too big for its own good. The coppers will know about Cod and his sister Shell, of course, but they probably don't give a toss. There are always going to be drugs in the city, and the police will tolerate them, to an extent. Kasia wants to see how it is herself. She's not been out this way since she had a cleaning job in the primary school a few streets north of here.

She gets off her bike in front of North Point shopping centre and is about to lock it to the railings, when she sees one of the moped drivers moving out of the car park. The rider is dressed in a black North Face jacket with grey joggers and a black helmet. This is why she's here, so she gets back on her bike and cycles in the same direction, she doesn't go fast. Kasia doesn't want to catch him, just to have a nosey at what's happening; and nobody ever notices a pretty young lass on a shopper bike with short red hair and a white summer dress. She gives an old woman a wide smile as she cycles past Bransholme Methodist Church and into the maze of the council estate. There's still the high-pitched, angry revving of the moped in the distance, all she has to do is follow that.

It doesn't take long for her to get to the cul-de-sac that is Dalwood Close. She stops at the end and looks down past the little garages to a small group of mopeds parked outside a brown fence. Two of the riders are chatting to each other in the morning sunshine. This is the place.

There's a sharp voice from next to Kasia. She turns to see a woman carrying a plastic shopping bag with a topknot in her thin blonde hair. Her eyes are red and her nostrils are flared. She's thin and gaunt.

"What the bloody hell are you looking at?" she calls. Kasia does not know the woman, but she is Cod's sister Shell. Shell has been up most of the night worrying that she is going to get a visit from the coppers for shooting that bloke just off Spring Bank, so she's pissed off. In the plastic bag, she carries seven bottles of nail varnish remover that she bought from the chemist, Shell is going to dissolve the plastic gun she used to shoot the man, and, according to Google, acetone which might be nail varnish, is supposed to do it.

"I asked you what you're looking at?" repeats Shell. Her voice has a nasal quality to it. Kasia reaches down into her shopping basket and pulls out her wide sunglasses. Without saying anything to this woman, she puts them on and gives her a smile. She sets her foot on the pedal and turns round to go back the way she came.

Kasia has seen everything she needs to see.

Gaz's phone buzzes. It's nine o'clock in the morning. The pain in his shoulder is fierce as he sits up in the right-hand side of Kate's bed. She's gone already and he is surprised he didn't hear her get up. He picks up the phone. There's a message from Our Dave.

'How you doing, kid?' The kid is what people say around here. It's a term of affection, sometimes. That's how Dave will mean it.

'All good, mate, you?' Gaz presses the send button. He is not at all good. Gaz swings his legs over the side of the bed and feels the soft carpet on his bare feet. The curtains are drawn and weak morning light bleeds through the cracks and sides. There's an orderly dressing table with a hairbrush and straighteners, her wardrobe is open to reveal clothes neatly hung up, there's the smell of lavender from a diffuser in the plug socket – it's not overpowering. This is a comfortable place. Last night she brought him up here and his shoulder did not hurt when she touched him, and when she sat on him, he felt close to her with her lips on his. He holds his head in his hand for a minute because the memory of it is powerful for him, nothing like the things that Lilly does with the men who visit her.

He stands up. He can't afford to feel at home. The only thing he has to wear is the towelling dressing gown that Kate gave him the night before and he puts it on over his shoulders. He'll need to go home to get changed. On the landing he hears Kate upstairs in the loft room chatting online to her client or her teacher. There's a post-it-note on the bathroom door with her big and curly smooth writing on it. "I'll be busy till 9.30 – don't go without saying goodbye." Gaz reads the note. His normal steel has returned. There'll be no goodbyes, he was foolish to let it get this far. He walks quietly downstairs and finds his jacket. There's a hole out the back where the bullet passed through but it's not ruined. He puts it on and finds the keys to Ela in the pocket, then puts on his shoes. Gaz opens the latch on the front door to let himself out. It feels wrong to leave like this after what she did for him but Gaz consoles himself as he closes the wood gently, that this is for the best after all. He walks the short distance to the Capri with the dressing gown covering his bits.

Ela is not as dirty as he thought she would be. There's dried blood on the dark leather seat and the steering wheel but it's blended in well, the smell is rich. He gets in and winds down the window, then puts the key in the ignition. The engine splutters in front under the bonnet. He tries again and the spinning sound does not catch once more. He takes out the key. Ela is not happy with him. It must be the lack of sleep and the loss of blood. He's seeing things that he could not normally see, like his eyes have been opened since he told Kate that he loved her.

"I can't be with her," he whispers down at the steering wheel. "It's not fair. I was wrong to come here last night. I know that. I made a mistake." He hangs his head to his chest. "I don't want to leave like this, but it's gone too far, for me more than her." He gives it a minute, gets the rag out of the glove box, and wipes down the steering wheel and the gear stick. A man in bright workman clothes on a tatty mountain bike passes and looks in the front window with a crumpled, confused expression. Gaz gives him a solid stare back, then starts the engine. This time, Ela roars into life.

Dilsha sits in the office of Avenue Cars. They're all there. Our Dave taps on the laptop, Bev has just come inside from vaping out the back door, Liz is leafing through a knitting book that she found in the charity shop across the road. On Thursdays, Dilsha has taken to bringing in breakfast for all of them after they've done the first drop. It's just after 10, Dilsha delivered two Congolese kids to school at the end of Beverley Road, Liz did a care home hospital run for an old woman in a wheelchair, and Bev took twin boys to the institute that kids go to because they are too difficult to be schooled anywhere else. Our Dave and Bev like Dilsha's cooking, they think she does it because she's sweet and kind, and while this is true; Dilsha likes their compliments. It reminds her of home, where the girls would get together and eat then chat at the same time. Breakfast is flatbread and homemade humous or pomegranate molasses mixed with tahini – easy food. Dilsha says it's all Kurdish but you can get the same thing in Turkey or Iran, probably. After all that went on a few months ago, Bev is Dalsha's sister, she's just learning how the Hull woman behaves – those that she likes she gently abuses, and those that she doesn't she is plain rude to, there is a very fine line between the two, and every time Dilsha thinks she understands, she doesn't. Liz is the same as always, happy all the time, Our Dave looks after her more than he used to.

The landline phone rings and Liz picks it up. She listens for a minute and then passes it to Our Dave. He wipes his mouth with a napkin and puts the receiver to his ear.

"Avenue Cars, Dave here."

"Now then, Dave." This is the voice of Rose. Far away down the M62 and over the bridge across the river Ouse, the square man sits in his office high up on Leeds Dock, opposite with his face in his laptop is Saif, it's sunny in West Yorkshire. "I would ask you how you are, Dave, but I don't give a toss. Did you get those letters my company sent you, about that payment?"

"I did," says Our Dave. "Have you got my response?"

"I have." In his hands Rose holds a legal type letter that Our Dave has sent him, it's a stalling tactic he's seen before where the client asks for more details. "I'll have all the information back to you in a week or so. I just wanted to ring and tell you that the door's still open for you to settle this without any need for legalities." Dave sighs down the phone.

"We both know you made the debt up, mate. I've got hard evidence to prove I paid that loan back. Your case is dead in the water, you know that as well." Rose smiles and shows his little row of bottom teeth. Saif listens to his gaffer talking in front of his computer with his eyebrows raised.

"We can make whatever we like stick, Dave, that's why I'm so good at what I do."

"I'm a busy lad, as I've told you before, anything you have to say to me, you can put in writing." Dave looks up and sees that Bev is staring at him. She's got that mother's sense that knows things just from the way you hold your face. Our Dave turns his head and stands up. The man in Leeds continues.

"You think that I don't know who you are or what you do?" explains Rose. "I know about the booze that you bring in through Hull. I know who you sell it to as well - it's my business to know things like that, and you know here at Sanderson's we're about protection as much as anything else. I could offer you my services even." Dave makes his way through the office to the galley kitchen at Avenue Cars, the back door is open to the car park.

"I thought you liked to speak face to face, anyone could be listening to this."

"My end's encrypted, mate." Rose is speaking to him through Saif's laptop, anyone else listening will just get hiss from his side.

"You'll not get paid, son. By fair means or not, you won't be getting anything from me."

"I haven't even started yet, Dave. I'll give you a few more days to think about it. You can settle the two hundred grand debt and that will keep me off your back for a while, at least, or, you ignore it and I'll have to come down on you."

"This is tiring, kid. I've been in this game a lot longer than you, and I've dealt with bigger lads than you too. I've got friends as well." Our Dave has stepped outside. He rubs his face with one of his big hands in worry. "I don't get it, what is it you want? From what I understand you're rich enough, you drive a posh car and wear a smart suit. Isn't that enough?"

"It's never enough though, Dave. I have to be the best at everything, and I will be."

"You'll drown, kid. I won't do it, you'll do it to yourself in the end, somehow." Our Dave is a nice man, and even to those who would do ill toward him. It wasn't always like that. In times past he'd have paid one of the men he knows in Leeds to blow off this Rose's kneecap, or he'd have done it himself. Now he can't understand why people aren't better to each other, and themselves. We're all going to die anyway.

"I'm going to send someone to see you, Dave."

"Really?" His tone is more of exasperation than anger.

"You, or maybe one of them lasses who drive your taxis. I'm not sure yet." Our Dave sighs and he feels sickness in his legs. He's not sure he can go through all this shite again.

"It's happened before, kid. Don't you think people have tried to rattle me already? You crack on with what you've got to do and we'll expect anyone you send."

"I won't have to send them, Our Dave, he's already there." Rose hangs up. He means Gaz. The traffic is slow on Chants Ave behind and he can hear the beeping of a rubbish truck backing up somewhere, there's the sound of a car radio in the next street. Our Dave does not want to get it wrong again with Gaz. Bev comes out the back door with a frown on her face. She folds her arms as she approaches.

"What's going on?" she snaps.

"Nothing."

"You promised me, Our Dave, you promised me after all the trouble last time. You said it was done."

"That was done."

"What's this then?"

"When you're successful you get folk who want to try and take you down a peg, or they want what you've got."

"I want it sorted," she says. It was not three months ago that Bev shot a man in the office here, a man who was about to batter Our Dave to death. It's been covered up all well and good, but Bev has not forgotten. She has nightmares still. "You owe me, Our Dave." He frowns down at her and nods in agreement.

"I'll get onto someone," he says. "I'll get them to sort it."
"See that you do."

Leeds is a funny city. Not as in laugh out loud funny. It's got all sorts. Factories to the south and east make electronics, process food and chemicals, in the centre there are huge insurance companies and banks. Some of the city is run down but there is investment here, wealth and the smell of success. Our Dave sells a lot of liquor that way, there are the chain pubs, the posh new craft beer outlets, the vegan cafés, and then there are the strip clubs, nightclubs, pool halls and bingo centres – there are a lot of drinkers there. If Our Dave didn't do any more business than just Leeds, he'd still make a fortune and just because he makes a lot of money, it doesn't mean that other folks don't as well.

Our Dave looks down at his smartphone and the list of people on his contacts. They are friends some and business associates others. He scrolls down to the letter P, goes past Patrick, Paula, and Penny to a picture of a skull and crossbones with the name Pickles next to it. His finger hovers over the icon. It would just take one touch to contact this man. Many years ago, when Our Dave was first someone to be reckoned with, he knew Pickles. He was a boxer out of Barnsley, a real tough nut who came to Hull a few times to fight in the eighties. He was more a nutter than a craftsman, and so any gifted fighter could take him apart in the end, if there was a referee to stop young Pickles biting his face off. When he ended up losing many more fights than he'd won, Our Dave went in halfway with him on a Leeds boozer, it was maybe only ten grand, but a lot back in those days. It turned out that Pickles wasn't as much of a nutter when there was money involved and he did well, better than well. He took over another pub and then another, and then a club. These days his son runs the bigger nightclubs he has in Nottingham and Bristol, he brings the vibe while Pickles brings the business. Our Dave would only have to call him and explain what's gone on. That would be it. Pickles knows that Our Dave does not call unless there is something wrong, and there wouldn't be any small talk. This Rose fella, whoever he is, would go through some sort of unpleasant experience, maybe he'd lose a thumb or an eye. Pickles wouldn't do it of course, some faceless goon might deliver the message.

Our Dave is unsure. Conscience needles him.

Maybe he's gone soft, but he doesn't know Rose at all. What if he's a family man trying to do the best he can in the only way he knows how? What if he's a good man? Maybe they could work together somehow. Our Dave has done things that he wishes he hadn't in the past too and he promised himself he wouldn't do them again. However, there are people to protect. There's also Gaz. Our Dave does not know how it will play when he is sent to visit him for the money, not after how they left it. The old man sits down in the chair in Avenue Cars in front of the laptop screen. He'd give anything to talk to Hazel about all this. She'd know what to do. She always did. He holds his face in his hands as he thinks. He'll try this on his own. Just for the time being, maybe only a few days. If Gaz comes calling, he'll talk to him, they have history, and if it all goes tits up, he'll phone Pickles and call in a favour, and something unnatural will happen to this Rose.

It'll get sorted whatever.

It always does.

CHAPTER NINETEEN
Gaz

It's night already. Gaz hasn't visited anyone on the spreadsheet today since he left Kate. He's patched up the gunshot wound in his shoulder with stuff he bought from the chemist. It doesn't look too bad to be honest. He's lucky.

Gaz parks the car in the street beside Clarendon Bikes in the darkness, he's been for a drive to clear his head. He turns off the engine and kills the lights. Loneliness settles in silence on him still sitting in the car. None of this is right. Not his cold flat with nothing in it above, not the protection job. Gaz thought he could do it alone, like he's always done, but he's lying to himself again. He's always had someone - it was his mother once upon a time, then it was Wilkinson, now it should be Kate. The fantasy of working alone that he's always told himself is wearing thin. The fathers he imagines he might have had are slipping away too,

The phone on the seat next to him buzzes. He picks it up. It's Lilly. He answers.

"Gaz, can you come round?" Her voice is clipped and to the point.

"What's happened?"

"I can't say." Lilly would normally ramble on.

"Are you in trouble?"

"Yeah." She sounds shaky. "It's the truth this time, Gaz."

"You there alone?

"No."

"How many?"

"Three that I can see."

"Do they know you're making this call?"

"They're listening. They're expecting you, Gaz." He thinks for a moment. He wonders where she is in the house. Maybe she's on the cream white sofa or upstairs in the bedroom or at the kitchen table with her elbows on the pale wood. This is a trap for Gaz. "Are you still there?" she asks.

"Yeah."

"I'm in trouble, Gaz. I need you here. Will you come?"

"What if I don't?" He hears her sniff on the other side and her voice breaks as she speaks:

"Something horrible will happen, Gaz. They said they'd do something horrible." He swallows and blinks. There he is, once again that twelve-year-old boy watching as the big man strangles his mother, with blood running down his chest from his mouth, and his heart banging in fear, locked and frozen because he's too scared to move. Gaz grits his teeth. He feels his hand on the ignition and he turns the key, Ela fires up in front with a roar. He won't let it happen again.

"I'll be ten minutes," he says.

The curtains are drawn and there's soft lamp light from underneath. Gaz has parked at the top of Grove Street and turned the car facing the main road, in case they have to leave in a hurry. It must be after ten at least. Black wheelie bins stand guard outside each front gate ready for collection in the morning. The air is warm and there's a breeze. Gaz walks up to the front door and taps on the glass with his knuckles, he doesn't want to just go in. His heart is beating lightly in his chest as he steps back – he has already considered who it could be, a disgruntled punter, a rival, the coppers, another pimp, those dickheads from Bransholme who tried to kill him the other night, the list could be endless. There's not much point in thinking too deeply about what to expect, because he will have to face it head on.

The door opens. It's Lilly in her shabby dressing gown. Her eye makeup has run down one side of her face and she looks pale. Her eyes are afraid.

"Come in," she says. Gaz takes a deep breath as he steps through the front door.

"Who?" he whispers, but she shakes her head and retreats

inside. He follows into the front room. There's a young blonde man relaxed on an armchair with a crew cut and tribal style neck tattoos, he's wearing a loose blue tracksuit and brand-new white trainers that shine. There's a look of arrogance in his flared nostrils. This is Dylan. He works for Rose like Gaz does, only he's actually nasty.

"Now then, Gaz," says a man coming in from the kitchen. It's Rose. He carries a spirit glass with ice in his fat hand and he smiles to show those tiny bottom teeth in his false grin. Rose is overdressed in a light blue jacket, a pink shirt, dark pants and expensive-looking smart shoes tied tight. "We were just talking about you," he says. Lilly sits down alone on the end of the cream white sofa and her eyes go to the floor. She looks small. They've already done something to her.

"Sit yourself down, Gaz," says Rose.

"I'd rather stand. What's going on?"

"Patience, Gareth," says the man as he sits down at the opposite end of the sofa to Lilly. He's not called Gareth. Gaz can see that Saif is at the little table in the open plan kitchen, tapping away at the keys on his laptop. Lilly does not look up and there's an uncomfortable silence as Gaz stands next to the flat screen TV waiting for someone else to speak.

"This here's Dylan," says Rose. Gaz has heard about him. "He fights out of Morley BTT club, second on the card at the last MMA North at Manchester Apollo. A proper Leeds lad. They call him Animal. He's as hard as they come." The blonde man with the crew cut and neck tattoos looks up to Gaz without emotion. "He's here to give you a hand tonight."

"Oh aye?" says Gaz. This translates as 'is he now?' and he manages to add enough sarcasm to make Dylan's face sour slightly.

"Why have Lilly ring me?"

"A bit of theatre, Gaz. Just something to get your attention. We need to have a word as well, about how things have been going." Rose does not mean that Gaz got shot in the shoulder.

He won't know this. "I'll let Saif explain it to you, shall I?"

"If you like," says Gaz. He's getting better at the sarcasm.

"I got a call from the madam at the brothel on Anlaby Road, her name's Maryanne," this is Saif from behind them in the dining room area next to the open kitchen. His voice is smooth and calm, business-like even, it sounds reasonable. "She likes you. She says she gave you a thousand pounds, yet there's no record of this on our systems at all." Saif looks up from his computer screen at Gaz in accusation.

"That's what you wanted me to do, isn't it?" Gaz answers. Rose does not take his beady eyes off the Hull lad. The big man is enjoying himself. He likes that Gaz looks nervous.

"You're not to keep the money though, lad," says Rose.

"I didn't." Gaz grins. "I gave it away." He hasn't had time to yet, but he will. Rose lets out a sigh before he begins the speech he is there to deliver.

"Saif told me that you were no good for the company. He said you were too nice, and there are people in my line of work who would totally agree with him. Look at the way you rushed to get Lilly here from that hotel, see how many people you haven't managed to threaten. Maybe I was wrong, maybe not, but I'll tell you, the worst people I've met in my life started out like you, and things happened to make them see the world in a different way. You can't teach someone to be soft, you see, but you can teach them how to be hard." The speech is unnecessarily long.

"Tonight," explains Rose, "I've got a job for you to do, and I do want it done, properly. I've brought Dylan over to help you out, and also to show you how it works. Right? And to add to all that, if I'm not satisfied when you get back here, we'll let Dylan have another go on Lilly. He's got a nasty streak see, he's not well mannered at all like you are, Gaz."

Gaz feels his fist clench at his side. He examines the room. There's a big lamp he could pick up and throw. He'd have to take the man with the crew cut first, then Rose, Saif would be a pushover. Gaz has had tussles with MMA sorts and karate experts before, they're fast and savvy fighters but not trained to be dirty, he'll go for the man's eyes with his fingers and there'll be no referee to call time.

Dylan with the crew cut and neck tattoos, AKA Animal, who was actually third on the card at MMA North in Manchester, takes a smooth black pistol out of his tracksuit pocket. He looks up to Gaz. He lost the match that night, and his career as a fighter was effectively over – until he found out it gave him credibility in another line of work.

The weapon changes things a bit. Gaz remembers the pain in his shoulder and he narrows his eyes.

"There's a fella I want you and Dylan here to deal with," says Rose. Gaz looks at Lilly at the end of the couch in her dressing gown. She's rocking backwards and forwards in tiny movements as she stares at the carpet with her eyes wide. One of her false nails has come off to reveal a bitten jagged tip. Gaz understands what she said before – you never get out of this.

"Who?" asks Gaz.

"He's kind of a local businessman, likes to think of himself as a bit of a hard nut, he runs a taxi office on Chanterlands Ave up the road. Name's Dave. They call him Our Dave, like he's some sort of uncle. You might know him."

Gaz swallows and he is sure Rose can see his neck bob. His hands are clammy. He doesn't know where to look so he stares straight ahead.

"What do you want me to do?"

"Remind him he owes me money, then batter him. A good job too. Something he'll remember." Gaz's brain goes fuzzy.

"What if I say no?"

"Dylan here'll take Lilly upstairs and he'll do his thing. Then he'll put a plastic bag on her head and tie it tight, and he'll watch as her eyes bulge out and she suffocates."

"What's the point?" asks Gaz.

"You're going to be a good operative for me, Gaz. I just

know it. We need people like you who are calm and smart, but you need to follow rules. This is training. It'll be easier for you in the long run, I promise."

All this time, Gaz thought he was playing with this man. It's been the other way around all along. Perhaps the only way out for Gaz really is that blister pack of Adderall in the drawer in his bedside cabinet.

It's a warm night outside.

"How much was the car?" asks Dylan. He stops to check out the shape of the bodywork in the glow of the streetlight from behind. He's more interested in what it's worth than anything else.

"Three and a half grand," says Gaz as he goes to open the driver's door and gets in. Dylan walks round to the passenger side and tries the handle. It won't open, so he pulls at it harder. Gaz leans over and opens the door from the inside.

"You have to be careful - it's an old car," he says after Dylan's climbed in and slammed the door. The blonde man with neck tattoos is rude and quick. This is why, on that sticky night in the Manchester Apollo, he lost against an unseeded lad from South London – he went too fast into the fight and the kid clobbered him with educated jabs that he ate rather than dodged. Dylan pulls hard on the seatbelt so that it sticks.

"The car's had it," he mutters. Gaz doesn't tell him to pull it slowly, he couldn't give a toss if they have a crash and this nasty blonde thug gets his head smashed into the dashboard. Gaz starts the engine and Ela splutters and coughs into life. His mouth is dry, this is a difficult situation. He pulls off and joins the light, late night traffic of Beverley Road.

"You've got the address, right?" asks Dylan. He has a slight lisp when he speaks.

"Aye," says Gaz. He heads right off Beverley Road onto Queen's Road, it's just past nine. He's on his way to Westbourne Ave, to the address Rose told him. Gaz knows it well. Our Dave lives there. His hands feel sticky on the big wheel and the pedals feel too big to drive. He will not hurt Our Dave, but he cannot let anything happen to Lilly either, he has no plan as they drive over the roundabout past the Queen's Hotel alehouse, he will have to make this up as he goes. He drives along Princes Ave past the big park and stops at one of the zebra crossings for a drunk to stumble past. Dylan drums his thin fingers on the dashboard in front of him, he is impatient also.

"We'll have to stop," says Gaz.

"What for?"

"It's too early, Our Dave won't be back till later. He knows my car, so if I park up in front of his house, he'll know I'm there."

"So what?"

"He'll do a runner if he sees me."

"I thought he was an old bloke."

"He was handy back in the day. He's still fit."

"Listen, Rose has already told me, that if you piss about I'm to do you first and then go onto fill in this Dave prick. If we're gonna waste time then I might as well just handle this myself." Dylan will be a well-trained and unpleasant fighter. He's slightly smaller than Gaz, but that means he'll be faster. It wouldn't be wise to take him on head to head.

"He won't be there. He gets back at eleven usually." Gaz does not know this. He wants to buy himself more time. Dylan looks at his chunky black watch.

"That means we've got fifteen minutes," he says. "I need to get into character anyway."

"What do you mean?"

"I usually have a smoke beforehand, it calms me down, and I'm less likely to kill someone. A man with my sort of abilities can do that if he's not careful." Dylan is arrogant. He grins and Gaz can see that his teeth are wonky with the lower molars sticking up like strange fangs.

"Not in the car though," says Gaz.

They lean on the side of Ela and look into the darkness of Pearson Park through the railings, it's a playground and the swings look eerie at night. Dylan puffs on some sort of pre-rolled blunt. He takes a big lungful and blows out the blue smoke into the night air then passes it to Gaz. He takes it in his fingers and pauses before he puts it to his mouth. Gaz doesn't smoke this stuff for the same reason he doesn't drink, the unsteady feeling of not being in control makes him scared. He passes it back to Dylan.

"I don't smoke it anymore," he says. Gaz wonders if he should start the fight now – he will have to go at it with Dylan, he's got no doubt about that, and he is not sure how he will fare against him. The only advantage is that Gaz gets to decide when and where they will scrap – that could be the difference between winning and losing. There's more. If Gaz doesn't manage to stop Dylan, then Our Dave will get a battering, and maybe Lilly as well. The tattoos on the MMA fighter's neck expand as he takes another toke.

"Saif thinks you're a soft bastard," says Dylan. "I agree with him. If this were Leeds, we'd have the job done already and be on our way home," he tosses the spliff on the grass in front of him even though it's not halfway smoked. "You better give me the key, son," says Dylan. "It'll take a grown up to get this done." He grins. There's the security of his training behind him and the swagger of knowing that he could kick Gaz on the side of the head and knock him out. Gaz can wait. He hands him the keys.

Dylan tries to adjust the seat to his smaller frame and curses as he looks to find the pedals. He turns the ignition and the engine splutters in front of him then cuts out. He huffs and tries again. Ela coughs a bit longer this time before the engine gives in.

"What does Rose want with me? If they think I'm soft, why bother with me at all?" he asks Dylan. The blonde man turns to him with his lip raised in a snarl.

"They know how people work. Rose says he can make you into a bastard, and he needs someone who knows this town." He tries the engine again and it doesn't even catch this time.

"How long have you worked for Rose?"

"Bout a year now," says Dylan. "He likes a lad who can get stuff done and isn't afraid to get dirty doing it either."

"You mean battering people?"

"What else do you think I mean?" There's the tinge of hatred on Dylan's voice. Like he's locked permanently as a teenager and all that anger in his chest is ready to explode at any minute. "Have you done something to this car?" asks Dylan.

"She won't start if she doesn't like you," says Gaz. It's the only explanation he can think of. Dylan hisses in disgust.

Gaz drives up to Westbourne Ave in the darkness and the trees on either side cover some of the streetlights to give it an eerie feel. The houses along this road are big and roomy, built in an age before the car, they are expensive and it's here where you'll find university lecturers, bohemian GPs, beekeepers, local historians and in the flats that you can rent out there are skint filmmakers and pot smokers, musicians, and teachers. Our Dave lives nearer the other end on the left-hand side.

It's well past eleven and the streets are dead. At the little roundabout Gaz takes it slowly and they pass the new fountain with a circle of mermaids around the bottom blowing water through shells. He drives another three hundred yards and finds a parking space next to a big oak. At this end, the houses are smaller terraces but they're still posh. Our Dave moved into his at a time when a normal person could afford a mortgage. Gaz puts on the handbrake. He could lie about where the man lives, but Dylan knows the address and he's been looking at his phone at regular intervals. Gaz opens the big door and gets out. There's no more time to play. He walks a few steps up to the house and waits for Dylan to follow. This is the little road through the houses that leads to Richmond Garage where Gaz bought Ela.

"We'll go round the back," he says as he goes down the path into the darkness.

"No, we won't," says Dylan. "We'll knock on his front door and take it from there."

"He's got a shotgun, you know." Gaz is tiring of the man. If he was going to batter Our Dave, he really would go round the back.

"You're stalling," says Dylan. "You can knock on his door and I'll stand behind you and watch while you do it." Gaz turns to him and his nostrils are flared. "Or you can run if you want. I'll do the job and then I'll go back and have another go on that lass."

Gaz is out of options. He should have led Dylan somewhere else because if he goes at it with this man, he will lose. He has a bullet wound in his shoulder and his stomach is worried, he is frightened for Our Dave and for Lilly too. Dylan approaches him with a swagger in the darkness. The clouds in the sky move over the moon above.

"You think you can have me, do you? Have a go, why not? Whatever happens, that old bloke is getting a kicking, and I'll be on top of that lass with her head pinned to the floor as I do her from behind." Gaz doesn't want to be led into a fight, he's bounced too many doors for that. He wishes he was quicker with his put downs, and he could rattle this little man with clever talk and insults. Gaz channels his airline pilot dad, a man who he imagines is always well presented and secure, someone who would be able to think and talk their way out of a fight. It's no good. The fantasy is running dry and Gaz doesn't have anything up his sleeve. He looks over his shoulder at Our Dave's house a hundred yards away. It has to be now.

He whips his arm up and clobbers Dylan with a right hook to his chin - anyone else would go down with the speed and the shock. Little Dylan, however, has got a face made of Leeds gritstone and his head moves but he comes back with a grin.

"I knew you'd try something; Saif said you would. Thought you'd have tried a bit harder than that though." As Dylan finishes the last word, Gaz's left hand connects with the centre of his chest, he can feel the wire bones and muscles underneath his knuckles. The little man slides backwards at the blow, brings his fists up and bends his knees slightly – it's the fighting stance, just like he's been trained. Dylan throws a leading foot strike to the back of Gaz's leg to weaken him, it's the kind of leg kick used in Thai boxing. It doesn't look like much, but it hurts like hell. Enough kicks like that and Gaz won't be able to stand up. This is fighting beyond his capabilities.

Dylan was a little scrawny kid at school. He lived with his mum and his grandma in a council house in Lincoln Green where his mum drank white lightning cider most days. He got picked on too because he was little and his clothes were dirty. The day before he started secondary school, the kids on the park opposite his house told him that the dinner ladies licked the cutlery clean rather than wash it and so, disgusted by it somehow, Dylan used his hands to eat his dinner that first day, and then every day after that. They called him Animal in the dinner queue but it wasn't because he was a hard lad at all. The name stuck. He joined the Karate club after classes because it was warmer than going home in the winter, and at first it was a way to defend himself, then a way to dominate. MMA was the same. Dylan knows the katas, the kicks, and punches, he's a grappler too, once he gets you on the floor he's like a crocodile in the water with a deer – he'll spin you around and put you to sleep.

Dylan throws a wide hook – it's not designed to connect, but to make Gaz dodge to the right and allow Dylan to move in like he's practiced a thousand times on the fighting mats in the gym; in two steps, he's hooked his leg around Gaz's calf and tripped him. The Hull man lands on the floor with an oof out of his lungs and Dylan is right on top of him with his arms working around his neck. Gaz struggles back. MMA fights are more like chess games. You can move to counter your opponent, you can give him something that will allow you to take something else, and all this happens in between the space of a heartbeat. Gaz doesn't even know the rules and before he understands quite where he is, the blonde man with the crew cut has his legs hooked firm around his waist and his head in a tight hold. Dylan rolls onto his back with Gaz above him, like all the best fighters do. Somewhere in his ears he can hear the roar of the crowd at the Manchester Apollo, only this time they are cheering for him. All he has to do is squeeze hard enough and Gaz will pass out from the pressure on his neck. Dylan grunts in his ears, and he sees the future – he'll batter some old git and then drive Gaz's car back to Beverley Road, jump the lass and collect his money from Rose. A job well done.

Gaz has fought a lot of people. There's no fear of fists or a broken nose, no worries about bruises either. The adrenalin that most feel when their blood is up is usually lost on Gaz - like it will be on Dylan. He relaxes as the thin man from Leeds strangles his neck and squeezes his stomach – he is held tight with Dylan on the ground behind. The world is beginning to dim around his eyes. Perhaps this is the way it's meant to be. Perhaps he is not meant to be with Kate, perhaps Our Dave is meant to get a battering, perhaps Gaz was meant to stand there as a twelve-year-old boy and just watch that man strangle his mother. He bars his teeth in rage. A while ago when Lilly was kidnapped, Gaz took the little taser from the top drawer of her bedside table, he's not sure it'll even work but he manages to get his hand to his inside jacket pocket. It's still there. This isn't MMA whatever Dylan thinks, this is not the Manchester Apollo on a Saturday night with the smell of beer and the roar of the crowd, this is Westbourne Ave, on the mud in front of the big terraced houses in the darkness. Gaz hits the red button on the side of the taser, it splutters and fizzes in failure but he doesn't have anything to lose here, so he rams the prods into one of Dylan's thighs around his waist and pushes the button again. It works. Dylans leg spasms outwards and Gaz feels the man shiver in shock and pain below him. He keeps the taser on his legs and the man's arms relax. You never quite know when something will come in. Gaz rolls off onto the grass.

The Leeds man has lost the momentum and the electricity dances around his nervous system. It's been a while since anyone has actually hurt him and the blunt he smoked ten minutes since has dulled his wits. Gaz is back with a heavy blow to Dylan's neck, this time, the punch stuns. Before he can take a breath, bouncer style, Gaz has pulled him to his feet and twisted one of his arms around his back. He staggers forwards as Gaz pushes him towards Ela. There's no referee to stop the fight. They pause. For good measure, he takes Dylan's head in both his hands and slams it against the dark metal of the boot. It makes a hollow dong sound and the blonde man is stunned again, Gaz uses the time to unlock the back. It creaks open and he lifts and pushes Dylan into the dark space within, the man starts to come round, he gets his hand on the lip of the boot to pull himself up, but Gaz is too quick. He slams the heavy door closed on his fingers, and Dylan roars in pain inside. Gaz puts his weight on it so it clicks shut and locks. They made cars heavier in 1982, sturdier as well. Dylan shouts and boots at his prison in the back of the charcoal black Capri. There's something feeble in the way he yells. It's not often people get what's coming.

Gaz drives down Westbourne Ave again, then past the Queens and north up Beverley Road. His neck hurts from where Dylan nearly broke it and there's periodic banging from the boot, although this is getting fainter. He's got a good idea about where to drop Dylan.

Clough Road is almost deserted, he drives past the big warehouse stores and the bright new police station on the right. When he's gone over the massive iron bridge, Gaz turns left at the roundabout. He's heading to the Bransholme Estate to replay the little group who shot him in the shoulder a few nights previous. He drives on past the tile warehouse and the service station and the heavy industry melts away. Bransholme is cut off from the rest of Hull by A roads and patches of woodland and grass. Gaz has been before, he bounced the door at the Nightjar pub a few times, and there are a few rough types but it's no worse than any of the other streets in this city. The houses are mostly council owned and so there's poverty, and in between the old ladies and boarded up bungalows, there are a few bad ones growing like weeds. He means Cod. North Point shopping centre is nearly deserted like the streets, a moped appears from a side road and takes off into the night with the red brake light blazing in the darkness. Gaz turns the big car round a corner and then another. The sixties prefabbed terraces look the same from any angle. It's a good job Gaz knows where he's going. Dalwood Close. He knows this because Cod yelled it at him while he was chained to a fence like it was a war cry. Gaz just needs to find the muscle car.

He goes over a speed bump and there's a yelp from the boot where Dylan must have hit his head. Gaz goes down one of the cul-de-sacs and turns round in the street in front of the houses so he's facing the way out. In the corner is the battered blue muscle car that Cod used to visit Lilly. This must be it. This must be Dalwood Close. He opens the driver's side door and gets out. Gaz doesn't know how this will play, but it will piss Cod off and hopefully, get rid of Dylan.

He walks a few steps down the little road in the darkness and under the streetlight, he can hear voices from the house opposite. The number 107 is painted on the wall. There's the heavy drumbeat of music from within and on the curb outside are four mopeds parked at random. The gate is open. This is the place. Gaz casts his eyes around him for something to chuck, in the doorway of the house opposite is a plant pot resting on a couple of bricks. These will do. Gaz lifts off the plant and grabs two of them. He does a little sprint and lobs the first brick over the fence with force, he hears the smash as it goes through the kitchen door. As quick as, he throws the next, this one falls short somewhere in the garden. He hears shouting from inside and voices moving towards the street.

If he gets this wrong, he'll get shot again. He might get shot again anyway. He turns back to Ela and bangs on the boot with the fat of his fist.

"You in there, Dylan?" he calls as he looks towards the figures moving through the open gates to their mopeds. There's a kind of angry, muffled roar from within. "I've got some Hull lads out here, they're gonna give you a little tickle, you ready?" Gaz imagines Dylan circling the octagon of the MMA ring wearing a mouthguard and yelling at the crowd as he beats his chest. This might be his biggest fight yet.

Behind, Gaz can see the bald head and bulging eyes of Cod come out through the gate, next to him, there are three young lads with their hoods up and dark tracky bottoms with black trainers. Gaz walks to the driver's side, gets in and closes the door. He starts the engine with a little whisper for Ela to come through for him and she thunders to life. Just under the steering wheel is a handle, he yanks it and the boot opens up behind. On cue, out comes Dylan. He staggers and yells a string of obscenities as Cod approaches with the little group of his hooded moped riders.

Gaz eases the handbrake down and accelerates off out the cul-de-sac. As he turns the car out into the main road, he looks to see Dylan executing some sort of axe kick on one of the lads, Cod himself is about to wade in. Their numbers will overpower Dylan eventually, Cod's ratty sister might even take a pot shot at him as well. Gaz has other things to deal with.

CHAPTER TWENTY
Goodbye #1

It's so late that even coppers will have gone home. Gaz stops to fill up at the garage on Ferry Lane. It's self-service and apart from an ambulance at one of the far pumps it's deserted. Once the petrol gauge looks like it's empty, you have to fill Ela up right away. Gaz has never tested this theory, and he wants to get to Rose, even though he does not know what he'll do when he gets there. He puts in his bank card and then fills her up with thirty quid. It might be more than enough, Rose might finish him off before he gets to use it all up. He sits in the driver's seat and looks down at his knees. His shoulder hurts, like his neck and his stomach rumbles in hunger.

A police car whizzes past on the other side of the road, and he looks up. Dylan was easy. Rose won't be. The phone buzzes on the seat next to him. The letters of the name are bright on the screen in the darkness. It's Kate. A spark of hope. He picks it up and holds it to his ear, a smile settles on his face. Her voice is sharp:

"You're a pimp," she says. The smile falls. She does not sound like the same woman.

"Yeah. I'm not doing it forever though."

"You live with a prostitute." He looks down to his lap in shame perhaps.

"That's not true. I just work there. I'm protection."

"Just to tell you, Gaz, it's impossible for me to be with someone who does what you do."

"What do I do?"

"You hurt people."

"I don't. I protect them. Who have you been talking to?"

"I just heard a few things. I put two and two together, Gaz." What was he thinking? Of course, this was going to happen. People know each other in this town, and Gaz never made a secret of what he does.

"I thought we had something," he says. There's a pause on the other end.

"You mean sex."

"Not just that."

"It's the beginning of me being used, again. You turn up in the middle of the night covered in blood. You don't tell me anything about what you do, and that's because you don't want me to find out. You disappear without saying goodbye. I'm ending this before it gets any worse." Gaz swallows. She is right.

"I didn't want you to know. I don't like what I do, and I don't like who I am." This is the truth.

"You can't fool me with that, Gaz. I've been used before. I'm not getting used again. If you'd just wanted something physical, then that would have been fine, but you had to add all that emotional shit onto it as well." Gaz is not a player. His palms are wet on the other end. He closes his eyes.

"I'm not like that, Kate. I can't be with just anyone."

"I've heard it before, Gaz, I've been fooled too," her voice wobbles like she's about to cry. She fights it. "Where are you?"

"On a job," he says.

"There you go again, sounds like lies to me."

"It's not, I've had trouble. I've just got something to fix and I'll be done. I'll be out of the protection business, and I'll go back to driving for Our Dave. This is it. Tonight. After tonight it's all done." He hears her sniff on the other end.

"Are you so damaged, Gaz, that you have to lie to me, again and again? Do you not see what it does to other people?"

Gaz looks at the dark night above the lights of the petrol station. He is tired. His throat is dry. He has not eaten anything since yesterday. His throat hurts where Dylan strangled him, and his shoulder stings constantly from the gunshot wound. She is better off without him. He knew this. Whatever he says, this is over. Gaz is shite at lying anyway.

"Are you there?"

"Yeah."

"I didn't lie to you, Kate. I did mean it. I've never said that before, not to anyone, and I couldn't help myself. If I'm being honest, you're better off without me, but I didn't lie to you." There's silence on the other end. "I'm just glad I met you. I'm just glad I spent the time I did with you," he adds. Gaz feels all the colour drain from his face. His fingers tingle. His stomach tightens. This hurts him.

"Where are you?" she asks again.

"At a petrol station. I've just come from Bransholme."

"I thought it would be easy. I thought you'd feed me all the same lies other blokes do. Maybe you have already."

"I just need tonight, Kate. I have to get rid of something."

"What?" He hears his own breath. His heart beats shallow. He's been straight with her this far, but perhaps the idea that he is going to kill a man is too much.

"I can't say."

"Why?"

"I'm mixed up in stuff, Kate. I'm mixed up with horrible people."

"Don't do it," she whispers. Her voice is low and commanding, it's the soft sound of reason and comfort, she is intelligent and brave, simple, and true. "Whatever it is, don't do it. Drive your car here, drive here to me." Gaz's head hangs deeper into his lap.

"I can't," he whispers.

"Why?"

"Someone needs me."

"You need yourself, Gaz. Don't you realise that?"

"If I don't sort it, then someone will get hurt."

"Is it the whore?" There's no point in lying, Gaz has lost this game, and his way too.

"Yeah." There's a pause on the other end.

"What is she to you?"

"Someone I look after," comes the reply.

"Can you leave it?"

"No. That's what I do, Kate, I look after people. That's what I am. That's all I do, and if I leave it now then there isn't any of me left." Gaz has not heard himself say this before and until now, he did not know. For his mistake all those years ago, he pays every day. He cannot get it wrong for anyone. Not like he did for his mother.

"Gaz, I don't know who you are. I don't know what you do even, but if you don't leave it, we're done."

"I'm sorry, Kate, we're done anyway. That's why you called isn't it?"

"I called because I wanted answers, Gaz. I was worried, but you're right. You can go off to her if that's what you want." Kate sits on the top of her stairs in her pyjama bottoms and a vest top.

"Good luck, then," says Gaz. His voice is monotone. Like Wilkinson says, Kate is way out of his league. He hears her sigh.

"I always fall for the wrong ones," she says.

"I've never fallen for anyone before."

"You told me you loved me."

"I do."

"I can't be mixed up with someone like you."

"I know. I'm sorry."

The line goes dead. Gaz puts the phone down on the seat next to him and rests his forehead on the steering wheel. He'll do the best he can for Lilly, and then he's out of this town, forever, he'll set up somewhere new and he won't work doors. If he has to, he'll crack open that blister pack of Adderall in his bedside cabinet, and there'll be no more bad dreams or mistakes, and his heart will not rattle when he thinks of Kate. He starts the engine and Ela fires up below him with a dark rumble.

He just has to deal with Rose.

CHAPTER TWENTY-ONE
Goodbye #2

He drives down Clough Road in the darkness. The streets are deserted. A taxi angles past him. There's a chance that Dylan text Rose while he was trapped in the boot. He could have called him even, so Gaz is not sure if the man will be expecting him or not.

At the crossroads on Beverley Road, he waits in front of a silent red light when nothing is coming in any direction. Rose will kill him, he has the means. Perhaps that would be the best thing all round. Kate can find a new man. Lilly will go back to work. Wilkinson will be in Spain. He'll collect no more money and stop no more fights. He looks down at the black phone on the passenger seat – he could call Our Dave. It's gone past that. He doesn't want to drag him into this, and anyway Our Dave would probably tell him to clean up his own mess. This one is for Gaz to sort out alone.

He drives along Beverley Road and there's the smell from the cocoa factory in his nostrils, burnt and sour at the same time. His shoulder stings, his neck does too. Gaz parks Ela at the little supermarket opposite the house on Grove Street and gets out. The light in the living room is still on. At the front door he turns the handle and steps inside, it's not locked. In the front room, Lilly lays on her side with her knees up to her chest still in her dressing gown. Her face is pale and her black hair is knotty and unbrushed. She looks up to Gaz as he walks in. In the little dining room, Saif sits behind his computer screen and opposite is Rose with the top button of his pink shirt undone. He too watches as Gaz paces into the room.

"Did you get my job done, son?" he asks. Gaz shakes his head. "Where's Dylan?"

"Probably face down in the river," answers Gaz. "Lilly, get up, we're going." The woman stares at him with frightened eyes. She does not move.

"She's not going anywhere, Gaz. She works for me, she has done for a long time." Saif glances up from the laptop.

"I told you he was the wrong person for the job," he's talking to Rose. "You just can't ever be wrong, can you?" The big man stands. He's more than six foot, taller than Gaz and with muscular shoulders and powerful arms despite the gut.

"We can still make an operative out of you yet, Gaz. What happened to Dylan?"

"Like I said, he's probably face down in the river. Some people I know took care of him."

"You don't just take care of Dylan. He's an animal. You'd have to put a bullet in his head to stop him."

"Maybe he came out on top. I didn't stop to watch. There were quite a few of them."

"This Dave? I told you to batter him."

"I didn't."

"Why not?"

"He's a mate."

"That's not how it works, son. I tell you to do something, and I want it done."

"I don't work for you anymore." The man pulls a tired face.

"You don't get to choose, Gaz. Once I look after you, that's it. Lilly here knows that. You should too."

"I never did work for you. I didn't collect for you. Your mate, Saif, there is right, I'm the wrong man for your organisation. Now. Me and Lilly are going to walk out this front door and then drive away and you're going to watch us do it." There's a pause. Gaz stands blinking across at Rose. He can see the wrinkles on his brow under his bald head and the wispy hairs from his chest through his unbuttoned pink shirt. He points over at the table behind him, just in front of the laptop is that same handgun that Dylan passed to him earlier.

"Do you know what that is, Gaz?"

"You're not going to shoot me," he says, "and even if you did, it might be the best thing to happen to me all night." Rose steps back and picks up the pistol.

"I'm not gonna shoot you, Gaz," he holds the weapon in his right hand, then points it down at the girl laid on the sofa with her knees up to her chest. "I'm gonna shoot Lilly, because when I break you, Gaz, you'll be a loyal little servant, just like she is." Her eyes are wide and lost as she stares at the far wall through Rose.

Here he is again.

He is that twelve-year-old kid watching, in his mother's bedroom, as a man strangles her. He listens as she chokes and the meathead with the tracksuit grunts as he kills her. This is Gaz. Impotent, weak, and frightened. This is why he protects people, in the hope that he can redeem himself for what he didn't do that day. He feels ice in his veins, and then, the blaze of anger and hatred.

He's not that little boy anymore.

Gaz bursts towards Rose. Perhaps he gave away his intentions in his face, or with his arms, maybe Rose has just got more experience than him, for as Gaz approaches, he brings the gun up in an arc, catching him in the side of his head with a crunch. Gaz stumbles across the room and his temple hits the flatscreen TV making a huge spiderweb dint in the screen.

"You're just a kid," bellows Rose. "I've been doing this shit for forty years, night and day." Gaz isn't good at starting fights, he's not trained for that. He comes back at Rose with a left hook, but the big man is too long in the tooth, he steps to the side and Gaz's punch whizzes past into thin air as he crashes into the little dining room across one of the chairs. Gaz is slow, and the bullet wound has begun bleeding through his shirt under his jacket. Rose steps to him, grabs him by the neck and hauls him upwards. He holds Gaz's face next to his as he whispers in his ear, the stink of his mouth is rotten:

"I think me and you had better take a little drive, Gaz, because you are going to work for me. We'll take a ride to see

Dave, only this time, you will go in and batter him." Gaz struggles as the man holds him tight, his nose wrinkles and his hands in loose fists flail while Rose controls him. Usually, it's Gaz who holds the drunks as they swing wildly with the emotion they've kept bottled up spilling out, and he will hold them till they run out of steam – it's the other way around tonight.

"Are you gonna calm down?" whispers Rose. Gaz nods, he will stop fighting but he won't calm down. Rose manoeuvres him to the cream white sofa and dumps him on the other end. Lilly has not moved during all this.

"This has all gone too far," says Saif from the table. He's stood up. Rose turns to him.

"What do you mean?"

"It's half past two in the morning. We seem to have lost an operative in Dylan, and this one has gone completely mad. Don't you think we should call this a night? It's quite clear Gareth isn't going to participate, I say we get rid of him while we're still ahead. We can come back another day to fix this Dave character, or better still, pay someone reliable to do it." Rose paces the room with the pistol held down in one of his big hands. Saif is right. This has gone too far and he's lost some of his emotion to it. He looks at Gaz on the sofa with the bruised cheek and blood down his white shirt, anger burns in his eyes. Rose knows how hard men are, he spotted grit in Gaz, but now he's sees that he won't be able to train him. Like always, Saif is right.

"Good call," he says. "What did you do with Dylan?" he asks Gaz. The blonde man was a real pain in the neck, but he could fight and he was easy to control, he might still be useful.

"Like I said, I left him with some friends," says Gaz.

"I gave you lots of chances, son. Too many even. If he's been hurt, you'll pay for it."

"Then I'll pay for it." Rose scoffs at this.

"We'll get back to Leeds," he says. "We'll have someone

else deal with our issues here." Saif nods, taps a few buttons, and closes his laptop.

"What about these two?" asks Saif.

"Gaz is coming with us. What about you, Lilly? Are you coming too or are you going to stay here?" She is pale and wide-eyed on the sofa, like some sort of ragged doll with her long messy black hair around her.

"I'll stay," she says. "Back to work tomorrow." Her voice is faraway and her eyes do not move from the wall in front.

"Lilly," whispers Gaz. She does not turn to look at him. This is the girl he drove to Leeds for, and the one who cost him Our Dave's van, and the reason he has returned to this house. "Are you there, Lilly?" he asks again. Rose looks down on the both of them with a half-crooked smile.

"I'm here Gaz," she says. Her voice is louder. "You should have got out while you could. Now you'll never get out at all."

"You're going to stand up, and we're going to walk out of here, the two of us." This is what he said before. Her eyes blink, she stretches her arms out above her and gives a big yawn, then sits up. She claps her mouth as if she's thirsty.

"I think I'm going to bed," she says. She turns to look at Gaz for the first time since he walked in. The eyes are red.

"Good luck, Gaz," she says, "I'll see you around." There's the zip of Saif's laptop bag, and then the sound of him putting on his jacket. Rose looks down on the sofa.

"She never did need saving, Gaz. The one who was always in danger was you." He grimaces up at the man with a beard. For the first time, Gaz sees that he's right.

"I'll drive, shall I?" asks Saif.

"Aye," says Rose. "Gaz can give me a lift in that car of his, we might as well get something out of this trip. It'll be worth a bob or two."

It's three o'clock in the morning. The silent time. House burglars and car thieves have signed off for the night, drinkers and clubbers have made their way home, the baby who will be up at half five has finally gone to sleep. This is the time for foxes to root through bins, it's when slugs leave their silvery trails and when traffic lights change in the dark streets even though there are no cars to care about them.

Gaz drives slowly down Beverley Road and towards the centre of town. Ironically, this is the quickest way out of the city from here. A couple of miles east of the main square along the river are the docks; cargo comes in from Europe, food stuff, booze, clothes, furniture and it all rolls out across the new main road through town and out down the M62 to Leeds or Manchester or onwards.

Ela's engine is quiet as they wait at the streetlights on Ferensway. At the green signal, Gaz eases down on the accelerator. They move through the deserted city past the train station and the old cinema. This big old car suits Rose, he takes up all of the passenger seat as he relaxes back. Gaz knows that he's got the pistol in the door well. He hasn't been as friendly as he usually is. Perhaps Gaz is past his best.

Gaz's eyes feel like they're full of grit. His chest hurts when he breathes in. The wound on his shoulder is gently weeping blood. He has a red mark on his cheek. If the coppers should stop them now, they would be questioned, but Rose does not seem like the kind of man whose luck is troubled by coppers at the wrong time.

Ela's tyres squeak as they drive the big bend out of the roundabout. This is the start of the flyover that takes the traffic out of town. Gaz speeds up.

"How much was she?" asks Rose. He means the car.

"Money in fair words," says Gaz. There's no more need for the pretense of civility. Gaz is not going to make it through to the light of day, and strangely, there is a sense of freedom in this. The game has been lost and won already. Wilkinson is off to Spain, Our Dave will get a new van, Kate will find a good-looking man, Lilly can go back to the punters and getting pissed at her mam's at the weekend, Rose here will go back to being whatever sort of big man he is. Gaz does not know where he'll end up, but he is glad it will not be the cold flat above Clarendon Bikes or another nightclub door.

The motorway opens up in front of them, it's two lanes on either side of empty space under the streetlights. Gaz puts the pedal down and the circular eighties speedo on the dashboard climbs. Rose's face is impassive as it looks through the windscreen.

"You'll take the next turning on your left," he says. This could take them to Hessle or the line of bright new superstores, the hardware centre or the furniture showroom. Gaz indicates so and the lights make a clicking sound against the silence of the engine. "When you get to the roundabout turn left and then go straight on."

"Where are we going?"

"Lord Line." Gaz gives a grin as he pulls the big Capri off the motorway. They are heading for somewhere only a local would know, for just beyond the shopping complex with PC world and Stonehouse furniture, and sat on the side of the huge river, are the ruined docks of St Andrew's Quay. Gaz drives past the chain restaurant that is closed at this time, and the bright neon of the computer store blazes out from the top of a glass fronted building; this place is often deserted in the daytime, in the early hours of the morning there's just a nightwatchman asleep in the office upstairs. Gaz knows the ruins of the docks where kids come to spray paint the walls and clamber around the fallen down buildings.

"Park in one of the spaces." Rose's voice has a gravel quality. In the growing light of the morning the pock marks on his face seem deeper. Gaz rolls Ela into one of the painted spaces on the concrete floor. The car park is deserted and the 2.6 engine hums idle under the bonnet in front. They sit, the two of them, looking across at the buildings of the crumbling docks in the distance. To the left is the biggest, and the words

Lord Line stand out in faded white glory across the top. Once upon a time this was the heart of Hessle Road, where trawlers brought in boatfuls of gold in slippery cod and haddock. Gaz has wandered through the shells of the once great meeting rooms and offices, he's climbed the ruined lift shafts and staircases and imagined that there really was an apocalypse and he was all that was left. The council have threatened to pull it down for years and periodically they board the buildings up, but kids and druggies return with crowbars and open the metal sheeting faster than it was fixed in place.

"You know my dad did a season on the trawlers out here. In the seventies." Rose looks out through the windscreen at the morning with his nasty eyes narrow. "I don't think he could stomach more than a couple of trips. He said the lads were bastards. He was as well."

"Whatever it is you're going to do, Rose, you better get on with it. I'm not here to listen to you natter shite about your old boy." Now there is nothing to lose, Gaz finds the voice of this ruined dock in him, it's irreverent and with the sharp cut of humour.

"You'll choke in the end, Gaz. You'll cry as well. They all do when it comes to it." Rose is being serious.

"There's kids and dog walkers all over this place, fella. I'd be found."

"We'll have a walk out by the river," says Rose. "You and me. I'll work it out as I go. It's not like I haven't done it before." Rose goes to the handle on the door next to him and gives it a hard pull to open up. It doesn't budge.

"It's an old car, you have to be patient," says Gaz. Rose turns with a clever look.

"I can shoot you in the car if you like," he says but there's no music to his voice. This is why all those years ago, his father did not get on well on the trawlers here – it wasn't that he was from Leeds, it was his personality devoid of humour – like Rose.

Gaz has had enough of this.

Time to take it into his own hands.

He hits the accelerator hard and Ela's engine grunts in response from below. The car lurches forward as the pistons inside drive the shaft to power the wheels, Rose thuds back in his seat from the acceleration. Gaz is heading for the path towards the ruin of the Lord Line building. In twenty yards he's got Ela up to thirty and he snaps the gearstick into second. Rose reaches down for the pistol he has in the well of the door. Gaz is going for it. Cars don't come this way anymore, the old road is full of holes. The dock that was once crammed with trawlers now sways with reeds and cattails, algae and old tyres, shopping trolleys and plastic bags. The car surges forward along the old tarmac, and the big ruin of the dock building up front begins to get closer.

Gaz gets Ela up to fifty and he throws the gear stick into third. Ela is built to do this, she's a muscle car from an age that did not know about global warming and conservation – the idea was to make a car that sounded like thunder and could move like lightning. Rose retrieves the pistol and brings it level with Gaz's temple as he drives. He pushes the barrel into the side of his head under the dark hair. There's the rush from the early morning world outside as it streams past the window.

"What are you doing?" he roars. Gaz grins. He's free. "Pull over," yells Rose, "now!" Gaz narrows his eyes and keeps his face fixed on the road. He's not going to oblige Rose by walking to his death and making it easier for the man to kill him. The game is over already. He's lost so many times that once more won't make any difference. He pushes the clutch and reaches for the gear stick faster than Rose can grab him. Ela surges into forth and the round speedometer pushes toward seventy. Ela's tyres bump on the uneven, disused road as she picks up speed. The sun is just breaking the horizon of the river Humber to the east, and the Lord Line rises to the west. Gaz is going for the smaller building on the right, the one shaped like a triangle with smooth sides that looks out directly over the Humber. Rose's finger hovers over the trigger of the gun that points at Gaz.

"Pull over," he yells again. Rose has let this get out of hand, for should he blow this young man's head open they would crash for sure. Rose was not sure if he would have killed the lad, he only wanted to hear him cry and weep, maybe beg too. He misjudged Gaz. Ela picks up speed still and Gaz turns the steering wheel to come off the old road, the tyres respond to the bumpier ground and the cab rattles, Rose's grip on the gun wavers.

"Pull this car over, or I'll put a bullet through your head," he's red faced and angry. He should have shot this kid already, for the car is now dangerously close to the building, and rattling over the bumpy ground so that the seats judder. Rose grits his little teeth – he should have stayed in Leeds, he should have listened to Saif, he had enough already with the business and the whore he extorted, why did he feel the need for more. Rose thought Hull would be easy, but he hasn't even got his fingers into the town, he hasn't even got past this dickhead kid he was sure he could use.

Gaz holds the wheel steady. He feels clarity, finally, as they speed towards the water's edge next to the tumbling down dock office. The suspension rattles and the engine in front roars. He is past worrying. Gaz is not that twelve-year-old boy anymore, he is not the one who stands and watches as his mother is murdered, he does not have to let Rose kill him. He can fight back. This will be better than the blister strip of ADHD drugs he found on the toilet floor of a Hull nightclub.

Ela clips a metal railing, the speed rips it from the wall and puts a deep scratch down her right-hand side. She does not slow as the dial touches ninety on the dashboard. Gaz knew that she was only his for the meantime, he knew that the minute he sat down in her. The dock wall approaches, and it is crumbled through age and the battering of the elements.

Rose tries the door handle again with his left hand, he pulls hard and Ela does not respond. There are some doors that can't be opened with brute force. The gun in his right-hand falters as he feels the intensity. His father hated this dock, he told him never to come to Hull, and never to have anything to do with the people here, but Rose didn't listen then, like he doesn't listen now. He feels his finger on the trigger and pulls. The pistol kicks back in his hand but with the juddering of the cab the bullet misses Gaz and puts a hole through the driver's side window. The young man does not take his eyes off the dark waters of the Humber rushing towards them. He's nearly home.

Ela breaks the crumbling wall of St Andrews Dock at nearly ninety, the front-end takes a battering but she does not slow significantly, not at this speed. Ela climbs into the pale sky and takes a moment there, majestic with the waters of the Humber some twenty yards below. Gravity takes over and she crashes into the water nose first with a splash that slows her and makes her serene all at the same time. Rose smacks his head on the passenger window in the fall and the gun tumbles from his hand, clattering under the seats. The thick freezing water swallows them into darkness.

The world goes black for Gaz.

Time loops round itself and dreams become real then dreams again. Voices swim around him from the past. There are faces he remembers but not from where, there are noises too and shouts from the old dock as it used to be. The cold water in his trousers wakes him, and he draws in a breath before it swallows him up and sucks Ela towards the bottom.

Under the water, Gaz feels the driver's door open, it catches a swirl in the current. He unclips his seatbelt gently as the car begins to angle down from him towards the riverbed - it's like he is being pulled out as he drifts, his eyes open in the gritty brown water and the freezing cold of the Humber – the ice and mud hurt his eyeballs. Gaz is not going to fight this.

He's got to let it all go, his mother's death, the dreams of Kate, the car that everyone loved and that blister pack of Adderall that he will not need now. He was born to lose after all, that's what life has taught him, that is all he has been good at. Below, the current and weight drag Ela and Rose down to the darkness of the river as Gaz rises. There is a lot he does not know. Ghosts are around him in the darkness of the muddy pitch black, they are those who lost their lives in this water, those who worked on the ships and boats above, who stacked and cut the fish, those that lived and died on this river, and it's their hopes for the future and for their sons and daughters that ripple through the ice-cold water. He can hear their easy banter and the shouting across the decks. Like his grandmothers and grandfathers, Gaz belongs to this river, but she will not take him back, yet. He breaks the surface as he lays there on his back with his face to the sky.

She doesn't want him. Not today.

CHAPTER TWENTY-TWO
Our Dave

The Humber is calm this morning. The sun is bright over the water and Mike squints through the visor of the orange safety helmet. He turns back to Ned behind in the lifeboat - there are always two of them. Mike has forgotten his sunglasses, it's never bright like this usually but then again, he didn't expect to be out at this time. In the early morning at half four, the boat was scrambled from just under the Humber Bridge in response to a call from the south bank near Barton. There's a lonely café on the river called Viking Way and you can hire their back room for weddings and reunions, there's a late bar and never a copper in sight. The talk over the radio was that a couple managed to wade out as far as their waists into the muddy water and then got lost in the darkness at about four. Humber Rescue were called, and they backed the boat out into the river on a tractor and were off. Mike and Ned have searched the south bank for a good hour to no avail. Fifteen minutes ago, they got a message over their headsets that the couple were found asleep in their car. It's good that nobody got hurt even if they wasted a ton of fuel crossing the river. Mike has been at this game for a little more than eight years, and though he grumbles, this river is his home. Ned's voice crackles over the intercom between their helmets.

"I could still be in bed with the misses," he says. Ned is a white-haired volunteer who used to drive ambulances until he retired.

"Dodged a bullet there then, Ned," says Mike. He looks over his shoulder and the man with a white moustache grins back at him. They have been through a few things, these two. They've rescued boats from crashing on the rocks, pulled sheep out of the freezing water and people too, they've fished out dead bodies as well, with their faces puffed up and swollen. Mike turns back to the steering wheel and sees, just out the corner of his eye, something bob in the water between the waves. He eases off the revs and the boat coasts for a minute, skipping over the current below.

"What is it?" asks Ned.

"I saw something," he answers. He keeps his eyes narrowed into the brown water to the left and he sees it. It's the smooth head of a seal some twenty yards away in the water, just the head. The wide black eyes are looking at him. It's telling him something. The waves wash between his view and when the water moves, the seal is gone. Mike looks back at Ned.

"There's something happened," he says.

"What?"

"I dunno, something. I just know it has." In any other walk of life, superstition and gut feeling are cast aside as nonsense. These men of the sea and the river, with their safety procedures and life jackets, sitting in a boat with twin two hundred horsepower Mercury engines that could easily get them home; these men trust their own instincts. Ned looks out at the flat water, above their heads and to the left is the mighty Humber Bridge, behind the sleepy south bank and ahead in the distance is the city of Hull. The iconic point of the Deep aquarium juts out into the early morning sky and there's Hull Minster not far away. Ned narrows his eyes at the detail of the cityscape in front.

"There," he says. "There's something in the water."

At first, they think he's dead because he isn't moving, his legs are bobbing on the surface and his arms are outstretched by his side. It is how Gaz thought it would end, but like everything else, he's wrong about this as well. The men from Humber Rescue yell at him over the water with shouts of 'oi' and 'hey'. Gaz manages to raise a hand so they can see him.

It's a struggle to get him onboard because he's weak. Mike and Ned take him by both arms and drag him on, there's blood down his front, he's hit his cheek. He will need to go to hospital. They sit him up against the side and Mike covers him with a silver survival blanket and passes him a clear bottle of water. Gaz's lips are colourless and he is shivering.

"Don't talk," says Mike. "Save it. You'll be okay now." He always says this, but he's never sure. He recognises the lad from when he came to collect on Harold's debt the other day, he remembers they talked in riddles and there was mention of Our Dave.

"I'll call the ambulance," says Ned. Gaz raises his hand as he looks up at them with weak eyes.

"No ambulance," he whispers. "Call Our Dave." Mike looks back at Ned. They have done things for this man before that they perhaps shouldn't have, they rescued a pleasure boat loaded with cases of whiskey and towed it to shore, Humber Rescue gets a heavy donation from him every year, he sends them a hamper at Christmas. Ned is not as deep in as Mike, but they both know that should anyone look into what they've done for the man, they would get nicked.

"You're not going to die, are you?" asks Mike. It's a daft question.

"Not yet," whispers Gaz.

"What's your name again, son?"

"Gaz," he says. "Tell Our Dave it's Gaz."

Just under the great towers of the Humber Bridge, and set off the road is the Humber Rescue shed. Next to the ramp leading into the water there's a tractor and the engine is running. Mike radioed ahead to let the driver know they were inbound, he sent a text to Our Dave as well. He looks down at the face of the lad sitting on the back seat of the boat with the silver blanket wrapped round him, his face is steady and his lips have some colour to them now.

"You're a lucky bastard," calls Mike out of his helmet at the kid. Gaz could give a cocky response to this, like 'I don't feel lucky', but he keeps it back.

"Thanks," he replies.

When they get close enough to the shore, Mike drives the boat on the carriage that the tractor has reversed deep into the water, he cuts the engine and gets out into the muddy river to clip the bottom to the carriage. When he's done, he gives a tap, the kid driving the tractor eases the big wheels out of the water and up the bank to the road. It must be half nine now. A dog walking couple with a red setter stand and watch the boat come out of the river with the water dripping off the orange bottom and sides.

Our Dave has parked up opposite the little playground and he stands leaving against his grey Ford with his hands in his bomber jacket pockets and a black beanie hat on his head. Gaz comes down the steps from the boat, the lad is wobbly but ok with the silver blanket still around his shoulders.

"Who's the bloke?" calls the kid who's driving.

"A swimmer got into trouble," answers Mike.

"Shall we get the ambulance?"

"No need," says Mike. "He's fine. We won't bother reporting it either, I think it'll be ok." Ned clambers down the steps from the boat finally. "We'll have a tea in the shed," adds Mike. "You can get yourself cleaned up as well, Gaz." He makes his way to the back of the boat to check the engines and the propellor like he always does. Ned heads off to the shed and the tractor driver climbs out and follows.

Our Dave walks over to stand in front of Gaz. He looks washed out with a pale face and hollow darkened eyes.

"What happened?" he asks.

"Rose. The guy who runs Sandersons," he says.

"What about him?"

"I drove him into the river." Our Dave blinks at the lad. He would think this was some sort of piss take from anyone else.

"Where is he now?"

"Twenty feet under the water, I should think, like that car. I went in over the old St Andrew's Dock." Our Dave looks out over the waters of the Humber and across to the south bank. Gaz is a tough one. He should have kept him closer. He feels regret.

"You could have called me, Gaz. I would have helped."

"I didn't know if you would or not." Our Dave looks down at the mud of the car park under his feet. He's failed this lad, you'd think he'd have learned enough about people at his age.

In the shed at Humber Rescue there's a long office next to where the boats are kept. Inside is a row of computer terminals and there are radios, headphones and complex maps that you can write on with dry wipe markers. Mike leads Gaz down to the end, and on the wall are hung up wetsuits, coats and helmets, there are rubber boots neatly in line by size order and at the far end, a wet room shower.

"We've got a box of old clothes in there too, kid," he says. "Get yourself sorted, and I'll make you a brew." Gaz walks to the end and steps into the wet room. He closes the door and slumps down on the plastic stool in front of a long mirror, he doesn't recognise the figure that looks back at him. He slips off his shoes and removes his muddy white socks, then his jacket and peels off his black t-shirt, robot slow. He sets his dripping wet wallet in the sink, and looks at his cracked, lifeless mobile phone. He's lost Kate's number now anyway. Fitting.

The shower water is hot on him, it streams down over his hair and shoulders and the warmth is divine. The open wound on his shoulders that is too cold to bleed begins to weep once more. Gaz looks down at his feet with the bones showing thin and his long toes as the brown water runs down the drains. He's just going to wash this all away and keep going. Isn't that what everyone does? Isn't that what Wilkinson did with her cancer, just wash the thing away and carry on? That's what Kate has done with him too. That's what he has to do with all of this. Gaz will have to start new. He will have to start again, afresh, and though he won't forget what has happened to him, he will have to accept that it was not his fault. He could never have stopped the man who killed his mother that night, but he can stop himself feeling guilty for it. Even if it's not true, if he believes it enough it might be. He packs the bullet hole up with toilet paper and wraps a sock around his shoulder to keep it in place. The pain feels sweet.

Next to the bin where he put his wet clothes there's a box. He finds grey tracksuit bottoms and a black jumper, right at the bottom is a dark brown flat cap. He stands in the mirror and fits it over his messy hair, looks at himself for a moment and then pulls it low over his eyes. He'll have to be stronger than he was. He'll have to be more open too. He'll have to let himself get hurt because he's been given another chance.

They drive back along the river, under the bridge and up through the streets of Hessle with big houses on either side. Gaz does not have anything to say. Our Dave is quiet and careful as he drives, he feels like he ought to break the silence:

"You can't wear a cap with it over your eyes like that," he says.

"How come?"

"It makes you look like you've got something to hide."

"I have," answers Gaz.

"We all have, Gaz. With your cap pulled down low like that you just advertise the fact to everyone. Pull it up a bit, let them see a bit of forehead, let them think there's nothing there but smiles. That's how you hide stuff, in plain sight." Gaz looks out the window.

"I'm sorry I screwed up with you, Our Dave. Whatever you have for me to do, I'll do it. I'll clean floors or shovel shite, I'll do your garden, I'll drive a cab, anything. I'll do it for nothing as well. I just need to get myself straight. I just need to forget all this."

"I'll get you back on the books." At the lights on Hessle Road, Gaz adjusts his cap, he lifts the tip so that his face is showing. He doesn't have to ignore advice.

"Can you drop me at the motorbike shop?" he asks.

"Not yet," says Our Dave. "I've got something at Avenue Cars."

"What?"

"You'll have to see."

"The coppers?" Our Dave does not respond as the lights turn green.

They drive down Pickering Road and Gaz looks out the windows at the semi-detached houses on the right side with cars parked in their driveways and the sky a bright blue behind them. He wants to look at Our Dave and ask what is waiting for him, but he knows the man will not answer. His stomach grumbles.

They pass the Five Ways pub with a huge England flag flapping in the wind pinned to the roof, and then on to Anlaby Road. There's a kid riding his orange BMX yapping into a mobile phone, an old woman dragging a shopping basket and a pug dog on a short lead, there's a runner, then a spice head staggering and two Kurdish men walking side by side with their black hair sleek and perfect. Life is normal and bright to Gaz's eyes. If Our Dave has had to do a deal with the police, Gaz will take it, he will go without a fuss and he'll say whatever it is he has to. If he goes to jail for what he's done, then that's the way it has to be.

They drive over the railway crossing and turn right into Chanterlands Ave. The traffic is thin in the morning and Our Dave parks his grey ford in the space outside Avenue Cars – it's not normally free. Dundee Street Fisheries across the road is closed at this time, and there's the metal sign for Steve's Cycles creaking in the light wind. Our Dave does not get out of the car right away, he turns to Gaz as if he wants to say something. His face is pale with a light frown of worry. Gaz stops him before he can:

"It's okay, Our Dave. I've got this. I can handle it," he says. The man nods. He wishes he had something that could prepare the young man.

They go in the front way. Our Dave opens the door and they walk through the waiting area that never gets used these days. He slides his key into the yale lock and yanks open the heavy door to the office. The girls will be out on their runs at this time, but there's still some of the pancakes that Dilva made in a plastic tub on the table. Gaz expects that whoever he is there to see will be out back.

"Do you want a brew?" says Our Dave as he opens the door to the galley kitchen. Gaz moves behind him and looks out the window. Parked long ways in the back yard is a white transit van with rust on the wheels and on the back arches. Gaz does not answer. He hears the door on the other side of the van slam shut and sees feet on the underside move to the back into full view. A figure walks around the front of the van, and there, scrubbing the windscreen with a sponge, in a long skirt with trainers and no socks, is Kate.

"I'm sorry, Gaz," says Our Dave. "She called me last night. She told me all about it." Gaz steps backwards into the office before she can see him and Our Dave follows.

The young man unravels quickly. The steel of washing this all away down the drain is replaced by fear. The one thing that Gaz has never learned to do is win. His stomach turns over and his nose begins to water as he steps back into the bright room. Our Dave looms over him.

"The van was the best I could get at short notice, Gaz. I need you to make a run, like you always do, to Scotland. The stuff's already in the back. We had it all planned for the end of July."

"What's she doing here?"

"She's going with you, Gaz."

"She can't."

"Why not?"

"She just can't."

"She talked to your Lilly this morning too, the one you've been looking after. She knows more than I do." Gaz's eyes flash.

"Me and Kate had a thing and it's done. We had something and I screwed it up. I don't want to see her." Our Dave moves closer as Gaz steps back, his eyes have begun to water with emotion, his heart is beating heavily in his chest, his legs ache.

"You have to," says Our Dave.

"I don't."

"You have to lay low after what's happened. You said you'd do anything?"

"Not with her." Gaz has nowhere left to step back; he is against the door at Avenue Cars with the smell of Bev's perfume from the chair where she sat a few hours previous in his nostrils. Our Dave is on him.

"There's something there, Gaz. She told me. She told me what you said." Gaz's eyes glaze with yet formed tears. His chest feels tight. He's afraid.

"I can't do it, Our Dave, I can't do it. I'll mess it up with her, I'll hurt her. I'm not good enough. She's better off without someone like me." The man puts his big arms on Gaz's shoulders and holds them tight as he looks into his eyes.

"This is what it's all about, Gaz. What you've got with her. That's it. Everything else means fuck all compared to that. This is a fight that you're not going to win, however it plays out, you'll be ruined and hurt, but before that, there's what you feel for her and what she feels for you. I can't let that go, and neither can you. If there's any way you can have what I had with Hazel, even just for a year, then you've got to take it, son." A tear runs down Gaz's cheek. He's prepared for it to go tits up, but he is not prepared for this. Kate is all he wants. Our Dave grits his teeth. Once upon a time someone gave him the same advice he is giving Gaz. "You need to accept that she likes you, son. You need to pretend that you're good enough, and it'll be true." Gaz has heard this advice before, Our Dave's grip on his shoulders is tight, and he holds him there for a few seconds. It's as intense as he has ever seen the old fella. Our Dave stands back then wipes the tears from his face with one of his big hands. He takes a minute to gather emotions back into him that should never have spilled out.

The door to the kitchen swings open and she appears, her hair is down to her shoulders and she wears a nervous smile. It's Kate.

"Our Dave said you'd be ready straight away," she says.

"He is," says Our Dave. Gaz looks to the big man and then to Kate. She gives him a weak smile.

"I talked to Lilly. I found her on Facebook. She said you might not be back. I'm glad that you are."

"Now you know about what I do."

"I know about what you've done," she says. Our Dave walks to the filing cabinet and pulls open one of the drawers. He takes out an envelope and passes it to Kate.

"She's got a full tank, but that will get you filled up for the way back," he says. Kate has a big key fob in her other hand.

"I'll drive," says Gaz. "I've done it before."

"Not this time," says Our Dave. "Not after what you did to my last van."

Gaz grins and his smile is wide and bright.

EPILOGUE

It's Friday night. Our Dave is in the queue at Dundee Street Fisheries. He just gets fish these days, Hazel never did like chips anyway. He likes the people he sees there and the folks who are in the queue with him. It's a community thing. His phone buzzes in his bomber jacket pocket so he steps out of the queue and outside.

"I'll save your space," calls a white-haired old lass. Our Dave shakes his head. He needs to take this call and he doesn't mind queuing again. Outside, he turns into the top of Newstead Street and stands next to the twenty mile an hour sign with the phone to his ear.

"It's me," says Wilkinson.

"I've got your name in my phone, lass. I knew it was you. What is it?"

"I just wanted to tell you I'm here and I got the money."

"Good. How is it out there?"

"Hot." Wilkinson has that same dead tone to her voice. Our Dave has known her for a long time. The woman wouldn't be talking to him if they weren't friends, and she's short with him because she trusts him. That's how it is in this town. "I wanted to say thanks."

"What for?"

"Buying the flat."

"I'll make a killing on it," he answers.

"Make sure you do."

"When are you back?"

"Probably never, Our Dave. I'm in a state, you know how it is." Our Dave swallows as he looks down the street. He took her to the hospital out at Castle Hill more than a few times. He watched her lose her hair.

"I know, lass. If there's anything you need, please let me know."

"That's why I'm calling. That lad, Gaz, I've been worried

about him. He's not messaged me for a good few days. Have you seen him?"

"I have," says Our Dave.

"How is he?"

"I think he'll be okay. You know what lads are like, they lose their phones all the time. I'll tell him to message you when I see him next, Wilkinson."

"You used to call me Ruby back in the day." Our Dave is probably the only person who ever called her that.

"I'll let him know, Ruby," There's a pause on the other end of the line, it must be a thousand miles or more to where she is in Valencia.

"Would you look after him, Our Dave?"

"Aye, I will. I've got a feeling he's been looking after me." Our Dave is not sure why he says this.

"He has to take care of someone, that's how he is, bit like you." Dave grins, Wilkinson knows him well.

"Are you off getting pissed somewhere?" he asks.

"On the beach right now, watching the sun go down." Our Dave hopes this is true.

"See you soon, Ruby Wilkinson," he says.

"Love you, Dave," she answers. She's never said this to him before.

It's way past three in the morning on Friday night. This is Dalwood Close, Bransholme. There are scooters parked up outside number 107, the music has died down over the last half an hour but it's still on, it never stops. Bob Marley reggae thuds out through the broken window taped over with cardboard from when it was broken and the sound is muffled in the street. Cod is having some smoke time with his boys, or rather, his mean-faced sister, Shell, is getting them to sample the next batch she's managed to sort from the weed dens. Cod's knuckles are split from where he hit the blonde nutter from the other day. He turned up out of nowhere and knew how to handle himself. In the end one of the scooter rider delivery boys hit him with a spade and he went down. They dragged him off to the phone box on the corner, and left him slumped outside before they called an ambulance. Cod isn't an animal.

It's been another good night. They take orders via text on one of Shell's many burner phones and she sends the lads out on their scooters. She has a good feeling about all this because, for the first time, she has enough money for her habit, and so the hunger for it doesn't bother her so much. She thinks back to the Polish girl on a pushbike with her short dress and red hair, and the flowers on the basket of her bike. For the first time Shell has found something she can do, and there's nobody going to stand in her way.

An online delivery van turns the corner and the electric motor makes almost no noise as it slows to the end of the road. There are two in the front. It makes a three point turn as if it is going to drive away again, but the lights go off and the buzz of the engine cuts out. The driver yanks the scarf up over her nose to cover her face then pulls the black cap further down over her eyes and red hair. Kasia would rather do a job like this herself, that way she knows it will get done properly and with no mistakes. The woman next her is bigger, she's Lithuanian ex-Russian special forces, Kasia met her when they worked in the fish factory on Hessle Road a few years back. Her name is Laura – pronounced in the European way. They've been through what they're going to do many times, they know the layout of the house and who will be there. They know the getaway plan. Nothing has been left to chance. A week ago, one of Kasia's dealers knocked a teenage roadman off his moped, and while he drove the kid to casualty for the broken ankle, he found out all about Shell, and he told Kasia.

This is what Kasia is best at – getting things clean.

Laura walks down the little path through the open gate to the front door and checks the handle with her black surgeon's rubber glove. It's not locked. No need to knock. Laura works at the spray can factory on Sutton-fields and she's married to a big blonde man and has two daughters under ten. She cooks most nights but sometimes her husband does the girls an omelette – like tonight. She steps into the house and the thuds from the reggae music are louder inside. Kasia follows.

They carry light plastic pistols held pointing upwards as they enter. The teenage delivery boy who spilled to beans on Shell's operation, also told him about the Vietnamese gun maker on Spring Bank West. The idea of 3D printed guns is appealing because these would not be traceable and neither would the bullets if you could make them yourself. Kasia had him found, and then moved to just near her warehouse off the old docks, turns out he can do much more than 3D print weapons, especially with better equipment. The pistols they carry were finished yesterday, then tested; they hold eight shots in a clip and the girls have two each. This should be easy.

Laura gently opens the door to the front room and the three men on the sofa look up at her with wide, stoned eyes. Cod is in the middle with two of the roadmen delivery drivers beside with their hoods off. She opens fire with both the pistols. Six shots. The snapping of the bullets isn't even as loud as the music.

Kasia moves into the kitchen and there's Shell on a stool with the open laptop in front of her and a cig in her right hand. She sees the black cap and the scarf over the face; she draws in breath with shock. Her default training is to swear and bellow rather than get out of the way or attack. Kasia delivers three shots into her chest, a fourth goes through her neck and puts a bullet hole through the window on the back door. Kasia stands over her on the kitchen floor and fires another one into the side of her head so the skull jerks. There's no emotion in this. Kasia does not feel slighted by this girl's attempt to step on her business – it's more like getting rid of a big spider's web in a corner, or scrubbing at a tough stain on a baking tray – it's just a job that needs to get done.

Laura sweeps the rest of the house. She's smooth and efficient, she's been trained to do this. In the upstairs box bedroom, there's a lad sleeping on a bare mattress, she stands at a good angle so that his head exploding doesn't splatter her. You only get this kind of knowledge from experience.

It's all gone well so far.

They unload the petrol from the back of the delivery van. Kasia stored it in anything she could find – empty two litre cola bottles as well as a big five gallon can that Laura carries. It doesn't take long for them to douse the front room and the kitchen as well as the stinking mattresses upstairs. Kasia wheels three mopeds in from outside the house and they leave them in the hall.

Kasia waits in the van with the engine on while Laura offers a lighter flame up to a packet of firelighters and then leaves it in the front room under the armchair she just covered in petrol. When she gets back to the van, Kasia does not drive off straight away – she waits until she's sure the fire has caught hold. In a few seconds, there are red flames flickering in the front room window through the rear-view mirror.

Kasia drives the van all the way to the edge of Bransholme and the deserted roundabout at Wawne, then on into the darkness of the countryside. At the Beverley and District Model Club Airfield, they abandon the vehicle near some bushes and set it on fire. It's a twenty-minute walk across the open fields to the deserted bridge at Weel, they don't cross, but keep to the road towards the village of Tickton where Laura parked her car behind the Crown and Anchor pub the day before. There's a change of clothes and footwear for both of them. They have tickets to a Micheal Bublé tribute act that was on at Bridlington Spa up the road. This is their cover story. Like it never happened, they are on the bypass back to Hull in five minutes. Laura gets home in time to say goodnight to her blond husband as she slips into bed next to him. Kasia's babysitter gets paid well for staying behind at the Dairycoates Inn till half twelve. As she gets into bed, Kasia lets out a relieved sigh.

It's good to get things clean.

This is Grove Street off Beverley Road. Our Dave stands at the end terrace house and rings the doorbell. It takes a minute for Lilly to answer. She's wearing her pink dressing gown and she's done her make-up but the black hair still has a few rollers in it. Her face is sharp as she looks down at the man outside. She's ready to start work again. It's all she knows.

"Yes?"

"Are you Lilly?" he asks.

"I might be. Who's asking?"

"I'm a friend of Gaz, my name's Dave. I run the taxi office on Chants Ave."

"I know you," she says. "Is he OK? I mean Gaz."

"Aye." Our Dave smiles. "He's fine."

"Do you want to come in?" He nods.

In the front room, Lilly has tried to straighten up, but the TV screen on the wall is still spidered from where Gaz hit his head against it. They both stand facing each other. Lilly has had a word with herself, she'll just have to forget what happened last night and get on with business as usual, that's why she's up and dressed and ready to turn on the green light for the punters on the app. This might be her first job of the day.

"Have you heard from him?" she asks.

"Aye. He's out of town now though, on a job to Scotland. Thanks for speaking to his lass, Kate. It made a difference."

"I wish he'd told me about her," says Lilly. Kate called her, it's not hard to find Lilly's number, she doesn't hide it in her line of business. She did not mess around in the phone conversation in the early morning. She told Kate exactly the kind of man that Gaz is, and it made her sad to do so, for it gave it all a kind of finality as if she were saying goodbye to him.

"Why are you here?" she asks Our Dave. "Are you looking for something?" This is Lilly's lead in. She has heard about Our Dave, although this is the first time she's met him, she knows he's got money and is not a bad sort. He would make a good regular.

"I am as it happens," he says. She smiles to show those white veneers.

"What did you have in mind? An hour?"

"Nothing like that," says Our Dave. "I'm looking for someone to work up at the taxi office." The smile fades and she cocks her head as if she doesn't quite understand.

"I can't drive."

"It's a social media position. I need someone to look after all the accounts and give them the same kind of feel, take photos and stuff like that, write the blurbs for posts and that kind of thing." This is the best shite he can come up with. He doesn't actually need anyone to do this. Lilly looks at Our Dave deadpan. Her first instinct is that he is taking the piss. She holds his stare just long enough to realise that he isn't.

"Are you offering me a job?" she asks.

"Aye."

"Why?"

"I heard that your previous employer went out of business."

"Rose?"

"That was it."

"What happened?"

"Gaz sorted him."

"For good?"

"Aye." Lilly does not know where to look. She steps backwards and sits down on an armchair with a vacant expression on her face. It's a shock.

"He's really gone?"

"Yes. Like I said, I need a social media person. Gaz told me that you're good at that sort of thing. He said you post a lot online, and you know how to take a good photo." She nods. There is a possibility, she thinks, that she may never have to sleep with another man for money ever again. It's a foreign concept to her. She looks up at Our Dave and he can see that she is confused.

"I'll give you a bit of time to think about it, shall I?" he asks. Our Dave passes her down a business card with Avenue Cars written on the front. "Give me a call when you've had a think."

"I will," she says.

When Our Dave has gone, Lilly stands in the front room looking at the punter app on her phone. Her thumb hovers over the switch to turn her green available light on. What will she do if she doesn't do this? How will she get by? It takes her a minute of looking at the screen before she sets it down on the kitchen table and goes to the back door for a cig. She opens the backdoor and the summer morning sky is blue and wide above the terraced roofs into the distance.

She doesn't know what she'll do, but it looks like it might be a beautiful day after all.

Printed in Great Britain
by Amazon

It's Hull's gangland streets… again.

Gaz Lockwood is a tough kid, but he's not cocky like other bouncers. He looks after people. Way back, he tried to look after his mam before she ended up in a box and they put him in care. Our Dave gets him to drive sometimes because the lad can handle himself and he knows how to keep his mouth shut.

With Leatherhead on holiday, things are changing. There's a Bransholme gang shifting weed and whatnot all over the city on mopeds, and a Leeds firm are trying it on with Our Dave.

Gaz has got into the wrong business for a young fella like him. It's protection. He's looking after a working girl because the firm know they can trust him, and then use him as well.

Kate works at the library on Chants Ave. She doesn't look old enough, but back in the day it was a bottle of sherry every afternoon before the pub. She's doing a master's in counselling these days. She's been through enough to know a few things.

You wouldn't put them together. Not in a million years.

Not unless you were Our Dave.

FLAT CITY PRESS

ISBN 9781739330859